# THE NEW KING

## CASTLE SERIES, BOOK 3

## J. H. WEAR

ISBN: 978-1-68046-965-3

Melange Books, LLC
White Bear Lake, MN 55110
www.melange-books.com

Published in the United States of America.

Cover Design by Ashley Redbird Designs

*To my grandsons, Ben and Mathew.*
*The three-hour trip to see them is always worthwhile. I just wish they would stop beating me at chess.*

# PART ONE

*Men are hopeless about planning events, unless it's war.*

# ONE

Sir Jon McKinney, Dragon Slayer, leaned over the heavy oak table. His thick arms supported him as he peered at a large map filled with small lines and comments. The map was unrolled, held into place by a sword on one end and two rocks on the other.

He muttered a curse under his breath and slowly stood up straight.

"Sir Jon, how's ya doin'?"

Jon turned to the doorway of the library where Gilbert entered, sporting a toothy grin and gripping a tankard of ale. The library on the second floor of Lord Perry's castle was nowhere near the size of the main library, although it still held hundreds of books and rolls of paper along the shelves that reached to the ceiling.

"Ah, just a little frustrated in trying to figure out all the possible routes an army can travel on. We not only have to defend the kingdom but also have to attack and engage the enemy. It's hard to figure out where the enemy might be traveling. This map is so detailed that it's difficult to figure all these markings."

Gilbert wandered over and peered at the map. "Lots of little lines be there, Sir Jon."

"I noticed."

"I helps you, Sir Jon."

"Yeah? What advice do you have, Gilbert?"

"Army don'ts like to travel over hills, hard on horses. So that cuts some routes out."

"Good point, but I did take that into account."

"Army also has to travel near water. They don'ts like to carry a lot of water. So looks for places near rivers."

"That makes sense. Gilbert, thanks for your help." Jon smiled, knowing Gilbert wanted to feel that he was contributing. "Now what brings you here? I thought Lord Perry had you doing some work in town."

"I is, Sir Jon, I is. Learns some more rumours and went to tell Lord Perry right aways. How come you here? Thought you had a room at Lord Troy's castle."

"I did too. But Liz was under the impression I would have too many distractions there."

Gilbert grinned. "She means the ladies there."

"I suppose so, but it seemed to me to be unnecessary." He thought of the women living at Lord Troy's castle and their habit of walking around topless, or sometimes nude. "I guess I see her point though." He put his hand on the small man's shoulder. "It's time to have some lunch. Come with me, Gilbert. You too, Reesler." Jon spoke to the gnant waiting in the corner.

Reesler quickly shuffled over. The gnant was made available to Jon by Lord Perry to retrieve items from the shelves in the library. The creature could easily climb to higher areas. Gnants were vaguely human in form but their facial features of elfin ears, sharp teeth and forked tongue made them look demonic in appearance. A hooked nose and a hairy face, coupled with claws on their hands and feet, completed their odd appearance.

Jon, unlike most people, was friendly toward gnants and even befriended a few. Still, he was aware most gnants disliked humans and would like to see all people leave Domum.

They reached a second-floor dining room and a servant quickly inquired what they desired to eat.

Jon gave his order for a sandwich and a pint of ale. He pointed at the gnant. "Bring Reesler something too."

The servant, a heavy middle-aged man with thinning chestnut coloured hair, didn't change his stoic expression and quickly complied. The last time he balked at serving a gnant, Jon admonished him, and the clearly worried servant begged for forgiveness.

"So Gilbert, what is going on with you and Donna?" Jon gave him a wink.

Gilbert gave a sheepish smile. "Well, Donna and I are getting alongs pretty good. Her family likes ol' Gilbert now after I tooks her to the ball at Lord Troy's a couple of moons ago."

"Going to marry her?" Jon recalled the wedding of Lord Troy and Patricia in the castle located at the edge of Horstruff. Gilbert, as a citizen of Vegrandis, the district located within the city of Horstruff, was not normally invited to gala events of royalty. However, Gilbert had befriended Lord Troy and began to be included in some of functions at the castle.

"Oh, I don'ts know, Sir Jon. Gilbert has his eye on a few women." Gilbert held back telling Jon that Donna had turned down his first proposal because of the lack of approval from her father. That problem had disappeared when Gilbert received an invitation to the wedding of Lord Sussex and Lady Patricia. As a result, Donna's parents saw him in a new light, although Gilbert now wasn't in a hurry about asking her a second time.

"I'm sure you do, but how many of them have an eye for you? I think you're lucky to have Donna interested you. Someone may sweep her off her feet if you don't act soon."

Gilbert squinted at him. "Donna have someone else after her? What do you knows?"

Jon spread his hands. "I don't know for sure, Gilbert, but a pretty girl like her? It just stands to reason."

Gilbert nodded his head slowly. "You may be rights there, Sir Jon."

"Just think about it, Gilbert. She may not wait for you forever."

Jon felt good about giving advice to Gilbert. He liked him and had seen the good side of him unlike many others, but Gilbert was also devious and selfish at times. Jon thought Gilbert just needed to be prodded in the right direction, and in this case to marry Donna rather than just keeping her hanging around as a girlfriend.

"Hello." Liz sang out in greeting as she stood in the doorway.

Jon broke into a grin. "Hi, how are you doing?" He stared at her in admiration. Her long blue dress with white frills billowed out at her hips, but the body of the dress was tightly fitted, making it appear that she would have trouble breathing in it. The front of the dress had a low scoop neckline and her bosom looked ready to burst out of the top.

"I feel great. I looked for you in the library, but you were gone, so I come to the only place you seem to have time for and that's where food is." She walked to the table.

"Sorry, I've been busy."

Liz patted her hand down in his direction. "That's okay. I'm going back to Lord Troy's castle for a girls' night. As soon as a carriage is ready, I'm going to pick up Nicole as well. I thought we should include her and make her feel welcome. She has had a tough time making friends."

Jon nodded, knowing that Nicole was originally a barmaid who made a quick ascension in social ranks when she became involved with Sir Anthony Graham. Despite the family's acceptance of her, she was excluded from most of the social circles in Horstruff.

"I'm sure she'll enjoy the company of the ladies."

"Yeah, it'll be fun." She partially sat at the edge of the table. "I've been thinking about the wedding and figure we have to have the wedding in Ballymiller, but your parents will probably want a second reception in Boston."

"I suppose they will."

"That's what I figured, but what about Domum? Do you want to have a reception here too? You know a lot of people here, so it makes sense to have one here too."

"I guess a reception here would be okay."

"Have you figured out who your best man is going to be? How big of a wedding party do you want? I like three bridesmaids and groomsmen, though we could go for four."

"I think three is more than enough." *Is she serious? Three wedding receptions?*

"Well, start planning about what you want for the wedding and who we need to invite. I guess I should check with your mother about some of the people on the invitation list back home. Anyway, we have a lot of work to do. Flowers, invitation cards, decoration, catering and music. You go back to work with your battle stuff. We'll talk more about this later."

"Sure, but I think you're better at details for the wedding."

"That's true. Men are hopeless about planning events, unless it's war." She walked to him and gave him a long kiss. "See you later."

After she left, Gilbert looked at Jon. "Ya still think Gilbert should marry Donna?"

Jon slowly nodded. "Just insist it's a small wedding. Better still, elope."

# TWO

Lord Darius leaned back in his chair, tilting it on its back legs. He crossed his black leather boots on the desk and turned a black handle knife in his hands. "So how is our friend Sir Nolene doing?" Lord Darius was tall but light of build. He favoured black leather garments and keeping his black hair and beard long. Together with his narrow, dark brown eyes and olive skin, he had a menacing appearance. That was backed up by his reputation for being an excellent swordsman and the occasional ordering of the torture of prisoners merely to make sure the population feared him. He smirked as he looked at the large man standing nearby.

Sir Sadon grunted. "He is doing what we expected, sire, and creating a nice bit of havoc." Beads of sweat glistened on his forehead and he used the palm of his hand to push back a few strings of long hair from his face.

"And his army?"

"Growing rather well. One of the nobility is helping him on the chance of future favours." The big man grinned, shifting weight that caused a strain on the belt holding his dark blue pants up.

"Good, perhaps we can start the next stage of our plan." He swung his feet to the floor, causing the chair to land with a bang. He stood, tossed the knife on the desk, and with his hands clasped behind his back, strode over to the open balcony. "I want you to organize the troops for an attack in a fortnight. I want you to personally lead the attack on the king's castle."

Sir Sadon gulped. "It will be a difficult assault, sire."

"That's why I want you to lead it. You're familiar with the need to improvise during an attack."

"Yes, sire." Sir Sadon lowered his head. "I will do my best."

"Good. But if the king doesn't fall, it will be on your life."

———

Sir Sadon stomped into the main royal stables. He looked around for the stable master, and after spotting him at the far end grooming a horse, bellowed at him. "McTeer, get your ass over here!"

The old man hobbled over as quickly as he could. "Yes, Sir Sadon?"

"I need your best horses ready in two days time."

"Yes, of course. How many horses do you need?"

"All but the hags." He turned to leave.

"But what of the need for protection of the kingdom?"

"I don't give a rat's ass. If I'm going to put my neck in a noose, then I'm taking every advantage I can." He grabbed the old man's tunic in his fist, hissing at him. "Not a word of this to anyone, or I'll cut off your balls." He pushed the old man away, almost causing him to fall, and walked out of the stables.

Sadon made his way back across the street, kicking at a dog that was slow to move out of his way. The canine yelped, and with its tail tucked, hid behind a food stand. Sadon entered a brick structure that contained his living quarters and office. The building was part of a group that belonged to Lord Darius and used to house the higher-ranking members of his staff. Wheezing, Sir Sadon climbed the stairs to his second-floor office that overlooked the courtyard. A female servant endured a grab on her behind before he ordered her to fetch him some food and drink. She hurried off as he entered the room and began his plan of attack using a map spread out on a table.

As his greasy finger traced lines on the map, he began to smile. *This may work after all.*

"Sire?" The servant girl approached cautiously from the doorway, carrying a tray of food and ale.

He looked up and grinned. "Put the food at that table over there." He pointed to a small table by a window. He watched her quickly set the tray down. "Now come here."

Her lips quivered as she slowly approached him and gasped as he reached out to grab her arm, pulling her close. He forced his mouth on hers as he jammed his hand over her breast. After a few seconds, he pushed her away.

"Unfortunately, I have to eat and too much work to do. But maybe next time." He laughed as she hurried out of the room, fixing her blouse.

# THREE

Liz climbed inside the four-horse carriage, painted bright red and yellow. Besides the driver, two guards rode at the back of the carriage with two more horsemen following. Liz sat on the black leather seats, padded with horsehair and cotton. Despite the cushioning, her body was jolted as the horses pulled the carriage over the rutted road.

The people of Horstruff stopped and stared at the carriage rolling by, recognizing it from Lord Perry's castle. Some of the common folk waved at the occupants hidden behind the dark lace curtains, while those on the street hurried to get out of the way.

The carriage rumbled down the street and out of the main town, turning down a well used road until it arrived at a private road that led to Sir Anthony Graham's castle. The driver stopped at the front of the castle where servants descended from two pairs of large doors. The castle was relatively new, less than two hundred years old, and was one of the largest castles in Horstruff. It was not as large as Lord Perry's, but did rival the castle of his father, Lord Kevin Graham.

The carriage door opened, and two male servants lent a hand on either side of Liz to assist her exit. She stepped forward, turning her head to look at the massive castle built with light and dark grey marble. She thought the hanging vines helped make the Graham castle an impressive sight.

She entered the foyer, where another male servant escorted her to a sitting room. A female servant immediately followed with a tray full of an assortment of drinks and pastries. As Liz selected a chair, another servant hurried forward to fluff the pillows behind her.

Liz tried to relax with a cup of tea, but she found that with every movement she was being watched. If she set the cup down, it was immediately refilled. She felt relieved when Nicole came into the room.

"How are you, Liz? It's so nice seeing you again." Nicole walked over to her with open arms.

Liz exchanged a hug and looked at her again, admiring her dark green dress with a deep V neckline. Like her own dress, the waist was pulled tight by a series of laces in the back. "You're looking very nice, Nicole. Life in a castle must agree with you."

Nicole smiled. "There are certainly advantages to living here. But…" she turned to look at the servants around them, "…it can be a little overwhelming."

"I see what you mean." Liz thought of her own quiet life she once had on Earth in Ballymiller. "But don't worry. Tonight you'll be able to relax."

"Yes, thank you for the invite. I haven't been able to garner many friends since I've moved in here. I guess that'll take a bit of time for the other ladies to accept me."

"I'm sure in time you'll have all kinds of new friends."

"Thanks, Liz. Could you give me a few minutes? I want to check on a couple of things before we leave. Why don't you say hello to Anthony? I think he said something about being in the central courtyard." She turned to one of the servants. "Grace, will you take Lady Elizabeth to see Sir Anthony?"

Liz followed Grace down a long hallway, decorated with coloured cloths and paintings, and to a second hallway that led to a courtyard. She saw several servants watching two combatants wield wood swords at each other. Both were without their shirts, their skin gleaming with moisture.

Liz walked across the manicured lawn. When she reached just past the servants, she called out, "Tony!"

One of the men turned his mouth open. Then a grin appeared on his face. "Liz! What a wonderful surprise." He dropped his sword and marched over to her.

Liz looked at him advance, staring at the muscles across his chest and shoulders. She looked at his high leather boots, military style of pants and back at his bare chest. When he stood in front of her, she grabbed his shoulders and gave him a kiss on his cheek. "Tony, it's so good to see you again."

"It's been too long." He turned to the servants. "Go. Practice is over."

"Playing with swords?"

He laughed. "You ignore my given name and insult my preparation for a possible deadly fight." He gestured toward a table holding refreshments.

She slipped a hand under his arm, finding his skin hot and damp. "Are you doing well, Tony? Happily married?"

He looked at her. "Yes and yes, but I often think of the time we spent together. I was very happy then too."

"Don't be silly. You were frustrated looking after the stables and having lost your title back then."

He took a long drink of water from a goblet on the table.

"Thirsty work I see."

"If I'm not tired after practice, then it wasn't worthwhile doing. Are you here to take Lady Nicole to Lord Troy's castle? I understand it's some sort of a private party."

"Just for women. We're going to have an all night party." She grinned.

"Pity for all the men." He stepped in front of her and placed a hand on her waist. "I truly miss you."

She took a half step back. "Tony, I miss you too, but…"

He pulled her close to him, leaning into her.

Liz lifted her hands, pushing them against his chest. "Tony, you mustn't."

He pressed his lips toward her.

For a moment, Liz turned her head away, before returning to face him. She pushed her lips against his, slipping her hands behind his neck. She broke apart from him again and lowered her head. "Tony, you have a wife. Behave yourself."

"I can't help myself when I'm near you."

She twisted out of his grasp. "I like you too, but we can't do this. Walk me back. I have to meet up with Nicole."

He put on his shirt and showed her the way back to the sitting room. "I'm sorry if I made you feel uncomfortable."

"Well actually you made me feel good, but we can't do that anymore. Here's Nicole, act proper."

Nicole smiled at Liz and gave Anthony a kiss. "I'm ready, let's go."

———

"So are you and Jon planning the big wedding? How's it going?"

Liz looked at Nicole sitting across in the carriage. "He's planning a battle and I'm planning the wedding." She grinned. "I think he's having more fun."

"Men do like to fight."

"How're things with Anthony?"

"Really good. He's treating me really well."

"I guess he'll be doing more sword practicing while you're away."

"He does keep himself in shape that way. I just wish all the women at the castle didn't find him so interesting. I'm guessing he has a couple of mistresses."

"Mistresses? Are you sure?"

"Of course. He's rich, good looking and has power. All these lords and high-ranking sirs have a woman or two on the side."

"Really? Have you talked to him about it?"

"What good would that do me? If he does, I'd rather not know. It's not as if I could do anything about it if he does. I'm not about to leave the comfort of being a lady of the court and end up back on the street. If I walk away, I walk away with nothing."

"That's horrible."

"It is what it is." She smiled. "I have a good life now. I'm not going to jeopardize it over some tart."

Liz thought about Jon alone at Lord Perry's castle.

Nicole spoke, as if she was reading her mind. "Jon is the exception, of course. He, of all the men I know, wouldn't stray."

Liz breathed a sigh of relief. "Thanks for saying that. I seem to be out my element here in Domum. Tell me more about what's going on in your life."

# FOUR

"Sir Nathan." Jon looked up as the big black man entered the library. Nathan favoured him with one of his rare smiles. "Hello, Sir Jon. How you be?"

Jon swept a hand toward the map on the table. "I'm getting a headache trying to work out a battle strategy."

Nathan shook his head. "I can't help you much there. I'm more for doing the battle plan on the field than on a table." He moved lightly for a big man as he walked over to the table. "The trouble in planning a battle on paper is you can't see what the enemy is really doing. Who knows how they have their maps drawn out?"

"That's one of the problems I'm dealing with." Jon gave a small sigh. "Also I want to make sure my decisions are not going to put our men in a bad position. I have their lives to consider here."

"Thanks for saying that. I can tell you, as a man fighting for his life in the battlefield, we always hope that those safely within the castle are not just tossing us to the wolves to get a worthless piece of turf."

"I hope I can earn the trust of the men in the battlefield."

Nathan nodded." You have mine, Sir Jon, but then I know you. I suppose the men will in time learn to believe in your leadership as well."

"Thank you, Nathan. I do understand that the common man must wonder who this Sir Jon is and why I'm planning this battle."

"You're a very smart man, Sir Jon, and that was why you were chosen for this task." Nathan turned to leave. "I understand what you said, Sir

Jon. Now it would help the men's confidence greatly if your title was that of a Lord." Nathan gave him a smile and a wink. "Time for me to get some food in my belly. We'll talk later."

———

Jon scribed some lines on his map and pondered the possibilities of the latest fictitious battle. *This is like an elaborate chess game. If they do this, what do I do? If I attack here, how will they respond?* He shook his head and pursed his lips. *If I was a warrior, would I trust a Sir Jon to make the right decisions for a battle? Confidence is as important as anything when it comes to a battle.*

"Sir Jon." The short, middle age servant waited until Jon looked at him. "Lord Perry and Lord Kevin Graham are here to see you." The servant gave a slow bow and backed away from the doorway.

Lord Perry stepped forward, grinning. "How are you doing, Sir Jon?"

"Fine, thank you." He looked over at the older, slim gentleman standing by Lord Perry. "It's nice to see you again, Lord Kevin."

"The honour is mine, Sir Jon. I understand you have taken up with the task to formulate our battle plan."

Jon nodded. "More like struggling with our battle plans, I'm afraid. Perhaps I wasn't the best choice for this. I'm not too sure what I'm doing here."

Lord Kevin walked over to his map and briefly scanned it. "It looks like you've accomplished some work here. I will let you in on a little secret, Sir Jon, and I hope Lord Perry will forgive me for being frank." He paused a moment to take in a deep breath. "You see, the kingdom has been in trouble for some time. Lord Perry has done a remarkable job of shielding us from the decay that has occurred in other regions, but the fact is that King Charles is not the leader he once was.

"We hear reports of the king's soldiers taking the law into their own hands, setting up artificial tax collections or highway tolls, and collecting money for their own pockets. Lord Bennett, as insane as he was, might have toppled the king if it wasn't for the quick thinking of Lord Perry and your own courageous work. Now we have yet another challenge to the throne. It is sad and traitorous, but this is what we are dealing with. Unfortunately, this latest attack on the king may succeed. King Charles is weak, physically and mentally. His two sons do not have the intellect to lead and are capable only of sending out distress calls for help. This is despite having more men and horses that those attacking. Such is the state of our affairs.

Lord Kevin continued. "So when you were asked to help formulate a plan, there were several reasons for it. One is that we needed to have fresh look on how we developed our strategies. For too long we always planned battles the same way, but now our stubbornness is costing us dearly. What worked so well against gnants has not proved to be so effective against men."

Lord Perry added his thoughts. "Our soldiers are questioning the leadership, wondering if they are merely being sent to their deaths. When some of the better informed men learned of your involvement, there was a sense of optimism."

Jon raised his eyebrows. "Because of me?"

"Indeed." Lord Perry continued. "You see, you are from the Otherside and men who arrived from there are held in high esteem. It is a common belief that those who lived there have been educated in ways that cannot be duplicated here. You have a reputation of a dragon slayer and helping to defeat Lord Bennett. You have the respect of several gnants, and they do not extend that honour to many men."

Lord Kevin added, "Many men have confidence in you, Sir Jon, including the lords, that you will find a way to win the battles ahead."

"Thanks, I appreciate that. I'll do my best."

Lord Perry smiled. "We know that. However, there has been a discussion among the lords regarding your status. It has been suggested that your present title of Sir Jon doesn't properly reflect your standing or responsibility. Therefore I am pleased to inform you that you have gained the title of Lord Jon."

Jon's jaw dropped. "Are you serious? Me, a Lord?"

"Quite. There will be a formal induction ceremony in three day's time, but in the meantime, you will have to do with the title of Sir Jon."

Lord Perry turned to leave with Lord Kevin but stopped at the door. "Oh, one more thing. A lord should have his own residence. You will be taking over the former Lord Bennett's castle."

# FIVE

L iz entered Lord Troy's castle with Nicole. Patricia, Lord Troy's wife, greeted them warmly at the entrance. As they were led down a hallway, Liz marvelled at how many paintings and statues Lord Troy managed to squeeze along the walls. Numerous alcoves held statues while paintings covered most of the stone walls. The head of a dragon mounted above one of the entrances startled her for a moment before she realized it was inanimate.

Liz admired Patricia's casual long white dressing gown with yellow trim. Although it was a bit transparent, it suited her. The two servant girls waiting at attention at the end of the hallway wore the traditional long skirts, and nothing else.

Patricia spoke as they walked. "There is so much to do here. We had to hire three girls for the castle and two men for the stables. One of the girls is also responsible for looking after Talker and Hairy. They're still acclimatizing to our world, but at least they seem content being here." Patricia referred to the two gnants that had been transported to Domum just before their world disappeared. "Here are your rooms. I'll let you both freshen up and we can get together with the other ladies later. In the closet there are some gowns you can change into to be more comfortable. Do you need help dressing?"

"No, I prefer to do that myself." Liz entered the spacious room and was drawn to the open French doors that led to the balcony. She walked across and stood by the stone rail to gaze at the manicured flowered garden beyond and breathed in the perfumed air.

After a few minutes she returned to the closet and chose a light blue, lacy gown. Then she began the process of undressing, working the tied laces at her back until they were loose. The dress finally came off and she took in her first deep breath since putting on the dress. She removed the petticoat and, after a moment of hesitation, her panties. *Maybe my Grammy would find these lacy things pretty, but these are big enough to use as a bedspread.*

She put on her gown and studied herself in the mirror. Liz worked her hair with a brush and satisfied with the result left the room. A few steps took her to another oak door, and she knocked.

"Nicole, are you ready yet?"

Nicole called out. "Come on in. I'm just doing up this robe."

Liz entered and looked at the sheer white robe Nicole was tying up. "Wow and I thought my gown was revealing."

Nicole blushed a bit. "Yeah, none of these seem to offer much coverage. I guess the tradition at Lord Troy's castle continues." She looked at Liz's gown. "That's pretty. Too bad there aren't any men here, other than Lord Troy, to enjoy the view." She laughed.

They walked together to a second floor lounge, where Patricia sat with several women. Liz recognized Angela, Alicia, Lena, Gwyneth and Juliana as part of the castle's servants, although it was rare for any of them to do hard work. Their main requirement was to look pretty and to make sure visitors, especially men, were taken care of. They sat on various large chairs in the centre of the room.

Lord Troy was standing by Patricia as he held a glass of red wine. There were two more women serving drinks, wearing long dresses that were cut high on the hip on one side and bare on the other side from the shoulder to the waist. Liz gazed at the women and smiled. *I'm glad I insisted Jon move to Lord Perry's castle. Despite what Nicole said that he was completely trustworthy, there is no need to lead him to temptation with naked females. The style of dress Lord Troy insisted on the servants wearing in his castle doesn't seem to be very functional.*

Lord Troy gave a small bow as he turned his attention to Liz and Nicole. "It is so nice to see you two again, Lady Elizabeth and Lady Nicole. Now that you have arrived, I will take my leave." He bent down and kissed Patricia, took a final drink of his wine and marched out of the room.

After Liz settled in a cushioned chair, Patricia introduced the two servers.

"This is Isabel and Rose." She first looked at the dark hair petite woman and then at a taller red head. "Maureen is working in the kitchen right now, preparing snacks."

Patricia grinned after Lord Troy disappeared. "He decided to travel around the town again. After being held hostage in the castle for many years, he is finally glad to be able to explore the outside world. That means we ladies have the castle to ourselves, except for the two stable hands working out in the back. By the way they're definitely worthwhile taking a peek at."

Liz sipped her wine, listening to the chatter around her. Angela was complaining that since they arrived on Domum, she had seen very little of Madoc.

"It's ridiculous. Gone at the crack of dawn and only returns late at night. He even didn't come home one night."

Juliana smiled. "Are you sure he doesn't have a mistress on the side?"

"If he does, she sure has him tired. No, he says he's working with Lord Perry to develop spells for protecting the kingdom from black magic. I just want to have more time with him."

Patricia reached over and patted her arm. "This is a time of war, and we have to understand our men have to prepare for battle. Their lives, and ours, depend on them being ready."

Angela gave a small smile. "I know. But I would have preferred it if he was still exiled on Earth. We would both be safe there."

"I understand how you feel. But we need Council Madoc and Sir Jon to help us. Right now it does not look good for King Charles." Patricia stood. "Why don't we go for a walk in the garden? That will help to lighten our spirits."

Liz followed the rest out of the castle and to the flower gardens. She caught up to Patricia along one of the small pathways that weaved among the potted plants, fountains and flowers. "Can I ask you a personal question, Patricia?"

"Of course." She smiled and took Liz's hand.

"Are you concerned about Lord Troy having all these beautiful and half naked women around him?"

"Not really. I understand he is a man after all, and before we married, he had taken all of them to bed at various times. But now I'm the only one who sleeps in his chambers at night. I suspect that during the day he may wander, but I own his heart."

"Nicole was telling me that lords often have mistresses, but there is nothing the wife can do about it."

"I suppose that is true. I know little of Earth and its customs, but on Domum women have little in the way of power except through their husbands. If you are married to a lord, then you have wealth and power. Unfortunately a lot of pretty women will tempt men of higher social standings to improve their own lives. The best way for a lady to make sure her man doesn't stray too far is to keep him occupied."

"I'm worried about Jon looking around."

"Do you have any reason to believe he would?"

Liz sighed. "When I first met Jon, he had another girlfriend. I was the other woman."

"When Jon was here the first time, when he was trying to get back to Earth and he didn't know if he would ever see you again, he didn't take advantage of the opportunity. He could have had any of the women here in the castle and he also refused Nicole's advances as well."

"Nicole, she tried to have him?"

"Don't get mad at her. She didn't know you at the time. But, yes, she made it plain he could have her at anytime. He was a gentleman about it but turned her down because of his commitment to you."

"Thanks, I feel better now. So how long have you known Troy? Did you fall in love with him right away?"

Patricia laughed. "Oh no, it definitely was not love at first sight. I was bought at the labour house and was required to do five years of service for him. At that time, I had a quick temper and often got in trouble with him for not doing my work. He had a lot of patience and rarely did he lose his temper with me. He offered to send me back to the labour house if I didn't like it here, but I knew this was as good as I was going to get. I have had experience in taverns and other homes and knew I was lucky to be here. So he would punish me by sending me to the dungeon until I learned my lesson."

"A dungeon? He sent you to the dungeon?"

"More than once. Come, I'll show you. It's not as bad as it sounds." Liz followed Patricia back into the castle and along a curved hallway. They reached an open arched doorway where Patricia took a lighted torch from a mounted wall bracket. She led the way down a set of stone spiral stairs.

Liz expected there to be only the gloom of a dirty dungeon, but as they reached the bottom of the stairs, she noticed there was light present. It was a soft light that reflected off the walls and floor, revealing an empty room with a series of cells along one wall.

Liz looked into one of the cells, through the iron bars. Light streamed in from an open slot high above in the centre of the cell, revealing a small bed made of wood planks.

"The light comes from chutes from the outside, so we don't always need a torch."

Liz nodded. "I expected this to be dark and dirty."

"We have the cells cleaned regularly, though it's pretty rare we use them."

"Except for you."

"Yes, well, I guess I deserved it."

"Because you didn't obey his every whim?"

Patricia smiled. "He owned me. He had the right to do what he wanted. He never whipped me, which is what some slaves receive from their owners for the littlest mistake. You have to understand that once someone gets sold in the labour house, they lose their freedom completely for five or more years. I made a serious mistake that got me into trouble and ended up in front of a judge. I was fortunate Troy purchased me. I could have ended up working in a tavern or worse."

"I guess that's some consolation. So Troy never actually hit you?"

"Well, I did get the occasional spanking, but it wasn't really a punishment." She blushed.

Liz looked at the far wall that held chains dangling from hooks and whips hanging from wooden brackets. "What about those?"

"Those have been there forever. The most Troy ever did was make some of us wear a slave collar for a day so that we understood what it could be like. He never hurt any of us."

Liz walked over to whips hanging on the wall. She touched one and found the leather hard and cracked from age.

Liz returned with Patricia to the upper level. Liz recalled her own experience when she first arrived at Domum and said she had been lucky to have been purchased by Lord Rosemore's family.

"I guess I'll never get used to ways of Domum, with people being owned and women depending on their husbands to achieve social standings. I like Domum to visit, but I wouldn't want to live here permanently."

Patricia looked at her carefully. "What if Jon wants to stay here?"

Liz shook her head. "No, he wants to live on Earth with me."

"He told you that?"

"Well, maybe in not so many words. But why would he want to live here? Earth is his home."

"I suppose you know him best. It's just that men are wanderers and believe they can have more than one home." She shrugged her shoulders. "Sorry, I was just curious."

# SIX

Freeman Colin Ferguson patted the horse's flank as he went by. "That's it for today. Maybe tomorrow we'll fit you with new shoes."

He strolled past the royal secondary stables for King Charles' kingdom, limping slightly from a broken leg that had never healed properly. Tall, but with a pronounced stomach on otherwise average frame, Colin had two main occupations. The first was taking care of the king's horses. The second was going to his favourite watering hole and speaking to those around him, enlightening them of his opinions. Two blocks past the stables placed him at the outskirts of the marketplace where taverns did a reasonable business from travellers and the local population.

He entered the Dragon's Egg tavern, found his preferred table where three of his friends already were drinking ale.

"How are you doing, lads?" He didn't wait for nods of acknowledgement before launching into a topic. "Have you heard the latest about the Princes?" He took a long swallow of the ale placed in front of him, the young serving wench not needing to ask what he wanted. She stood close by to capture the latest news.

He lowered his voice slightly as it was not wise to make disparaging remarks about the royal family. "It seems the young men were having a dispute about who got to ride Rex, the white stallion. It was an embarrassment. They didn't fight like men but rather like princesses, pushing and calling each other names. This is while their father is barely able to sit up straight in his chair. King Charles must be wondering which one of his fine sons is going to be the best to take over when he's gone. Technically Morley, being the oldest, will be chosen. But Harris, even though he is two years younger, has more brains." Colin glanced around the table. "But his old man can't stomach Harris's preference for young boys."

The server gave a small gasp and hurried off to spread the gossip.

Smitty, the burly blacksmith, nodded. "It ain't no good at all. It don't matter to me much whether it's the king or one of the princes, but I wish someone would get me some decent metal to work with. They want a hundred new swords but give me enough to make only half that. Low grade stuff to boot."

Colin tightened his jaw and leaned forward. Jabbing a finger on the table, he hissed, "I tell you lads, and you can mark my words, this kingdom is like a fat cat that had it easy too long. Someone is going to figure out she don't know how to fight no more. We're ripe for the pickings, I tell you."

Percy, who owned a shop in the centre of town, opened his mouth but then closed it, finding that this time there wasn't any argument on what Colin said.

———

Daniel swung the axe one last time at a log stump and dropped it by the pile of wood. He took a deep breath and wiped the sweat from his forehead as he stared off to the horizon. It was the direction of a full day's ride to Regius, where King Charles ruled, to the north and two hours ride to the west to the town of Treston. He wished he was a bigger man so he could handle the physical exertions of clearing land for crops better. He turned to Sarah's voice calling out at him.

"Twelve eggs! The hens laid twelve eggs today." She hurried carrying a dark brown wicker basket.

He grinned. "Food for the table and some to sell at the market." He watched her approach, her blonde hair glittering in the sunlight.

Sarah lifted the bottom of her grey skirt with one hand as she stepped over the uneven ground, smiling. Suddenly her smile disappeared, and he quickly turned to see six men ride up on horses, dust rolling behind them. He grabbed the axe again but wasn't sure what good it would do against them.

The horsemen quickly surrounded them, two of them with their swords drawn. One of the riders commanded, "They'll do. Bind them and let's be off."

Daniel stepped in front of Sarah. "Leave her alone I say!" He held up his axe in defiance.

A big, dark skinned man slipped off his horse. He laughed as he stood in front of Daniel. With his double-edged sword he swung down hard, shattering the axe handle in the middle.

Daniel looked in surprise at the useless axe handle, and suddenly a backhand across his jaw sent him toppling to the ground, landing him on his side. He moaned as he felt Sarah drop to her knees by his side, her hands on his face.

In a blurred vision he watched Sarah being hauled to her feet and a rope tied her hands behind her back. Next his hands were tied together behind him, and he was shoved to sit on the back of a horse behind another rider. He struggled to keep his balance as his head slowly cleared.

Daniel tried to look around but couldn't see Sarah, assuming she was somewhere behind him. Fear and anger raced around in his head, and he became increasingly frustrated as he rode to an unknown fate.

He watched as they were taken deep into the woods and to a large camp, full of horses and men. There was no doubt in his mind this was an army preparing for an attack. He was pulled off the horse and told to sit on the ground.

The sound of Sarah's voice, screaming to be let go caused him to turn. He saw her try to run toward him but was quickly grabbed by two men, one of whom slapped her in the face.

Daniel saw her swear at her attacker as she was gagged and dragged away to a far tree.

*What the hell do they want with us? Can I make a deal to protect her, get them to let her go?* He looked at the tall, chiselled-face guard standing next to him. "Can you tell me what's going to happen to us?"

The guard shook his head. "Just following orders." He looked quickly to his left and right and softened his voice. "Now you best be quiet."

Daniel sighed, surprised at the gentleness of the guard's voice, and looked over at Sarah's frightened face.

———

Sir Sadon grunted as he stepped out of his tent. "Where is he then?" he bellowed at the guard standing by a fire pit.

The guard quickly pointed in the direction of a young man sitting.

Even at thirty feet Sadon could see the sweat and fear on his face. "Bring him here then."

The prisoner was hauled to his feet by two guards. After being shoved over he was pushed to his knees in front of Sadon.

"I have your wife over there, and I have to say she is a very handsome prize indeed." He pointed at a gagged blonde sitting on the ground, her hands secured behind her back.

"Please don't hurt her. I'll do anything, just let her go."

"Of course you will, and here is what you're going to do."

The prisoner listened carefully to Sadon's demands.

"Do you understand?"

"Yes, sire."

Sir Sadon smirked. "Good." He turned to one of the guards. "Rough him up some, make him look like he just escaped from a battle and send him on his way." He walked back to his tent and turned to look at the woman, a smile creeping across his face.

Daniel looked at the back of the departing Sadon, loathing the man who would so casually take Sarah and himself as prisoners and use them like tools. Then he turned his attention to the tall guard who gave a small grimace.

"Sorry, you heard what Sir Sadon said. Nothing personal." He picked up a broken tree branch, hefted to test its weight and used it to beat Daniel.

Daniel tried to cover his head by rolling on the ground but soon was covered with cuts and bruises. Breathing hard, he was pulled to his feet and his hands freed.

"All right, on your way, you know what to do."

"Can I say goodbye to my wife?" He spat out blood from his mouth, guessing his nose might be broken.

The guard looked over at Sir Sadon's tent and nodded. "Be damn quick about it."

Daniel hurried over to Sarah. "I'll be back for you, I swear, and get you free." He kissed her over the gag, and he mounted the horse given to him. He looked one more time at her tear stained face and steered the horse out of the camp, followed by two horsemen.

# SEVEN

Liz leaned back against the cushion, exhaling as she observed the others around her. She wondered how Jon was doing and considered he was probably getting more work done than if she was around. *At least in Lord Perry's castle there aren't a bunch of underdressed, sex starved females to distract him.* She looked down at her gown. *I guess that includes me as well.* She looked over at the middle of the room where Lena had Gwyneth lying on her back. Gwyneth had her two hands pinned above her head by one of Lena's, giggling as Lena used a fingertip from her free hand to draw circles on her face. So far, their robes were closed but Liz considered it was only a matter of time before they came off. *They should just go and get a room.*

She looked at the table in the middle of the room with the metal box that contained the mood figurine. The figurine was inside the container, but with the lid open, some of its erotic effects reached out to the women. She was feeling the subtle pleasant influence and it concerned her of the eventual consequences. Liz took a drink of her wine and smiled as Patricia did an exaggerated dance around the floor. Her robe became undone during her dance as she whirled around.

Alicia and Juliana were sitting next to each other, looking comfortable with their close contact. Occasionally one would run a hand along the other's leg or arm. Juliana was bare from her neck to her waist from Alicia slowly undoing her gown. *I wish they would close that damn figurine box. She's starting to look good.*

"You okay?" Angela spoke softly as she stood by her side.

Liz looked up at Angela. "I'm fine."

Angela slowly dropped next to her. She gave Liz a careful smile. "You looked deep in thought."

"I guess I was thinking of Jon."

"Well, that's understandable. But we're here right now and you might as well enjoy the party."

"I am. It's fun watching Patricia dance."

"She has some good moves. Back home she would make a good stripper."

Liz laughed. "That's hardly an acceptable occupation for a lord's wife."

"Still, she flashes that robe open like she has done it before."

"I'm sure she has had some practice." Liz giggled.

Angela slowly slid her hand along Liz's arm, coming to a stop on her hand. "I guess they do things a bit different here on Domum, at least in Lord Troy's castle." She gave a very soft squeeze on her hand.

Liz responded with a squeeze back. She took another sip of her wine and licked her lips as she watched Patricia finish her dance. Patricia ended by sprawling on the floor, her robe open over her hips as she took in deep breaths of air. Liz felt Angela's fingertips slowly slide up her thigh over her gown and down again. The movement was repeated, and Angela carefully untied the ribbon at the waist.

Liz stopped breathing as Angela placed her hand on her bare leg. She turned to face Angela, not sure how to react to the advances that felt good but also wrong. Angela leaned toward her, her eyes closing as she tilted her head. After a moment's hesitation, Liz pressed forward, kissing Angela on the lips.

Angela gave a soft moan and ran her hand up Liz's arm to her shoulder. Her fingers grazed her neck and slowly dropped her hand down her chest, pushing apart the gown.

Liz felt Angela kiss her neck and move lower. She reached out and found Angela's hand.

"You want me to stop?" Angela spoke with a warm breath on her skin.

"Actually I was thinking that maybe we should go to one of the bedrooms."

Angela took her by the hand and led her out of the door.

———

"My head hurts." Angela groaned as she lay on the bed in one of Lord Troy's bedrooms. The morning light from the window hurt her eyes.

Liz turned to see Angela lying on her back with one hand on her forehead. "A bit too much wine last night?"

"I think so." Angela rolled out of bed and walked to the pitcher sitting on a table. She poured herself a tumbler of water and drank it slowly. She turned back to Liz. "Want some?"

Liz got out of bed. "Thanks, that looks good." She looked around the room. "What happened to my robe?" Last night came back to her in a fog. Her last recollection was going to bed with Angela, where they made a mutual decision just to go to sleep. She guessed that being out of the range of the mood figurine helped put their wants in check. She took the glass of water and quickly drained the contents.

"I don't think it made it this far." Angela walked over to the closet and pulled out a gown. "Here you go." As she handed her the gown she gave Liz a smile. "Look, about last night. I'm sorry if I pushed you and well…"

"It's all right. It takes two to tangle. But the next time I see them pulling out that mood figurine, I'm running for the hills."

"Agreed. Let's go and find some breakfast."

Liz followed her out of the bedroom after Angela found something to wear. *What is going on here? First, I get kissed by Tony, and then make out with another woman. And here I was worried about Jon getting into trouble.*

After breakfast, during which Lord Troy joined them, Liz reluctantly got dressed again. She needed to obtain help from Isabel to tie up the strings of her dress. *It's a good thing they have servants to help you dress in this world. I would never be able to tie this by myself. It sure is an extreme from last night with women partying naked to wearing three layers of clothing. This is hard to get used to.* Liz made her way downstairs to where Nicole was waiting in the lobby.

Nicole grinned at her. "Ready to go home and return to our quiet lives?"

"Now I am, but I'm glad for last night. It was fun."

"It was. The carriage is outside. Maybe we can have another girls' night out again soon."

"It would be nice." Liz stepped outside. "But now it's back to reality."

———

Liz smiled at Nicole sitting across from her in the carriage. "How come every party at Lord Troy's ends up with women losing their clothing?"

"It's because Lord Troy planned and designed his castle that way. He had been confined to his castle for a long time and used subtle, and not so subtle methods to get what he thought made a perfect world."

"He sure managed to get a collection of beautiful, young women to have around."

"As I mentioned earlier, that isn't uncommon for powerful men. They often have mistresses. Of course, the converse for poor men is true. They usually don't have any women at all."

"I think I definitely prefer Earth as far as relationships are concerned. More of one man for each woman, and one woman for each man."

Nicole smiled. "Here on Domum, we have more extremes between the wealthy and the poor than on Earth. So women on Earth don't have to rely so much on men for financial security. But remember, on both worlds women are attracted to powerful men. It's just that on Domum it is socially acceptable for such men to have a mistress or two. On Earth, they would have to be discrete about it."

"I guess it is what it is."

"Make the most of your time here. Jon certainly has adapted rather well to Domum. You have the benefits of being one of the wealthy here. You enjoy wearing the fancy dresses, right?"

"I do, but it is a pain putting them on."

"That's what the servants are for. You also have fancy balls you can attend, providing you can drag Jon away from his work. If he's too busy, you will have to find something to pass the time away."

"That's true." Liz blushed.

"Don't feel embarrassed what happened last night. We were just having fun. Of course when we do go to parties at Lord Troy's castle, we will have to keep what happens there to ourselves."

"What happens in Lord Troy's castle stays in Lord Troy's castle?"

Nicole grinned. "You got it."

# EIGHT

Daniel occasionally looked behind him to check if the two riders were still following him. He wasn't surprised to see they were still within sight and, as he urged his mount up a hill, he tried to formulate a plan. He had no doubt that as soon as he returned to Sadon's camp, Sarah and he would be killed, their usefulness at an end. He took another breath through his open mouth, his nose too plugged up from blood to take in enough air. Considering that Sadon would be preoccupied with the next part of his plan, he might be able to slip back to rescue Sarah. Sneaking into the camp would be dangerous and not of good odds, but he wasn't going to leave Sarah by herself.

At last a road appeared that made travel easier and he took the opportunity to relax a bit as the horse made its way toward the town.

As the horse and carriage traffic increased, Daniel could make out Regius, the town that surrounded King Charles' castle. He followed the wide, main road that went through the centre of town and straight to the open gates of the castle courtyard. He gazed at the high walls that surrounded the courtyard and the castle, marked by towers at regular intervals. Daniel increased the speed of his horse, galloping into the courtyard. He knew that when the iron and wood gates were closed it would be a formidable fortress to attack.

His horse closed toward one of the guards that blocked the entrance to the castle itself. "Help me! There has been an attack on the village of Treston."

Daniel slid off his horse as the guard approached him.

"Speak. Who attacked? How many?" The tall guard challenged him with his spike pointed toward Daniel's chest.

"I did not recognize their banner. There were perhaps a hundred, maybe more, horses and men. They took over the town, killing anyone who opposed them. I managed to escape after they beat me. Please, you must send help right away."

"Stay here, I will get someone."

Daniel expected the king would send out men right away for the rescue, but instead he had to repeat his story to increasing ranks before he reached a nobleman, who pondered the circumstances for several minutes. Daniel finally heard him send down an order for two hundred men and horses to take care of the situation.

Daniel was ignored after that, without even a thank you for his warning. He took a long drink of water and stole an apple from a table as he left the courtyard. He waited until after the king's men rode out, their red, gold, and black banner flying high above the lead horse.

He was told to return to camp immediately after delivering his message. But Daniel saw little advantage in doing so. It was apparent to him the attack on the king's men would leave the camp largely deserted. It would be the only opportunity for him to try to rescue Sarah. He hoped he wouldn't be too late.

———

The two riders that had followed him to Regius didn't wait for him. As soon as they saw the banner on the lead horseman, they turned their mounts and headed back to camp at high speed.

At Sir Sadon's main camp, a guard standing at the entrance of the tent looked up as the two riders hurried over.

"Tell Sir Sadon that the king has sent riders, perhaps a couple of hundred horsemen." One of the riders shouted out before he dismounted from his horse.

The guard nodded. "Wait here, he has that woman with him." He opened the tent flap and called inside. "Sir Sadon, the king's men are on their way to Treston."

A curse issued from inside the tent, and Sadon shouted. "Get the men on horses! We have to move quickly."

The camp suddenly came alive as men hurried to their horses. Sadon mounted his horse and yelled at a guard climbing on a horse, "Check on that whore in my tent. If she's still alive, clean her up. If she's dead, dispose of her."

The chiselled-faced man frowned. "Yes, sire." Sir Gavin slipped off his horse and turned to the tent. *There must be a special place in hell reserved for him, that fat bastard.*

Sir Gavin walked back to the tent and looked inside. Taking a deep breath, he approached the blood-stained body lying curled up naked on the floor. At first, he thought she was dead, but when he touched her shoulder, a shudder went through her.

"Tis all right, miss. I won't hurt you." He took a blanket to cover her and poured a cup full of wine. He kneeled next to her. "Drink this now." He spoke as gently as he could.

As he watched her try to sit up and take the offered drink, he wondered if he was really helping her. *I'm helping her to get better so he can use her again. She would be better off dead now. God help me, this is the devil's doing.*

"Rest now, I'll check on you soon." He left the tent, looking for any signs of trouble outside. Her husband, it struck him, was a man who would do anything to save her. Despite the near impossibility of rescuing his wife from a military camp, Sir Gavin considered the small man would certainly try.

———

Daniel crept through the woods, leaving his horse a safe distance from camp. He moved to the edge of the camp and past the first empty tents. A few armed men, cooks, and servants moved lazily about. He hid in tents whenever he heard anyone approach as he carefully moved to where he last saw Sarah. At last, he saw the large tent of Sadon's and waited at the edge of a supply tent until it was clear. Daniel looked at the spot where Sarah was sitting the last time he saw her, but as he suspected she had been moved. He wondered if she had been taken to Sadon's tent or one of the others and pondered his next move when he heard a sound behind him.

Daniel turned to see a sword pointed at him, the same guard who had beat him last time.

The man scowled at him. "You really do have more guts than brains." He waved the sword at the direction of Sadon's tent. "March over there."

Daniel put his hand on the knife tucked into his belt but reconsidered. There was little point in entertaining the suggestion that he could somehow overcome the guard with such a small weapon. He may die soon, but at least there was a chance he might see Sarah again or at least learn of her fate.

He entered the tent and saw the brown blanket covering a body, the slow rise and fall indicating the person was asleep.

"Sarah?"

"It is her. Wake her while you still have time."

Daniel looked at the guard who stood at the entrance with his sword lowered and hurried over to Sarah.

"My love, what have they done to you?"

———

Terran urged his horse forward. He knew the beast was struggling, injured by an arrow sunk into its flank. He understood how much it must distress the horse. He, too, had an arrow sticking out from his thigh. Terran had broken the arrow shaft off but left the head imbedded, fearing the removal would cause even more blood to come out of the wound.

He was near the end of the king's horsemen when they were attacked. The ambush was sudden and had caught the unit off guard. The battle was short, as first arrows poured from two sides of the line of the king's soldiers and during the panic from a full fledge attack at the front. Terran had at first managed to escape during the confusion and headed back to Regius and to the king to warn of the attack, but soon was aware of several horsemen pursuing him.

He passed the first small farms that lined the main road to Regius and considered going to one of the homes for refuge. His horse was barely doing more than a trot and he realized it was doubtful it would last the journey without rest if it survived at all. He turned back to look for the enemy when the short shaft from a crossbow punctured his side. He clutched at his ribs as he fell off his horse, moaning as he hit the hard ground.

Terran tried to crawl away. He looked back just in time to see one of the men dismount from his horse and walk toward him with the sword raised. He froze on the spot, watching death approach. It was the last he was to see.

———

Daniel stared at the bruised face of Sarah, one eye swollen and closed. She gave a meagre smile.

"I knew you would return."

"Don't speak. We need to get you out of here."

The guard walked over and handed Daniel her torn dress. "Put this on her and be quick."

Daniel put the garment on her as fast as he could. Sarah was scarcely able to help him, barely able to move her limbs.

The guard looked outside of the tent and returned. "Where did you leave your horse?"

"Up in the woods, north of the supply tent."

"Go there. I'll bring your wife to you."

Daniel looked at Sarah and turned to the guard, a question on his lips.

"You'll never get her past the others in camp. Leave that to me. Now go before time goes against us." He looked around the tent for a moment. "Best grab that sword sitting in the corner. You may need it later."

Daniel nodded, giving Sarah a quick kiss before hurrying out of the tent.

Sir Gavin looked at Sarah, who stared back at him with her one good eye. "Miss, you look half dead already, which is a good thing. I'm going to haul you out of here as if you were dead. Don't do anything, act like you are dead or surely you will be."

She slowly nodded and whispered, "I can do that."

He bent down, lifting her to a standing position and put her over his shoulder. "Okay now, here we go." He strode out of the tent and began to walk straight toward the edge of the camp. Near one of the tents, a couple of men were chopping wood for a fire pit, and he slowed down to peer at their work.

"Good, we'll need a fire for the men when we get back. They'll be hungry."

"What's with her?"

Sir Gavin lowered his voice. "Our great leader worked her a bit too much. Died when I tried to give her a drink. Bloody waste if you ask me. I would have wanted her all night."

One of the other men retorted. "Probably better for her this way. All night with him would be hell."

Sir Gavin began walking away. "I'll make sure her body is far enough away so it don't draw any scavengers here."

When he reached the edge of the woods, he spoke softly. "Are you all right? We're almost clear."

"I'm okay." Her voice came out in a ragged whisper.

The guard puffed as he climbed a small hill and spotted Daniel and his horse. "Almost there, miss."

Daniel hurried from his horse to take Sarah from the guard, but the guard held up his free hand. "Save your strength, lad, you're going to need all of it later." The guard continued to carry her and lifted Sarah onto the horse's back.

"I suggest you lead the horse so it don't get tired out by having two riders. Don't go on the main road to Reguis, avoid that at all costs. I suggest you make your way out of this area altogether, maybe head toward Horstruff. Lord Perry keeps that kingdom safe, at least for now." He reached into his pocket and pulled out a few coins. "Take these. You will need to buy her food soon."

"Thank you, but why are you doing this?"

Sir Gavin smiled. "The chances of me surviving these battles are not great. If I should perish, maybe this good deed will let me go through heaven's door."

Sarah spoke, a whisper against the wind. "I will pray for your survival. What is your name?"

"Gavin. Now hurry before dark catches up with you."

# NINE

"I really think you need to get busy now with the preparation of your castle, Sir Jon." Lady Beatrice sat across from Jon in a tearoom at Lord Perry's castle, carefully taking a sip of tea. "The whole castle has been in a state of neglect since Lord Bennett disappeared, save for the area used for the administration of justice and some areas of the grounds."

"What do you suggest? I'm a bit busy with battle plans right now and Liz is away. Also, I'm not sure she would know much on how to get the castle up to standards."

"Of course, she wouldn't, and I know you're preoccupied with other matters. But if you allow me to take charge of this, I can get things up and running very quickly. Then I'll show Lady Elizabeth a few things because I'm sure she'll want to be in charge of the castle's upkeep as soon as possible."

"That sounds all right." Jon tried to look interested in the conversation as much as possible, although his mind was drifting to maps and battle plans.

"Good. I will use some of my staff and Lord Perry's to clean the castle and establish the grounds back to their earlier splendour. I can also go to the labour house and purchase some staff. Lady Elizabeth and you can add more staff at a later date. Speaking of Lady Elizabeth, I will work with her when she arrives here to discuss the décor. I'm sure she will want to add her own flair to the castle."

"I'm sure she will." Jon gave a smile, hoping his visit with her would soon be over.

Lady Beatrice continued. "Now, I must let you get back to your work and I need to see Lord Perry about some social engagements coming up."

Jon thanked her and after wishing her well, hurried back upstairs to work.

At one time, he would have objected to hiring help from the labour house, essentially making them slaves until their contract was satisfied. Jon later learned that anyone without a place to live or with financial means to show they were independent, were picked up by the king's guards. It meant the homeless were sent to the labour house, where an employer would agree to provide them with shelter and food in exchange for services. Those unable to work remained in prison until such time they could fend for themselves. Jon considered the labour house now to be a method to reduce the number of poor and homeless and that it served as a sort of social safety net.

Jon returned to the library, sighing as he stared at the map he was working on. He began to mark it with a soft piece of charcoal when a servant at the entrance interrupted him.

"Pardon me, Sir Jon, but Sir Keith is here to see you." The servant stepped aside, and Sir Keith entered the room.

"Hello, Sir Jon, hello." Sir Keith beamed a smile and immediately approached the desk where Jon was working. "How are you doing?" He kept his eyes focused on the desk.

"Fine, Sir Keith. What brings you here?" Jon thought Sir Keith looked a bit too eager to see his work.

"Well, I happened to hear that you were working a battle plan, and I thought I would lend you my assistance. I am familiar with much of the terrain around here." He placed a finger on part of the map and traced a path next to a charcoal line. "Is this where you are planning to send the king's men?"

"It's only a possibility."

"I should help you plan your strategy, Sir Jon." Sir Keith gave a nervous smile and wiped his forehead with his sleeve.

"That's okay, Sir Keith. I appreciate your offer, but I have to work things out myself, and Lord Perry will take a look at my efforts later."

"Very good, Sir Jon. It looks like you plan to meet an attack near the Soultaker Hills by the River Animus. A good choice as the terrain allows for an attack from more than one direction."

"Thanks, Sir Keith." Jon felt increasingly uncomfortable with the attention Sir Keith was giving to his map. "Perhaps we can go and have a drink in one of the lounges."

"Certainly Sir Jon, it will be nice to renew our acquaintance."

Jon led the way down one of the wide hallways in Lord Perry's castle. It hadn't taken him long to figure out how the castle was laid out. After getting lost once, he now knew where the various lounges and dining areas were located. Lord Perry employed an abundance of servants and besides the foremost dining area on the main floor, he maintained several smaller ones throughout the castle.

Jon gestured for Sir Keith to join him, choosing a table near a window. He glanced out to see another part of the castle, the tower rising several stories above. Down below a flower garden was being tended to by several gardeners.

After a server, a long-haired brunette with a full figure, brought them two tankards of ale, Jon smiled at Sir Keith. "To you, Sir Keith, and our adventure together."

"Thank you. We certainly did have quite the journey with many perils."

"But it all came out quite well. I managed to reconnect with Liz, and you won the heart of Lady Karla." Jon gave him a wink and encouraged Sir Keith to take another drink.

"Yes, well, for reasons unknown to me she seemed to find me desirable." He gave a grin. "As a matter of fact she is currently living in my castle."

"Well, Sir Keith, that is good news." He raised his glass and signalled the server to bring two more ales. The server brought the large ales over, smiling as she set them down.

"Did Lady Karla originally come from this area?"

"No, she is from quite a bit north of here. I can't recall if she told me the name of it or not." Sir Keith frowned as he tried to recall a name. "No matter. She didn't have a place to live in Horstruff, other than a rooming house, so I offered to let her stay at my place. I know it's not strictly proper for ladies to stay in a gentleman's residence, but it seemed to be the right thing to do. Nevertheless, I suspect tongues will be wagging that I have an unattached lady living with me." Sir Keith gave a bit of a smirk before he took another gulp of his ale.

"I suppose there will be some talk, especially since you are known as an adventurer, and by extension, a bit of a ladies' man."

Sir Keith's cheeks turned slightly pink. "I do try to be discrete in my dealings with the fair sex."

"Of course, but I imagine there are a few ladies wishing they had been a bit more open with their feelings toward you. I have seen eyes turn in your direction when they thought you weren't looking."

"Really? I wasn't aware...of all the circumstances." He took another drink as Jon signalled the server for another round.

Jon took a coin, a bronze fern, from his pocket and held it between his fingers. As she placed his new tankard in front of him, he pushed the coin into her hand. She looked at him puzzled. He turned his head near her ear and whispered, "Flirt with him. I need him to drink."

She smiled and placed another tankard in front of Sir Keith. "Now is a big man like you going to make me come back for that half empty tankard, or are you going to finish it now?" She rested a hand on his shoulder and fluttered her eyes at him.

"Oh, I wouldn't want to be the cause of you having to do extra work." He drained his tankard and handed it to her.

Jon looked at her retreating figure. "She seems to like you."

"Must be my aristocratic demeanour." Sir Keith smiled. "Some ladies find the polished gentleman interesting, rather than the uncouth attitude of some of the working men."

"Perhaps that is what Lady Karla finds so attractive about you. Have you discussed the possibility of marriage with Lady Karla?"

"The subject has been broached, but no decision has been made yet."

"I would have thought she would be eager to formalize your relationship with her."

"I'm sure she does. However, she said it would look awkward for her to move into my castle and suddenly announce our engagement. She felt that Lord Troy's marriage to that former sex slave was not appropriate at all, and all proper etiquette had been breached." He hiccupped. "She told me she wants to protect my reputation by taking a reasonable time before we become engaged."

The server returned with more ale, and Jon noticed the strings of the collar of her top had been loosened and had slipped lower. She gave Jon an ale first and bent toward Sir Keith to replace his tankard. "Do finish your ale, kind sir. I don't want to get in trouble for serving drink that isn't up to standard."

Sir Keith's eyes focused on an area lower than her neck and gave a crooked smile. "We wouldn't want you to get in any sort of trouble now, would we?"

She smiled back as she took his empty tankard, and slowly stood.

"Thank you. Unfortunately, I have a bit of a reputation for getting into trouble now and then."

Sir Keith watched her walk away. "Nice lass, if a bit foolish in her behaviour."

"I would imagine Lady Karla is more careful how she presents herself."

"Oh, yes, a proper lady at all times."

"She must see a kindred spirit in you."

Sir Keith nodded. "Yes, we both strive to stay above the common riffraff. Unfortunately, neither of us seemed to have been judged always fairly by others. As she said, some promotions are based on popularity and not on fairness."

"Promotions?"

"Well, for example, I am a Sir. But Lady Karla brought to my attention that I should have arisen to that of a Lord. She said she had no objection to Sir Anthony being promoted so quickly after being a mere stable hand, or your own adoption of the title of Sir and, if rumours are true, your subsequent rise to that of Lord Jon, but surely, I should have had that honour bestowed upon me by now. It seems the administration of Horstruff is jealous of my reputation and refuses to pass my name forward for endorsement. As a matter of fact, that is one reason why Lady Karla wants to wait before announcing any marriage plans. She feels that it might hinder my chances for becoming a lord if we were engaged. She is always thinking of what is best for me."

"How very gracious of her. She does seem to understand the politics of the kingdom rather well."

"Oh, she does indeed. She has talked about…well, I best not reveal all that we talk about."

Jon grinned. "Of course not. I better be getting back to work. Let me walk you to the main entrance.

As they left the lounge, he mouthed the words thank you to the server, who gave him a smile back.

Jon waved goodbye to Sir Keith and immediately made his way to where Lord Perry's office was located, on the next level.

Lord Perry rubbed his chin as he sat back in his chair, listening to Jon.

"As I said before, I can't be positive, but it might be Sir Keith is providing Sir Nolene with information about our defence and battle plans."

"You said he was unusually interested in your map markings? How much information did he gather from it?"

"He gathered a fair bit from that one map, but I had two other maps with different scenarios in them. So it's not as if our plans were laid bare before him. I'm quite sure that Lady Karla is pushing him to do this. She has him convinced that he was wrongly passed over for a promotion to Lord."

"I see. What are your recommendations? I can, of course, have him either exiled from Horstruff or put under the king's custody under the suspicion of treason. If proven he would be put to death. Lady Karla would suffer the same fate."

Jon shook his head. "We don't know for certain he is spying. However, why don't we restrict access to the office by posting a guard in front? We can restrict Sir Keith, or anyone else, from gathering any more information. If Sir Keith asks about the guard, we can simply inform him we are increasing security in Horstruff. Next, I can talk to Sir Keith about the map and imply that this is the plan we will be using."

Lord Perry steepled his hands together. "That sounds like a good strategy."

Jon nodded. "Lord Perry, I'm not trying to defend Sir Keith as he is clearly acting suspiciously. However, I believe Lady Karla is the instigator behind this and is using him to improve her own lot."

"Yes, at one time I believed Lady Karla was a woman merely trying to improve her position, but now it seems she is also power hungry. I am concerned she may be using some of the dark arts to gain what she desires."

———

"Did you find out any of the battle strategies?"

Sir Keith nodded. "I did obtain some information." He leaned forward to kiss Lady Karla, who turned her cheek toward him.

"Were you drinking?"

"Yes, just a pint or two. I had to loosen up Sir Jon's tongue"

She sighed. "I suggest you write out what you learned while the information is still fresh in your mind. Drinking in the afternoon is quite uncivilized."

"I agree with you, of course, but it was an effective way to get Sir Jon off his guard."

"Sir Jon, that impostor. It doesn't matter. He will have short rein as Lord Jon, along with those other fools that support King Charles."

"Now dear, they aren't all bad men."

"I'm not sure they aren't anything but men who stumbled their way to power and wealth. Now you better get to work."

"Yes, I will. Perhaps afterward you would like to have a rest with me." He gave her a smile.

She gave a small smile back. "I would Keith, but if I was to share your bed, I fear I would succumb to the physical pleasures I want from you. Then I would be at risk of getting pregnant and that would put you in a bad light. No, as much as I yearn for you, it is best we continue to sleep in separate bedrooms."

# TEN

Liz hurried up the stairs and hastened down the hall. She was surprised to see a guard standing by the door where Jon was working.

After a brief discussion with the guard, who sought Jon's permission, she was allowed to enter the room.

She gave him a hug and a long kiss.

"What was that for?" He acted surprised at the passion in her kiss.

"I just missed you, that's all." She smiled at him. *That and my guilty feelings.*

"I missed you too." He gave her a kiss back. "How was your party?"

"It was all right. Well, the girls can get a little wild."

"Yeah, I remember what Lord Troy's castle was like. As long as you had fun."

"I did, but after spending the night with women, I'm glad to have a man like you for my own."

Jon nodded. "That's good to know. I have some news."

She grinned. "What?"

"I am going to be promoted to Lord Jon and we will be living in what was Lord Bennett's castle." He stood there beaming at her.

Liz forced a smile on her lips. "That is wonderful to hear. Does that mean you're planning to stay on Domum longer?"

"Well, no. Not really. I'm still planning to stay long enough to draw up attack plans to help the soldiers defend Horstruff. But if we do decide to stay here longer, at least we will have a place of our own to stay in. By the way, Lady Beatrice is helping with the cleaning and decorating of the castle, so you should talk to her about what you want."

Liz gave Jon a kiss goodbye and went to their room to change her clothes. She didn't feel good about the latest news. *While it would be nice to have our own place, is Jon really saying we're going to be here much longer than defending Horstruff? Is he trying to set things up so we could live here permanently? In Lord Bennett's old castle no less. And that reminds me, I better find Lady Beatrice and see what is being done to the castle.*

Liz put on a yellow dress with a low-cut front that required help from a servant to tie up the back properly.

"You look very beautiful, Lady Elizabeth." The young servant admired her as she fluffed out the dress.

"Thank you." She liked how the dress fitted her, and the tight bodice lifted and made her breasts appear larger than they were. *I guess there is one benefit for having your lungs squeezed tight.* She looked in the full-length mirror. *I still would prefer jeans and a halter top though.*

Liz left her room and found Lady Beatrice having tea with Lord Perry. Despite the cluster of servants around them and being separated by a large table, they acted as if they were alone sitting across at a small table and ready to hold hands.

"Lord Perry, Lady Beatrice. I'm sorry to interrupt."

Lord Perry gave her a grin. "Not at all. Please, will you join us for a bite to eat and some tea?"

Two servants rushed to the table, producing another setting in seconds. A third servant held out the chair for her. Liz soon had a teacup in her hand and chatted with her hosts. She noticed Lady Beatrice had her hair done carefully and her dress had glittering colours set inside blue fabric. She had a larger than average body but compared to Lord Perry appeared small. After a few minutes Lord Perry stood.

"Do excuse me, ladies. I have much work to do." He smiled as he spoke to Lady Beatrice. "I will be seeing you later this evening, my love."

After he left, Lady Beatrice asked for a bottle of wine and fresh glasses for their table. She waited for the last servant to carry away the tableware.

"It is so much easier to gossip when the help aren't listening and spreading every word around faster than the wind."

Liz laughed. "So true."

"Now how is your stay here so far?"

"Good, but I'm concerned Jon wants to live here. I like it here, but I have a life on Earth that I want to return to."

"I understand. A man who is given the responsibilities like Lord Jon will feel very powerful indeed. Servants appear at the snap of his finger with women smiling and flirting with him. That would be difficult for anyone to give up."

"True, but if he wants me, then he must be prepared to return to Earth before too long."

"Good for you to want to have your own destiny, but if I were you, I would be very careful about giving him an ultimatum. He wouldn't be lonely here long."

Liz took a drink as she thought about what Lady Beatrice said. She began to worry.

"I didn't mean to upset you dear. I just wanted you to be aware of how others perceive Sir Jon. Now, I hear you were at Lord Troy's castle."

Liz smiled. "Yes, I attended a ladies' only party. I knew a few of the ladies from the first time I was on Domum and it was nice to renew friendships."

Lady Beatrice agreed. "It is fun to spend time there." She gave a smile as she lowered her voice. "Every so often it is nice to get out of these confining dresses and relax wearing next to nothing, have a few drinks and talk about nothing with the other ladies. Of course, when they bring out that nasty mood figurine, things can get a bit out of hand."

Liz gave a small laugh. "When we woke up the next morning without the influence of the mood figurine and wine, we wondered what we had done."

Lady Beatrice grinned. "We just have to keep such information away from the men, or they'll want to join us."

"Has Lord Troy always been known for the parties at his castle?"

"As long as I can remember. When he throws a party, it is quite the event. Everyone wants to attend. The women have new dresses made, each trying to outdo their outfits worn the time before and each other. It is amazing how much women are willing to flaunt themselves. Then of course, he has these half naked females serving drinks. It makes for a very interesting evening."

"Doesn't Lord Troy get into trouble for making the women go around undressed like that?"

"Well dear, it is simply the case that some are horrified by it, but others wish it was more common. It's not illegal and certainly no one of importance has told him he should stop. Things may change now that he is married. I would imagine Lady Patricia will want to reduce that amount of temptation for her husband."

"I just find it odd that he can buy these women as sex slaves."

"Lord Troy is at least open about what he wants them for. I'm not condoning his appetite for young ladies, but he was the first lord to do away with collars and other signs of slavery. He also refused to use corporal punishment as a form of discipline. Other lords began to follow his example, and while there are a few lords who like to have their slaves identified as such, it's now a waning practice."

Liz smiled. "So you're saying he really is a good man?"

Lady Beatrice smiled. "I will say that. Now let us finish with our wine. We have some planning to do."

# PART TWO

*Now I know what the devil looks like when he's unhappy.*

# ELEVEN

Sir Sadon dropped off his horse and made his way back to his tent. He paused to look at Gavin, expecting an answer to an unspoken question.

"Sorry, sire. She passed away as I tried to make her drink." He looked at Sadon, noting that neither he nor his horse showed any sign he had been at a battle unlike the men around him.

"Damn. I thought the bitch was tougher than that. What about her husband?"

"He never came back, the coward. Probably still riding with his tail between his legs."

"I would prefer it if he was dead."

"It's a fool's errand to try to find him. I doubt he can cause us any trouble."

"All right. Get the men ready to ride tomorrow evening. Now I'm hungry, get me food and drink."

Gavin nodded and set out to find enough food for the two men.

———

The morning light showed the camp bustling with activity in preparation for battle. Sadon spat on the ground as he left his tent. He walked toward the centre of the camp and noticed Gavin putting a saddle on a horse close by. "Make sure my tent and belongings are packed. I'm going to get some breakfast."

"Yes, sire." Gavin frowned as he finished with Sadon's horse. A few minutes later, he enlisted help to pack Sadon's belongings.

"How did the battle go?" Gavin asked one of the men who had gone with Sadon on yesterday's fight.

"Not much of a battle, if that's what you want to call it. The ambush went well. The poor bastards never knew what was going on until it was too late. They tried to surrender, but Sir Sadon ordered them all killed. There is no honour in killing unarmed men." He looked at Gavin with irritation rising in his voice. "We even had to chase down those who tried to escape. It doesn't feel good killing the king's men that way, I'll tell you."

"We are but soldiers following orders. Save your anger for the next battle." Gavin gave him a stern look. "If Sir Sadon hears you talk that way you won't be in any more battles."

The other man nodded as he watched Gavin walk away with part of the tent's contents. *I wish he was leading this fight and not that pig Sadon.*

Gavin stomped on the packed ground, kicking at a rock along his path. He hated the position he was in. A few years ago, he had joined Lord Darius' guards and proven himself to be capable both as a fighter and a leader. As time went on, he became less enamoured with the rule of Lord Darius and considered resigning his post and the small promotions he had received. That would have meant moving to a different kingdom, such as Horstruff or even to King Charles' kingdom. But he hesitated giving up his position and the better than average pay he received. Then word came down from Lord Darius that battle plans were being drawn. As a soldier, he knew anyone resigning at that point would be considered a traitor or a coward. The sentence for a soldier accused of that was death.

Sir Gavin's stomach churned into a knot when he learned it was King Charles that they were going to attack. Even worse was Sir Sadon promoting him to a position where he would meet with others to finalize the battle strategies. When Sir Sadon saw that he was an excellent swordsman, he decided to use Sir Gavin as his personal assistant and for protection. Sir Gavin stood in line to get his breakfast, trying to focus on something other than his loathing of Sir Sadon. He thought of Daniel and Sarah, riding away and now presumably safe, and a small smile crept on his lips.

He ate his breakfast alone as he sat against a tree, relaxing, when a messenger came up to him. "Sir Sadon wants those in command to go with him to meet Sir Nolene."

"Bloody lovely. Start the day meeting a man who loves dragons."

The ride to where Sir Nolene waited took an hour. Sir Sadon led the way with the four other commanders following close behind. Sir Sadon normally didn't like to be in front even when they weren't in battle, but only he knew of the location to Sir Nolene's camp.

Sir Gavin smelled the dragons before they reached their camp. He knew that the dragons had a peculiar body odour of spicy vegetation, but that could pale in comparison to the food they ate, and it was the second smell of decaying flesh that assailed his nose.

Sir Sadon sneered. "Glad my stomach has digested breakfast long ago."

Sir Gavin didn't feel as fortunate and took a drink of water from a water pouch to help settle his stomach. He saw Sir Nolene on his horse appear from among the trees. The tall, lanky man had long, dark hair drooping from an egg-shaped head. He wore protective armour but with a bright yellow vest over it.

A pronounced Adam's apple bobbed as Sir Nolene spoke. "You have arrived at a good time. The dragons have just fed and won't get agitated when they see you." He turned his horse around and led them deeper into the forest. The trees suddenly gave way to a clearing of rocky hills.

Sir Gavin looked around, seeing perhaps twenty men and four dragons. Two of the dragons were adults with the younger dragons about half their size. The men all wore bright yellow vests and faced the dragons a good distance away. The dragons were grouped close together, standing lazily as their heads swivelled around. He looked at the creatures with their double row of teeth in crocodile-like jaws. He knew when mature the pony-sized Patiri dragons normally hunted by themselves or in small groups and their colourful scales of red, green and yellow showed they didn't worry about camouflage or stealth. Each of the four thick limbs ended in six razor sharp claws and the now folded wings had a bony front edge used to batter opponents. The tail and the neck were of equal length with each slightly longer than the body. The other unusual thing about the dragons was the black leather hoods they wore. The hoods restricted their vision to only what was straight of where their snouts pointed at.

Sir Nolene took a long bullwhip from one of the men and with a flick of his arm caused it to crack.

The dragons snorted and lowered their heads close to the ground.

Sir Gavin stared at the submissive dragons. *Now I know what the devil looks like when he's unhappy.* He heard a low growling that made his hair stand up. He went up to one of the men in yellow vests.

"Ugly beasts."

"We don't keep them for their beauty." The short, heavyset man shrugged. "We have four more dragons a mile from here. The beasts get agitated if you have more than four or five together, and believe me you don't want them any more agitated than you have to.

Sir Gavin snorted. "No doubt about that. Tell me, why are you and the others wearing a yellow vest?" He glanced at the nervous short man with blond hair who had problems with what to do with his hands.

"Part of the training of the dragons teaches them never to attack anything yellow. It doesn't ensure they won't attack so it's smart to always face the dragons to see how they're behaving."

"Maybe I should be wearing yellow too."

The blond man shook his head. "No worries there. They have been fed and Sir Nolene has given them a command not to attack."

"All the same I'm not going to turn my back on them. They must be hard to train."

"It does take a special skill that I'm still learning. You have to start when they're just hatchlings and establish your authority early. The dragons are actually quite social and will follow commands from the leader."

"How many dragons do you train at a time?"

"Not too many, usually around three. We get as many eggs as we can, but a lot of dragons don't train well. We have to kill off over half of them before they're a month old and a few more later. Patiri dragons can be stubborn."

"I notice two of the dragons are smaller than the others."

"They're younger and follow what the older dragons do. It's all part of the training process."

Sir Gavin looked on as Sir Nolene blew into a long, thick tube made out of a light coloured wood to produce a singular low note. The dragons raised their heads and stretched their wings. They turned agitated as if ready to attack. After a few seconds, they settled down, their large yellow eyes peering at Sir Nolene.

"I thought they were ready to take off there."

Freeman Owen tugged down his yellow vest and shook his head. "They won't go until Sir Nolene gives them permission by sounding the dragon pipe."

"How do you get the dragons to fly to where you want them to?"

Freeman Owen smiled knowingly. "We use a type of fish oil that has a strong smell. The dragons are trained to fly wherever we place a container of it."

"Well, you're doing a job I wouldn't want to do. I don't trust those monsters, yellow vest or not." He looked over and saw Sir Sadon walking back to where the horses were.

After Gavin made his way over to the horses, Sir Sadon spoke to him.

"Here, you can carry this. Careful you don't drop it, or the dragons will chase you." Sir Sadon handed Gavin a clay pot with a lid sealed with wax.

Sir Gavin secured the gallon-sized pot with a rope to the saddle of his horse and unhappily rode back to the main camp.

———

Sir Sadon pointed at the map rolled out on the table. His commanders stood on the other side and paid close attention as he spoke.

"We ride right to the front of the castle gates. They're expecting their own troops back so we will have the lead horse fly their banner." He looked at one of the commanders. The short, heavy weight man kept his black hair in a long ponytail. "Kaden, you will be in command of the first charge. You will make sure the gates remain open and kill as many of the king's men as you can. Once you have gained control of the gate, Connor will follow up with more men."

Sir Kaden squeezed his jaw tight, holding his temper in check. If he failed to keep the gate open or if help was slow to arrive, he would be dead. He stared at the drawing of the castle with the high stone walls surrounding it and centered within the town of Regius. Beyond Regius was another wall, a scattering of buildings and farmland. Farmland where his parents toiled, and he should have stayed to help them. It was now too late to change his destiny, but he longed for a time when his conscience was clear.

Sir Connor brushed away his blond hair that hung around his face before touching one of the two other castles on the map. The castles formed a large triangle on the map. "What about the troops there? They could overwhelm our attack."

Sir Sadon shook his head. "King Charles thought he was being clever by having three castles that each held part of his troops. That made most attacks difficult, but he didn't count on dragons. Sir Nolene is going to have dragons land between the main castle and the two others. I guarantee that neither horse nor man will want to cross their path."

Sir Connor, a slim man of average height, looked at Sadon and back at the map. "If you can keep those other troops away, we have a good chance against the main castle."

Sir Sadon nodded. "King Charles' days are numbered." He looked over at Sir Gavin. "What's the matter? See a problem with my plan?"

Sir Gavin shook his head. "No sire. Just that a lot of men will lose their lives before the battle is won."

"That doesn't matter, as long we have the castle." He laughed and reached for a tankard of ale.

# TWELVE

S ir Jon lifted up his chin as he struggled with the clasp that held the collar of his shirt together. "There, that is one tight fit. I hope I can swallow my dinner later."

Liz smiled as she watched him rotate his head to test the tightness of the collar. "Don't complain too much. This dress is so tight at the waist that I can hardly breathe, and my boobs are squeezed forward and up. It's as if someone was pulling on them to try to lift me up." She saw him look at her with appreciation, and despite the discomfort she was in, she enjoyed how the dress looked. The long dress billowed out below her hips while the middle accented the smallness of her waist. Her breasts seemed to gain a cup size under the confines of the ribbed fabric, with a modest amount of cleavage showing below the scoop neckline. She liked the how the dark and light green dress went with her fair skin and blonde hair. All in all, she felt pretty as she stood in front of him.

She did like how Jon looked now that he had finally shaved, cut his hair and cleaned himself up after spending too many days working. The white shirt was a nice contrast to the black suit he wore. As was traditional for formal men's wear on Domum, he also wore a small black cape that flashed a red underside as he walked. His thick-soled boots added even more height to him, making him a rather imposing figure.

She rubbed her hand on his chest, feeling the starch and rough cloth. "You look nice." Liz lifted her head and received a kiss from him.

Sir Jon held out his arm. "I guess we better get going. It wouldn't be good for us to be late."

She giggled. "Yeah, they may decide not to make you a Lord after all."

Lord Perry insisted that they use one of his carriages to travel to the ceremony, telling them their own carriage didn't meet the expectations of the formal event. The red and black carriage with four horses and four guards seemed a bit pretentious to Liz for a journey less than a mile through Horstruff. She did feel like royalty as the townspeople stopped to stare and even waved as they passed by. Other horses and carriages pulled to the side of the road to ensure they had easy passage as they moved down the cobbled street.

The carriage came to a stop only when they reached the front doors of Lord Perry's castle and there a twin row of twenty-four guards lined the way up the front steps and to the double set of large doors.

Two guards in their dress uniforms assisted Liz from the carriage where she took Jon's arm. She felt excited as she climbed the steps and grinned as they entered the castle. She watched in amazement as four men raised long trumpets and sounded a short two-note announcement.

A guard dressed in red and gold proclaimed in a deep voice what Liz thought must have carried across the entire castle, "Sir Jon and Lady Elizabeth."

As they moved into the ballroom, the other guests turned and applauded.

Lord Perry, accompanied by Lady Beatrice, stepped forward with open arms to greet them.

"Welcome, welcome." He gave Jon a handshake and clasped a hand on his shoulder. "This is a special day indeed." He turned to Liz and gave her a hug and stepped back to look at her. "The way you look my dear, we are fortunate that Jon didn't want to keep you for himself and stay at home."

Liz blushed and grinned at the same time, not knowing what to say other than a quiet thank you.

Jon and Liz made their way slowly through the room, interrupted by well wishers. After a few minutes, they stopped to talk with Lord Troy and Lady Patricia.

"I must say, you and Lady Elizabeth received quite the welcome, not subdued like it was for some of the other guests."

Liz listened to Jon and Lord Troy talk and gave a smile to Patricia as she shifted position to get closer to her.

As they complimented each other on their dresses, Liz observed that while Patricia's dress covered her, the material was light enough to show off her figure that attracted pleased looks from the men and a few stern looks from the ladies. She remembered back at university social functions being in the same position, trying to show enough to attract the men while not going too far as to receive nasty looks from the women. Her empathy was strengthened by the hospitality Patricia had shown to her and others when they were invited at Lord Troy's castle for a girl's night only party. There was also her attitude that challenged the norm of Domum society that Liz found rather stifling for women.

Liz glanced around as Patricia chatted and noticed how everyone wanted to say hello to Jon. She understood it wasn't just because he was going to be promoted to a Lord. Not only did everyone seem to like him, but there was a genuine respect for him. She wondered if he would be willing to give that up and return with her to Earth.

By extension of being with Jon, Liz was also greeted warmly. She did enjoy the attention but saw there was a definite division of those who were accepted and those who were not. Patricia, despite some less than welcome looks from other women, was generally accepted along with Lord Troy.

Liz also noticed those who remained isolated and ignored by almost everyone save for the servers carrying refreshments. She had little sympathy for Sir Keith and Lady Karla, not having a good feeling about either of them; and it seemed many others had the same sentiment about the couple. She looked past them and saw Lady Nicole, standing in Sir Anthony's shadow as he chatted with several other guests. Liz saw not only the plastic smile on Nicole's face but also the frustration of being ignored.

"Excuse me, I want to say hello to a friend." Liz walked confidently to where Sir Anthony and Lady Nicole stood.

Nicole smiled as Liz approached and looked surprised as Liz hugged her. Liz conversed with her as if they were best of friends and after a few minutes, Liz returned to where Jon stood with his cluster of admirers. Liz took a glance back and saw several women had filled the space around Nicole, chatting with her as one of their own.

———

A bell sounded and gradually the crowd drifted out of the room through a second set of doors. Behind the doors was an auditorium-size room with a raised platform near the back of the room, faced by layers of padded benches. As Liz entered the room with Jon, a guard in a red dress uniform escorted them to a reserved spot on the benches. Liz looked around the room, impressed with the abundance of gold trim, rich fabrics that hung like drapes along the walls and the elaborate throne that sat by itself in the middle of the platform. Dignitaries were seated on the benches while the rest of the guests stood behind them, waiting in excited whispers until Lord Perry strode forward among four guards to the throne.

Lord Perry sat down and using a mace attached to a long pole tapped the floor three times. A hush filled the room as the crowd waited for him to speak.

"This is the time of need. We want the strong, the noble and the courageous to lead the masses to help determine the fate of all of Horstruff and indeed, the whole kingdom. This is the not the time for those with their own agendas, those who worry more of their own self-preservation than of those around them, nor of those who are short sighted and see only the hours ahead and not the moons of passage.

These are dangerous days in which it will be easy for us to falter and to succumb to those who want to use force to take what is ours. Instead I say to you all, each and every one of us, we have an opportunity to repel the wickedness that wants to strike us and instead forge ahead to make this land wealthy and safe."

Liz listened to the powerful voice that held everyone's attention, recognizing it as a speech that prepared people for an upcoming war. She looked over at Jon, who was leaning forward as he listened, and realized he was one of the leaders Lord Perry was talking about.

"This is not the time for the faint-hearted or those who lack moral courage and seek only their own gains. This is the time for those who are willing to stand up and stand with me united in a common cause." Lord Perry stood and gazed at the people around him.

"Ladies and gentlemen, I have spoken to you of what we need. Our council has decreed that two openings of lordship be given to men who will help protect Horstruff and the kingdom. It is with the highest esteem that I will ask these two gentlemen to approach the throne and accept the honour of lordship." He paused as murmurs filled the room.

Liz was puzzled. She knew Jon was to be promoted to lordship but who was the second man? She tried to look around without obviously turning her head to see if there was any clue to his identity.

Lord Perry smiled. "I have the privilege of asking Lord Jon McKinney to step forward to accept the responsibilities of a lord."

Applause and cheers filled the room as a red-faced Jon stepped lightly to the throne.

"And I now ask Lord Madoc to step forward to also accept the responsibilities of a lord.

Liz noted as Madoc approached the throne the applause was reduced and cheering definitely subdued. She was shocked that Madoc had risen to lord status so quickly after his forced exile by Lord Perry. As she listened to them take oaths, she wondered how long it would be, and if Jon was going back to Earth.

———

A celebration followed in a ballroom after the ceremonies, and Liz found herself drinking a bit too fast as she accepted congratulations from others. As Nicole told her before, a woman's success often depended on the success of her husband. She held back expressing her feelings on that situation and graciously accepted their accolades. She gave Jon a quick kiss and whispered to him that she was going for a walk to catch some fresh air.

She quickly made her way to the set of French doors that opened up to a garden of flowers and green plants planted in circular design. Potted trees obscured sightlines along the curved pathways.

Liz sighed as she walked among the plants, glad she hadn't said anything that would have embarrassed Jon. She felt like telling a couple of well wishers who told her they were so happy for her that it was Jon who was promoted to a lord, not her. She considered she was being a bit unreasonable but knew it was really because she wanted to move back to Earth and not live in the chauvinistic, medieval world of Domum.

"Liz!"

She turned at the sound of footsteps and saw Sir Anthony run up to her.

"Tony, we shouldn't be seen alone together here. People will talk."

"I told Nicole that I was going to check to see if you were all right so it isn't a secret."

"I'll bet she wasn't too pleased to hear you say that, all the same."

"You may have a point there, but I don't think she was angry about it."

"I would be a little upset if I saw Jon chasing after Nicole to see if she was all right."

"Look, I am honestly concerned about you. I saw you going out by yourself and was worried if everything was all right." He spread out his hands.

"You didn't chase me to steal a kiss?"

He grinned. "Well, if that happens it would be a bonus."

Liz smiled. "An unlikely event." She turned to walk again. "Tony, I like you very much. Too much maybe. Part of me wants you more than a friend and it is tempting to take advantage of your offer. But I value Nicole as a friend and won't give that up in exchange for a roll in the hay with you. I also have Jon to consider. Even if he never found out, I would know and the guilt I would feel would be awful."

"Okay, message received. I will not press you again."

"Good, because there is something else you must now consider. Nicole knows you are sleeping around with other women. In fact it is common knowledge you have had several ladies since your marriage."

He gave a small shrug. "It is hard stopping being a ladies' man just like that."

"Women like you, Tony. You are handsome, well mannered and powerful."

He gave a small, restrained smile.

"But if you were a woman that slept around as much as you do, they would call you a whore."

He looked at her with an open mouth expression.

"That's right, Tony. You do not have a good reputation. You are an easy lay."

He rubbed the back of his neck as he walked in silence.

"Did you hear what Lord Perry said? This is the time to stand up and do what is right. How can others look up to you as a leader when you have one eye on who you will bed next? You managed to stop being a drunkard. Now it is time to stop being a womanizer. Become the man that Lord Perry and the rest of us need."

He nodded. "Your words sting like a sharp blade, but they are also on their mark. For you, and Nicole, I promise to be better behaved. My wife deserves to have a man she can trust."

They made their way back toward the ballroom and saw Nicole standing by the open doors watching them with her arms crossed.

Anthony walked ahead, quickly climbing the short steps to where she stood. He placed his hands on her shoulders, giving her a kiss that she didn't return.

Liz caught up in time to hear him speak.

"Nicole, Liz has told me an awful truth and what I have to do to amend it. Please come with me for a walk."

Nicole looked at Liz as she allowed Anthony to lead her away.

Liz smiled. "It's okay. It really is good news." She watched them leave and saw Jon talking to Lord Perry and began to hurry over. *That was fine advice I gave to Tony about not being selfish for his own needs. Maybe I should try and follow that as well. If I love Jon, I should be willing to support him on his desire to help Domum during its time of trouble.* She reached a smiling Lord Perry as he rested a hand on Jon's shoulder.

Lord Perry turned as Liz approached. "Ah, here is your wonderful lady."

Liz blushed as she wondered how Lord Perry managed to have such an effect on those around him. One compliment and she was back to being a schoolgirl.

"I was just about to explain to Lord Jon the reason for promoting Lord Madoc. When Jon first arrived on Domum, Lord Madoc tried to warn me of the danger of Lord Bennett. I was hesitant to believe what he said at the time. But I remember his final words to me at the time. He said, "It comes down to whether you trust me or not." He was right. It was a matter of trust. It was a good thing I decided to believe him. Now we are at another crisis and again I ask myself if I trust him. The simple answer is I do. Lord Madoc scares a lot of influential people because he possesses powerful magic. Regardless of our fear of him, I believe he has honour and when he accepted being a lord, he also promised to help save Horstruff and the kingdom."

Jon nodded. "I don't have a problem with him being a lord. He has the same magic whether he is a lord or not. Better to make sure he is on our side."

Lord Perry smiled. "I see we think alike." He turned to Liz. "I know you are unfamiliar with our music here, but may I have the honour of having a dance with you?"

Liz mouthed inaudible words until she nodded and took his arm. She looked back at Jon who gave her a friendly wave. *Great, two left feet and I'm dancing with Lord Perry.*

# THIRTEEN

Daniel tugged on the rope, making the horse follow reluctantly over the hilly ground with Sarah riding uneasily in the saddle.

Sarah looked around from her vantage point. She had been half asleep earlier but now found her strength returning. She was still in pain but focused on Daniel and how they had to get as far away from the battlefields as possible. The terrain was tough, but Daniel told her he wanted to avoid the roads until they were well away from Regius.

"Daniel?"

"Yes, love?" He turned around, worry showing in his eyes.

"It's okay. Just that I would like to rest a bit, off Evado." Sarah had named the horse, picking a name she understood meant escape.

He hurried to her side and helped her down. "Rest as long as you need."

"Do we have any food? I'm a bit hungry."

Daniel shook his head. "No, but while you rest, I'll go and find something."

She smiled. "My hero." She slowly shifted her position on the ground. "I'll be fine. I'm just a bit sore, that's all."

He started to leave but a cry high above caused him to freeze. The silhouette of four lupus dragons glided above him. He let out a sigh of relief. The Lupus dragons were small dog-sized dragons that hunted in packs, and while they were dangerous to isolated animals, they rarely attacked people. When Daniel heard the cry above, he was worried about another type of dragon. The Fornido dragon was the largest dragon, a fearsome predator that hunted alone. Daniel and Sarah were in one of few areas that the dragon was known to inhabit, and he hoped not to come across one as they journeyed.

Daniel let out his breath as he moved quietly among the tall grasses. He heard insects chirp and buzz as they flew out of the way. He ignored them and kept his eyes to ground, looking for the tell-tale signs of small game.

He was surprised to find instead the remains of a leather vest, the material badly torn and faded. He poked at it with his sword, turning the fabric over. Then his eyes widened as he stared at what he uncovered.

# FOURTEEN

Sir Gavin steered his horse just outside the town of Regius to one of the lesser used roads that took him up to one of the surrounding hills. He picked a small tree-less hill that gave a good view of Regius and the king's castle within. After dismounting from his horse, he carried the clay vessel a short distance away. Sir Gavin placed it on the ground, picked up a large rock, and paused after he lifted it up to his shoulders. *I don't see how this stuff is supposed to smell strong enough to attract dragons miles away.*

He hurled the rock down, shattering the clay pot. Seconds later the stench hit him, reeking like rancid fish. Covering his nose, he raced to his horse, which was already backing away. He jumped on it as he tasted bile in his mouth, his stomach wanting to heave anything inside it. The horse didn't need any encouragement to gallop away and a few minutes later he was able to finally draw in a few deep breaths of air.

"Well, I guess dragons won't have any trouble finding that."

———

Colin nodded with grim satisfaction as he crossed his arms. "What did I tell you lads? Didn't I say that we're in a heap of trouble?" He stared at each of the men sitting with him at the Dragon's Egg Tavern. When none of them replied, he continued. "Have you seen the guards running about, looking for better swords and other weapons? None of them are snoozing behind the stables anymore, I'll tell you that." He pointed a finger at Percy. "They had the nerve to try and recruit him and others to help defend the kingdom, offering a few coins as pay that would probably get their throat slit."

Percy spoke up. "They said it was my duty as a citizen to join up. I told them it was their duty to make sure they didn't need civilians in the first place to do their job. They didn't like that much but I was so mad I didn't care."

Colin slapped his hand on the table. "Good on you, Percy. Let's hope..."

The blare of trumpets interrupted his next words. Then shouts and the sound of horses running past the tavern filled the air.

Smitty was the first to the door and he cautiously peered outside. He closed the door quickly and turned to the others. "Better take cover. The battle is on!"

———

Sir Nolene stood in the open field that lay between King Charles' castle and Lord James' castle, one of the two castles that provided military support for King Charles. The field was split by the road that was used between the two castles and normally experienced steady traffic. To give Sir Nolene time to work, Sir Sadon ordered two roadblocks set up on the road, using trees dragged across the road. The king's men would soon remove the roadblock but not before Sir Nolene was to complete his task. He put on his yellow vest and two of his assistants followed suit as they tightened the reins on the horses. Sir Nolene took a long flute that hung from his belt. Slowly he scanned the sky and lifted the flute. He paused before placing the flute to his lips and turned to his assistants.

"Now remember the pattern of two sharp notes and one long lower note. Observe that I pause several seconds before repeating the sound so the dragons do not get confused."

Both assistants nodded vigorously and Sir Nolene began to play the flute. He repeated the series of notes three times and waited. Minutes passed as the men scanned the skies. Then four black specks began to form into the shape of dragons. The men watched the four dragons when Sir Nolene pointed to another part of the sky where four more dragons were approaching.

"I see the second group of dragons. They won't try to land once the first group has taken possession of the field. But it's good they are in the area. We will easily be able to lead them to the second location."

The first group of Patiri dragons circled the open field, slowly dropping lower as they cried out a warning growl.

Sir Nolene played his flute again and paused as the dragons dropped lower, only a few feet above their heads. The largest dragon landed first, growling and hissing at the men as it flapped its wings. The other dragons followed, standing a few feet behind him.

Sir Nolene continued to play his flute, a series of short, sharp notes. The dragons, with gleaming eyes, progressively settled down and eventually became quiet as they stared at the men. Above them the second group of dragons wheeled about high in the sky. Sir Nolene climbed on his agitated horse and blew on his flute once more, ordering the dragons to defend the area as if it was their nest. Then he and his assistants quickly rode away, lest the dragons get confused if defending their nest also meant attacking those wearing yellow.

Sir Nolene wiped the sweat from his forehead as he headed to the next location. He felt the dragons would now effectively block help to King Charles from Lord James. The next task was going to set up a similar situation with the second group of dragons near the remaining castle to block those men from helping King Charles. Then King Charles would unlikely be able to withstand a full assault from Lord Darius, and Sir Nolene hoped the promise of being made Lord and given his own castle would not be forgotten.

———

Sir Sadon sat watching the battle from a hilltop. His horse was nervous, wanting to move away, but he would have none of that. A couple of solid hits with his armoured covered hand on the horse's flank caused it to settle down. The dragons were making more than just his horse nervous and they had successfully stopped the men in nearby castles from sending assistance to King Charles' castle, despite trumpets blaring and bells ringing. Eventually the soldiers from the nearby castles would be able to drive the dragons away but by then it would be too late.

He leaned forward on his saddle and determined Sir Kaden had succeeded in penetrating the castle walls. He guessed he was no doubt battling for his very life and thus determined to keep the gates open. Sir Sadon raised his right fist in the air and brought it down in a swoop. Soon he saw the charge led by Sir Conner, as hundreds of horses raced to the castle, dust following in their wake.

Sir Sadon turned to Sir Gavin. "It looks like the battle is going to plan so far."

"It does. I feel I should be there helping."

"Maybe you do, but I want my best swordsman here for protection. You never know if someone figures they can make an easy attack."

Sir Gavin nodded. "Yes, sire. You are in vulnerable position away from the main battle." *You coward.*

———

Colin sat next to Percy at the table slowly drinking his ale. The noise of the battle broke through, causing the men and women to huddle inside and occasionally jump and gasp. "Didn't I say this was going to happen?"

Percy turned to him. "You did. But if you say I told you so one more time I'm likely to punch you in the nose."

Colin grimaced. "I only try to enlighten those around me about what was happening. I can't help it if I'm right."

"I sure the hell wish you was wrong on this one."

A soldier wearing the green and white colours of Lord Darius burst into the tavern with two more men behind him. He looked at the group sitting at the back of the room. "Any of King Charles' men here?" he bellowed.

Everyone shook their heads.

"All right. Stay in here or your lives will be taken." He stomped out and the group in the tavern let out a collective sigh of relief.

Smitty spoke first. "I hate to say this, but the battle must be nearly over. Lord Darius' men must be going building to building looking for the remnants of the king's army. For all the faults the king had, rule under Darius will be far worse."

Colin nodded. "Let us hope that someone will come to the rescue."

———

King Charles stood with the protection of his royal guardsmen. The throne room was the last refuge for the embattled king and his sons, which stood behind him as Lord Darius' troops pushed them into the corner of the room.

With weapons poised, the battle came to a stop. Sir Sadon came forward and spoke to the king.

"It is over. Surrender or die."

King Charles spoke in a raspy voice. "I will surrender on the condition you spare the lives of my sons and my men."

"No conditions. Lord Darius will decide later if they are allowed to live."

The king bowed his head and dropped to one knee. "Please, there is no need for further killing."

"Take their weapons, and lock them all in the dungeon." He turned to Sir Gavin behind him. "That went rather well. Let's make ourselves comfortable until Lord Darius arrives."

# FIFTEEN

Gordon Miller listened to Tuck ramble on about particle physics, adding a few comments of his own. It was the second phone call this week from the physics student and it occurred to Gordon that Tuck must be bored and lonely.

The reasons were quite clear to him. Tuck's best friend and fellow graduate at the university had fallen in love. Tom had met Marisa, a former sex slave on Domum, and managed to obtain her freedom from Lord Sussex. She quickly agreed to move to Earth and live with him in a small apartment.

That sudden change in Tom's personal life had suddenly given Tuck too much time by himself. The result being phone calls to Gordon to talk about physics. Gordon didn't mind the calls, but felt sympathy for Tuck, understanding what it was like when friends suddenly disappear.

He finally was able to hang up and made his way to the liquor cabinet to pour a glass of port when the phone rang again. Gordon stopped, muttered a minor curse, and turned back to the offending instrument.

"Hello, Gordon Miller residence."

The voice on the other end was hesitant and spoke in a low voice. "Hello? Is this Sir Gordon Miller?"

"This is he, but without the title Sir. Who is this?"

"This is Nadine Newman, Sir Jon's former girlfriend."

The name was familiar to Gordon, recalling Jon informing him

Nadine was actually a gnant at one time. The Adepts, the gnants leaders and higher thinkers, used magic to change her into a human to use as a spy. Her first task was to use Jon as a source of information, as the Adepts determined that he would have a large influence on the events on Domum. Nadine's use to the Adepts disappeared when she was unable to follow him to Ireland from Boston. They decided to eliminate her, but she managed to escape and live as a human on Earth.

"I remember Jon telling me about you. How can I assist you?"

"I need Jon's help. I fear I am dying."

"Dying? What is wrong?"

"My body is starting to revert back to being a gnant. Some of my internal organs are not stable."

Gordon heard the tremble in her voice. "I'm very sorry to hear that. Jon isn't here but is visiting Domum. Is there anything I can do?"

"Get Sir Jon. Ask him to help me. He is my only hope."

"I will endeavour to locate him, but I'm not sure how long that will take."

"Please hurry. I am not sure how much time I have. I feel very ill."

Gordon hung up the phone and rubbed his chin. Then he pushed a series of numbers on his phone.

"Hey there."

"Hello, Tuck. I need your help with a problem."

"Quantum mechanics? Time dilation?"

"Neither of those. Actually, a request for help from a young lady." Gordon explained the phone call from Nadine and how he needed to get in contact with Jon. "But the problem is I'm not sure how capable I am of traveling to Domum. Certainly, I can arrive on Domum using my crystal array but I'm not sure if I can move about there without difficulties. So I was wondering if I should contact Tom and ask him to go to Domum to find Jon, or perhaps you can think of another way to resolve this dilemma."

"I'll do it. I'll go to Domum and find Jon."

"You will? I'm not certain what the risks are. Perhaps we should contact Tom."

"No, there's no need. If he can travel to Domum and come back, so can I."

Gordon was surprised by the force of Tuck's voice and waited a moment before responding. "Very well. I will send you an airline ticket."

---

Tuck squeezed the phone. He remembered Tom making the journey to Domum months ago to help save Domum and to obtain the freedom for Marisa. Tom returned a different man and won the heart of the woman he fell in love with. Tuck replaced the phone on the table and placed a hand on the back of the nearby chair to steady himself. *What the hell was I thinking in agreeing to go to Domum?* He straightened up and released his hand from the chair. *Maybe the cowardly lion is looking to find some courage.*

———

Tuck talked to Tom over the phone from the Miller Castle, asking what he might expect to see on Domum and how to go about finding Jon.

"Honestly, Tuck, it might be better if I go. I'm not going to be surprised what I see there and probably can find Jon easier than you."

"I'm already here at the castle. I just want to know where I should start looking for him."

"All right, if you want to do this. Hey, I'm going to pass the phone over to Marisa. She knows Horstruff better than me."

A moment later he heard Marisa's voice. "Tuck, I'm surprised you want to go to Domum."

"I don't want to. More like I need to."

"Need to? Because you want to help Jon's former girlfriend?"

"I never met her. I'm doing this to stop living like a turtle."

"Tuck, there are easier ways to do that."

"Yeah, but fate has put me here."

"Men always pretend they're taking the high road to explain their irrational behaviour." She paused. "Still, I respect you for doing this. You're being brave."

"Thanks. I don't hear that term to describe me very often."

"The best place for you to start might be Lord Troy's castle. He's a good man and will help you. Tell him I sent you to see him. When you first arrive in Domum you will be near what used to be called Lord Bennett's castle. Lord Bennett is dead now, but his castle still has the court and judges to deal with criminals. So avoid going there as they may stick you in prison for being in Domum without permission."

"Okay, avoid Lord Bennett's castle. How do I find this Lord Troy?"

Marisa gave him directions. "When you arrive, you will come across a maze made out of hedges. To get through the maze you must use the pattern of left, right, right, left, left, right, right, then left and finally right."

73

"I might get dizzy going through that."

She laughed. "Call out if you get lost. Someone will come to get you. By the way, most of the women at Lord Troy's castle will be almost naked, so don't be shocked by their appearance."

"It might be the inspiration I need to do this. Thanks, Marisa, for your help."

―――――

Tuck walked around the Miller Castle, studying the paintings he had seen a dozen times before and took another swallow from the glass of port he was carrying. Tuck didn't appreciate why Gordon liked port so much, his own tastes ran more to beer, but he had to admit the drink was calming his nerves.

"Tuck I have the apparatus, that is the array, set up in the backyard."

Tuck jumped. "Good." He stuttered out his reply. "When do I step across?"

"Well, if we wait an hour or so then it will be morning on Domum. I assume you want to arrive during the daytime."

"That would be preferable."

"Are you quite sure you want to do this? I can't help but notice you seem to be a bit nervous. It was not my intention to pressure you into going to Domum."

"You didn't pressure me. I did that myself. One of the reasons I spend hours studying physics was so I can hide from the real world. It's time I stepped outside of my safe zone."

―――――

Tuck stood in front of the array and reached for the crystal hung around his neck by a leather string. He held the oval crystal between two fingers and placed it toward the centre of a sheet of plywood. A power cable ran to the plywood that contained several crystals in an oval that were carefully aligned and adjusted to resonate with the crystal Tuck held. As he approached the plywood, the centre and the edges of the plywood disappeared, replaced with the image of another world.

"Remember, Tuck, once you go through the array you cannot return back to Earth for at least half an hour until the crystals recharge."

"I remember. Thanks." He took a hesitant step through the opening and entered the warm, humid world of Domum.

Tuck took a last, backward look at where he stepped through, but the portal had disappeared. He began the slow walk to where he saw a street, or at least the medieval equivalent of one. Tuck wasn't too sure of the plan of action Gordon had suggested. Walking up to strangers and asking if they knew the location of Sir Jon seemed to him a dubious method of locating him.

Tuck walked through the open field with sweat already appearing on his forehead. He sniffed the air and was rewarded with the scent of horses and the weak aroma of decaying food. *Not exactly what I'd call a charming village.* He viewed the stone and wood buildings across the street, both styles looking old and permanent, and turned his attention to the castle next to the field. It did look like the Miller Castle, though with some minor differences such as the stone-wall fence. *Nice to see something familiar, but Marisa told me to avoid it.*

He continued his walk through the tall grass and crossed the cobblestone road, stepping around the horse droppings. He wasn't the only person navigating the road, pedestrians of various descriptions hurried across as they avoided the horses and the carriages. Tuck turned to his left and began the journey to Lord Troy's castle.

Some of the people gave him a second glance, but he kept his eyes forward and his walk brisk. As was suggested to him, he wore older clothes. Apparently, he didn't look entirely out of place as the reactions from the Horstruff residents were slight.

Tuck was glad he wasn't suddenly jumped on as some sort of strange looking alien but was troubled by a minor fact.

*Who would have thought that the common dress in a medieval world is much the same as a poor graduate student?* He felt the frayed sleeve of his shirt. *That might also help explain the lack of success I have with the ladies. Who wants to go out with a man who has the same fashion sense as a medieval peasant?*

He trudged along the wood sidewalks, occasionally glancing in the windows of the shops. They looked to him like merchandise sold at flea markets, a mixture of new and used. He noticed the traffic had decreased as he walked, and the buildings changed from largely stone and brick to wood. There was a narrow space between some the buildings, though the tall weeds indicated it wasn't used much as a shortcut.

The sidewalk came to an end and he walked along the edge of the road. He passed several other travelers, including a donkey pulling a cart. He also saw a gnant that ran up to him, stared at him and raced away into the brush along the side of the road.

*I guess he didn't want to stay and talk but did seem to know I wasn't from around here.*

Tuck was relieved he hadn't been questioned or challenged by any of the Domum citizens. He felt he could actually be just walking along a dirt road back home, except for the overly warm temperature, when he saw a group of dragons flying high above. Tuck watched the dragons make a long, slow circle. It was hard to make out details on their silhouetted bodies, but there was no mistaking that the crocodile-shaped head didn't belong to any bird he had ever heard of or seen. He felt a touch of fear and fascination with the creatures as he stared. After a few minutes, the dragons flew away in a V formation.

*I'm glad I don't have to face those up close.* He walked along the road wondering if there were other creatures that might be lurking about. He passed an older couple, the man pulling a small two wheeled cart filled with sacks of potatoes. They looked tired and didn't even seem to notice him as he passed by.

A few minutes later Tuck followed a bend in the road when a dark brown, wolf-sized creature landed on the road, its triangular shaped wings beating the air. Tuck stood still and stared at the gargoyle. It had an over-sized head for its body that looked similar to an ape's. He found the overall appearance disconcerting and wondered if the creature was dangerous. The gargoyle opened its mouth, showing off numerous small, pointed teeth. It growled at him and Tuck dived off to side of the road, sliding on his stomach on the grass and mud.

He twisted around to look back and saw the old couple come into view. Again the gargoyle growled.

The woman picked up a rock and threw it at the gargoyle. "Get!" She yelled at it.

With a quick beat of its wings the gargoyle took off.

Tuck slowly emerged from the ditch and brushed the dirt from his shirt. *Well, doesn't that make me look like an idiot.*

———

The road became less travelled after he arrived at an intersection and turned off, following Marisa's directions. A short time later he came across an eight-foot-high hedge that served as a maze.

*Okay, I better not get lost here.* He followed the path that Marisa told him, arriving at the large double doors of the castle. He pulled the cord by the door, hearing a dull chiming sound from behind the doors. Tuck looked behind him, observing the water fountain with marble nymphs playing within the large bowl, when he heard one of the doors opened.

He turned and saw a tall redhead staring at him, her face without expression. She wore a long dark green skirt and, other than her long hair to offer modest coverage, a bare top.

Tuck knew that the women of Lord Troy's castle were known to be underdressed, but the sight of Lena froze him.

"What do you wish? You have entered the property of Lord Troy without permission."

Tuck took a deep breath and pulled in his stomach, straightening out his shoulders. "I came here to see Lord Troy."

"Lord Troy is not available. However, if you wait a minute, I will obtain some food for you. Then you must depart immediately." She turned back into the entrance.

"No, wait. I didn't come here for food."

She paused at the doorway, tilting her head.

"I came here to ask for Lord Troy's help to find Sir Jon, not for a handout."

"Why do you think Lord Troy would desire to help you? By the way it is Lord Jon now." Lena detected an accent in his voice she found familiar. She also noticed that though his dress was that of a peasant, he did speak well.

"Marisa told me he would help me."

"Marisa? You know her?" She opened the door wide again.

"Yeah, she's with my friend Tom."

"You're friends with Sir Tom?" She grinned.

Tuck frowned. "He's hardly a Sir. But yeah, he's my friend."

"Please come in. Lord Troy will be delighted to see you."

He followed her into the castle and to a sitting room. He looked at the strange paintings and sculptures along the way, marvelling at their brashness.

"What is your name?"

"Tuck."

"May I pour refreshment, Sir Tuck?"

"Sure. Do you have a cold beer?"

Lena filled a tankard with ale. "I hope this is to your liking." She smiled and hurried out of the room.

Tuck looked around at the large furniture and the oversized paintings as he sipped his ale. He thought that the owner of the castle really liked to push the boundaries of art. He wondered if the size of the furniture indicated something about the man's ego as well. He heard a tapping noise mixed with footsteps and turned to see Lord Troy and a blonde woman enter the room.

Lord Troy gave a slight incline of his head and spoke. "It is so very good to meet you, Sir Tuck. Welcome to our castle and I hope we can be of assistance to you. This is my wife, Lady Patricia, and I am Lord Troy Sussex at your service."

Patricia stepped forward. "We understand you are friends of Marisa and Sir Tom. How are they doing?"

Tuck was surprised by Lord Troy's appearance, thinking he appeared like a showman from a century ago. He noted that unlike Lena, Patricia was at least dressed, though her full dress with a scooped neckline certainly showed off her assets.

"They're doing fine. Look, I need to find Lord Jon right away. Can you tell me where he is?"

Lord Troy nodded. "Of course. It is common knowledge that he has now taken up residence in the castle formerly used by Lord Bennett."

Tuck closed his eyes. "Damn, I walked over from there."

Patricia sympathized. "Oh, dear, if you only had known. No matter, we will have a horse and carriage take you back."

"Thank you."

"In the meantime we will get you something to eat and I will have one of the ladies clean your clothes. You don't want to see Lord Jon with mud on your clothes."

Tuck looked down at his shirt and pants. "They aren't that bad, are they?"

Patricia crossed her arms across her chest. "They are. We do have certain standards here before you show up before nobility."

———

Tuck stood in front of Lena and Gwyneth in one of the large bedrooms, staring at them. Both wore only long skirts and smiled at him as they waited. Lena held a burgundy coloured silk robe draped over her arm. "Is there a problem, Sir Tuck?"

Tuck tightened his stomach muscles. He felt embarrassed taking his clothes off in front of them. He also felt even more embarrassed if he were to ask them to look away, especially since they were half naked. "No, no problem." He unbuttoned his shirt and tried to act casually as he passed his shirt over to Gwyneth. He looked up at them, giving a forced smile as he removed his shoes.

*I guess I would never make it as a male stripper. I can't even take off my shirt without blushing.* He slowly unbuckled his pants, took a deep breath, and pushed them down to his ankles. He slipped them off his feet and with a shaking hand, passed them over.

Gwyneth took his pants and smiled. "Would you like us to wash your under-garments as well, Sir Tuck?"

Tuck blinked and looked down, wondering if a mysterious stain had suddenly appeared on his underwear. Fortunately the black briefs looked normal, except for a growing bulge. "No, I'm good. Thanks." He felt like grabbing the robe from Lena to hide his excitement.

Lena walked behind him and opened the robe. "Your under-garments are much more interesting than the ones normally worn on Domum, Sir Tuck."

Tuck stuck his arms out and put on the robe, tying the front up quickly.

Gwyneth carried his clothes out of the room while Lena stuck a hand under his arm, tugging on him to follow her. "Come, Sir Tuck, let us go for refreshments while we wait for your clothes to be cleaned."

Tuck walked with her down a few hallways and arrived at a large dining hall.

He gratefully sat down on one of the large captain chairs and surveyed the various foods in the dishes set on the table. He recognized potatoes, corn, green beans and a couple of other dishes. Although the sausages and other sliced meats looked mystifying as to their origin. That didn't prevent him from attacking each item with gusto, and his enthusiasm didn't go unnoticed by Lena.

"Were you a bit hungry, Sir Tuck?" She favoured him with a smile.

Tuck looked up at Lord Troy, Lena, Patricia, and another woman standing at the table slowly adding food to their dishes. "Oh, sorry. I guess I was a bit hungry. It's actually dinner time on Earth and I guess I worked up an appetite."

Lord Troy added food to his plate without looking up. "No need to apologize, Sir Tuck. If you are hungry, then you should eat until you are filled. Do ignore the stares and comments from the young ladies. I believe they are fascinated with the knowledge you are not from Domum. While they are staring and comments are impolite, they do not intend any disrespect." Lena said.

Tuck looked at the women at the table who immediately bowed their heads in unison as if he caught them playing a trick.

"That's okay. I'm considered a bit unusual on Earth too."

"Thank you for your understanding." Lord Troy gave a tight smile. "Rest assured I will address this issue to them privately later."

"Please don't get mad at them. I didn't mind at all."

"That is kind of you to say so, Sir Tuck." Lord Troy acknowledged with a smile.

"Tell me, how did Jon become a Lord?"

"Lord Perry himself nominated him for election. While any lord can propose a candidate, Lord Perry carries considerable influence. The rest of the lords accepted his promotion with little discussion and reservation."

"But why was he chosen?"

Lord Troy wiped his mouth with a napkin. "I believe there are a few reasons for that. First, if Lord Jon is going to help establish a secure defence for Horstruff, he needs to have the confidence of the fighting men that he is a man of stature. They would be less willing to follow him if he was a mere sir.

"The other reason is Lord Perry hopes Lord Jon will be willing to stay on Domum permanently. By promoting him to the status of Lord and having him take ownership of what was Lord Bennett's castle, Lord Jon is more likely to stay on Domum."

Tuck nodded. "Jon may like it here, but what about Liz?"

Patricia put down her wine glass. "That is an entirely different matter."

––––––

Tuck held his neatly folded clothes as he stood in the bedroom. They were definitely clean although still with a hint of dampness to them. "Thanks for cleaning them."

Gwyneth smiled at him as she stood in front of him. "It is no problem, Sir Tuck."

Lena touched his shoulder. "Are you sure you don't want us to help you get dressed?"

"I'll be fine." He watched them leave the room and sighed. *I think I know why Tom liked it here.*

The carriage ride was not a comfortable journey. Tuck was jostled side to side as they went down the road. Lord Troy and Patricia sat opposite of him inside the carriage and smiled after one large bump.

Lord Troy explained. "Sometimes the road develops a few holes. We will soon get to the main road which will be a lot smoother."

"I hope so. At least it's faster than walking."

A few minutes later, the travelling did become somewhat even, and Tuck stopped worrying about being tossed onto Patricia's lap. He looked out of the open window at the passing scenery and travelers on foot who were forced to stand at the edge of the road as the carriage passed. He looked at how they were dressed, in loose fitting and dirty clothes, and realized he had arrived at Lord Troy's castle looking very much like them. *No wonder they didn't want to let me pass through the front doors without washing my clothes first.*

Traffic, including other horse drawn carriages, increased as they entered Horstruff. A short time later, they reached Lord Jon's castle. Tuck sighed, knowing he arrived back at the area he had begun at.

"Come, Sir Tuck. We will make sure you do not have any hindrance entering Lord Jon's castle." Lord Troy stood outside of the carriage and offered his hand to Patricia to help her step down.

Tuck jumped down and walked with them to the front gate. The two guards didn't make any effort to stop them while a young man hurried to the front doors of the castle. Before Tuck reached the entrance, the doors had already been opened and a servant bowed to Lord Troy.

"Welcome, Lord Troy and Lady Patricia. Lord Jon has been informed of your arrival. Please follow me to the waiting room."

Tuck followed behind, noting his presence had been ignored so far. *I might as well have been a ghost.* He noticed the castle was almost a duplicate of the Miller Castle, though the main staircase spiralled to the second floor from the opposite side. He looked toward where the kitchen was located in Miller Castle and decided it had to be in the opposite direction in Domum's version of the castle. He sat in the waiting room as servants quickly offered refreshments to Lord Troy and Patricia before turning their attention to him. Tuck wondered if he was by himself if he would still be standing at the front gate.

An attendant, a few minutes later, approached the trio. "Lord Jon will see you now. Please follow me."

Tuck trailed behind the others, climbing the spiral staircase and entering a room with a guard posted by its side. He heard voices coming from inside, sounding urgent. He stepped inside the room saw Jon and

Madoc looking at a map on a table. Jon quickly stepped forward to greet him.

"Tuck, what are you doing here? Perhaps you can assist us with our problem."

"Well, actually, I came here to give you another problem."

# SIXTEEN

Donna slapped the broom on the floor, sending a cloud of dust spiralling away. "Papa, I don'ts know when or even if Gilbert asks me again. Remember before you says he not good enough for me? I tolds him then you wouldn't lets me marry him. He not asks me since."

"Fine thing. I just try to looks after me last daughter and she gets mad at me. You want me to ask him to ask yous again?" Edward leaned against a wall, glancing at the back where he kept a whisky flask.

"No!" Both Donna and her mother answered in unison.

Trudy shook her finger at Edward. "Papa, you does enough harm already. First insults Gilbert and when yous finds he has money, suddenly becomes his friend. Now maybe too late. Handsome man like Gilbert has choices." She walked over to her daughter and hugged her. "There, there my sweet child. Don'ts yous worries none. Gilbert ask agains, you'll see."

Edward took that as a sign he wasn't needed and disappeared into the back room of their shop.

Trudy heard Donna try to stifle a sob and whispered in her ear. "You shoulds invite Gilbert over to your house and makes him a nice meal. A man will speaks of love more often with a full stomach."

Donna nodded. "Maybe so, but I haves not much food in the house to fill Gilbert."

Trudy reached into her apron pocket and produced a silver fern.

"Yous not tells Papa. Yous buy some food and maybes a new ribbon for yer hair.

Donna hugged her mother. "Thank you. Yous the best Mama in the whole world."

Trudy smiled. "Remembers, it's okay to let a man knows you likes him. It's also okays to let him knows other men likes you too. Now yous go. Papa and me finish cleanings up."

Donna gave her mother a kiss and hurried out of the shop. She thought of her mother's advice, of perhaps getting Gilbert jealous. She knew he reacted quickly to perceived threats, real and otherwise. As she walked down the road to her home, she began to formulate a plan.

She picked up a few groceries and meat from a butcher that she knew didn't label dragon or horse for beef. Donna calculated Gilbert was likely to come by tonight. He had missed seeing her for two days and that was as long as he normally was occupied on his other activities. As she purchased a new ribbon for her hair she worked on her plan.

Peter opened his door to her light knock. A bachelor nearing middle age, he fancied himself as a ladies' man even though women didn't share that belief. "Donna, what brings yous to me home?"

"I needs help with me door. It gets stuck sometimes. Can yous come over to looks at it?"

"I cans do that for you, Donna." Peter smiled, showing off yellow teeth.

Donna gave him a shy smile. "Thank you, Peter, Yous is a good friend."

When she reached her home, a small affair converted from a business that had disappeared, she unpacked her groceries and opened the back door, dropping a small pebble by the hinge. As she expected the door resisted closing and she smiled her satisfaction.

Donna prepared dinner, wondering what time Gilbert would show up. While she was fairly certain he would come over tonight it was the time that was hard to determine. Occasionally it would be quite late into the night after he stopped to have a few pints of ale. She had given up scolding him on that and focused her attention on getting him to stop gambling. Donna wasn't sure why she had fallen for him. Part of her wondered about the truth of the tales he told, worried how much he drank and was annoyed how much attention he paid to other women. However, part of her fascination with him was the very things that annoyed her and there was no doubt he had her heart. A knock on the door startled her out of her thoughts. She hurried over to the door and greeted the smiling Peter who was holding a small wood box with a few tools inside.

"Hello, Peter, thanks for coming over to helps me."

"Me always happy to helps a lady in distress. Is it this door that's sticking?"

"No, the backs door." Donna led him to the back and pointed at the door. "I cans hardly close it."

Peter tried opening and closing the door a few times. He scratched his chin and looked at the door handle.

Donna held back from sighing and watched as Peter slowly investigated the door. To her relief he eventually began to look around where the hinges were located. With a sudden insight he spied the small pebble and produced it between his fingers.

"Aha! I finds the problem." Peter stood beaming as he gazed at the pebble.

"Oh, Peter, yous so clever. You must stays and have some wine."

Peter graciously accepted the wine and Donna poured two glasses, sitting with him in the living room.

Donna listened to his musings on the upcoming battle. "I tells yous, Donna, this battle is not going to be good for our little town. If Lord Darius wins, he won't be happy that Vegrandis pays no taxes. He will claim a pound of flesh from us."

"We best hopes Lord Perry wins."

"Aye. Buts I hears that some ain't happy we not pays taxes, yet we are protected by Lord Perry. Mights be trouble either way after the battle."

Donna had heard similar rumours in her parent's trading store but hadn't heard of any solutions, other than someone should do something. Vegrandis didn't have a town council, deciding main issues at infrequent meetings. The loudest voices usually carried the vote but rarely did anyone stand up and take charge of a problem. The king, and with Lord Perry now his representative in Horstruff, had given up on trying to enforce laws and tax collection in Vegrandis. Businesses and the population migrated about the town on a whim. Business was more often done on trade rather than the exchange of money. It was a nightmare trying to find anyone in Vegrandis who didn't want to be found and equally difficult to tax a business that could be in a new location every week. It was a great place for residents of Horstruff to find a bargain or to make a trade, providing they knew who to talk to.

A second knock on the door made Donna jump up. She opened the door slowly. "Oh, Gilbert, it's yous. I's didn't expect you tonight."

"I's here anyway." He waited until Donna swung the door open. "Peter is here?"

"Yes he is. I hads a problem and Peter was so nice to come over to helps me."

Gilbert frowned. "I woulds help you."

"I didn't know whens you woulds show up." Donna put her hands on her hips. "You just show up when yous feels likes it." Donna turned and smiled at Peter.

Peter stood. "I best be goings. Nice seeing you, Donna. Hello, Gilbert."

"Thank yous for yours help." Donna gave Peter a small hug.

Gilbert watched Peter walk away and turned his attention to Donna. "He comes over often?"

She shook her head. "He just a friend."

Gilbert opened his mouth to say something but stopped with his jaw open. "Something smells good."

Donna sighed. "Do yous wants to stay for dinner?"

"I woulds likes that."

"I knews you woulds." Donna headed toward the kitchen. Feeling annoyed at Gilbert's short attention to Peter's visit, she dropped a plate in front of him.

"Maybe I should've asked Peter to stay for dinner."

"What's for? More for yous and me."

"He was nice to me, helps me out. You never around to helps me."

"I busy working for Lord Perry. He trusts me to gives him goods advice."

"Yous rather spend time with Lord Perry than me." She put her hands on her hips. "Peter seems to enjoy me company."

Gilbert's face began to turn red. "I don'ts like him hanging around here. You me girlfriend."

"Maybe I is, but maybe I wants to be more than just a girlfriend."

Gilbert looked down and took a drink of his wine. "Your Papa not wants Gilbert to marry you."

"That was befores. He see yous different now."

"You thinks so?"

"I knows so. I also knows I not wait forever for you to ask. I likes you, Gilbert, but there are other men who likes me too."

Gilbert took a big gulp. "Maybe I ask your Papa 'morrow."

———

86

Gilbert stepped inside the small trading shop, immediately causing all conversation and action to come to an abrupt halt. He looked around at Donna, her parents and the two customers as they stared back at him.

Finally Trudy broke the frozen moment. "Oh, looks who here. Gilbert, whats a nice surprise."

Edward walked over to Gilbert and extended his hand. "How is my good friend Gilbert doing? He grinned. "Comes to the back room where we can talks. I gots a drink for yous."

Donna whispered to Trudy. "Does Papa have tos makes it so obvious?"

"Papa means well. I sure Gilbert understands that." She turned to a customer at the counter. "Two wood knives for a bag of corn? Not goods enough. Four knives or you gets half bag."

Donna took a few steps away from where her mother bargained with a customer. She strained to hear what Edward and Gilbert were saying but could make out only the odd word. Suddenly she heard a curse and Gilbert stomped out of the backroom, looking annoyed.

"That be an insult!" He walked out of the shop, ignoring Donna calling after him.

Trudy hurried to the backroom and shook her finger at Edward. "What dids you says to Gilbert?"

Edward held up the palm of his hands. "Hardly anythings at all." He looked down toward the floor. "I merely suggests thats since he a man of money thats he not needs any dowry to marry Donna, perhaps he pays us a bit for taking her hand."

Trudy pursed her lips and began to hit Edward with her fists. "Yous being an idiot, Papa. You offends Gilbert and now he runs off."

"Okays, okays." Edward turned away from Trudy's blows. "I goes and make things up to him."

———

Trudy and Donna waited in the shop, occasionally looking out of the shop doors for a sign of Edward or Gilbert. Then they saw Edward make his way back to the shop, looking upset.

Trudy stood staring at him with her hands on her hips. "Well?"

Edward shook his head. "Gilbert, he be coming back. Wants to marry Donna."

"Then whys do you looks so mad?"

"I had to give Gilbert the dowry plus another goat."

# SEVENTEEN

Daniel bent down and hesitantly touched one of the five crystals lying inside the torn leather. He knew little of crystals and magic, but he could feel the power at his fingertips, giving him a tingling feeling. He scooped up the crystals and carried them gingerly to Sarah.

"I don't know much about crystals, but these seem very powerful."

She looked questioning at the crystals. "Is it safe for us to be around them?"

"I think crystals need a spell to activate them." He frowned. "I know what you mean. But perhaps fate has led us to find them."

"You may be right. In that case we should take them to Horstruff and give them to Lord Perry."

Daniel nodded. "That's what we will do then. In the meantime I will go and find some food."

He hurried off, hoping he didn't come across any more surprises.

———

Sarah opened her eyes after nodding off to sleep. The slow rhythm of the horse as it walked made it easy for her to rest. She looked at Daniel, feeling he must be exhausted from moving from dawn to dusk, stopping only at night. Even then, he would go out in search of food, water and setting up a safe place for them to sleep.

"Are you okay, my love?"

He turned around and gave a tired smile. "I feel fine." He turned back to lead the horse.

"Don't you think you need to rest a bit?"

"No, we must keep going."

"Why, because of the crystals?"

Daniel paused and stopped walking. Without turning around he spoke. "The crystals. As soon as I touched them, I knew of their power. I don't know how to use them, but I am certain that their use by the right people will save the kingdom." He turned to Sarah. "Our lives are in peril. We have been given a chance by Sir Gavin to escape to Horstruff. Now these crystals suddenly show up. I think there has to be a connection, that we were meant to find the crystals and give them to Lord Perry. Maybe that is the key to save the kingdom and ourselves."

Sarah smiled. "Maybe, or maybe it's one more thing to get us into trouble."

He quizzed her, "You think we should just leave the crystals here?"

"No, I think we should do what you said. Maybe we can make a difference in this war."

After a day of travel, Daniel made camp by a clump of trees. He was thankful the night was warm enough to sleep in the open and that Sarah was gaining her strength back. Despite being a poor hunter, he was able to obtain enough food that they were not hungry. The exertions of the day taxed his energy and as soon as he stretched out on the ground, he fell asleep. His sleep was disturbed by Sarah shoving on his shoulder.

"Wake up. Something is around us."

It took a moment for Daniel to change from his dream to reality. He slowly lifted his head and reached for his sword. The horse was acting nervous, pulling on the rope that secured her to a tree. He peered into the darkness around him and at first, couldn't make out anything unusual. Then he saw the shadowy shape of a creature creep less than a stone's throw away. Seconds later his eyes made out the short wings of the flightless Tantus dragon and his hand became damp as he lifted his sword. He watched as the horse-size predator move quietly and suddenly roar as it sprung ahead startling a deer from the trees.

Daniel lowered his sword and quickly ran to Sarah and helped her on Evado. He climbed on its back as well and without any encouragement, the horse bolted from their camp. He knew the Tantus dragons usually hunted in pairs. The first dragon would scare the prey to the other dragon waiting ahead and a blast of dragon fire would disable the prey. Both would feast on the animals that the dragon fire had weakened, partially dissolving the flesh. Fortunately the dragons were after the deer and not them.

Daniel slowed the horse as there was a danger of galloping in the dark. He knew which direction Horstruff was and also where the closest road was that led to it. He turned the horse and tried to calm her down.

"I think we're far enough away now that we can use the roads. We'll make better time and there will be less danger from dragons."

"I think that is a good idea, Daniel. Maybe we can come across some farms that will give us some food. You have done your best hunting, but I'm getting tired of the small animals you have caught."

He laughed. "I know. We need a dozen just for one meal. Sorry, I'm not quick enough to catch a deer."

"You did fine. You have us both alive and well. You're my hero."

The progress through the woods was slow, as they made their way at night. But neither of them was tired or wanted to rest with the knowledge that dragons were in the woods. When they reached the road, a dirt path just wide enough for two carts to pass one another, they stopped to rest. Daniel wrapped a rope from the horse around his wrist, figuring any disturbance would cause the horse to react and he would wake up in time.

He understood what Sarah meant about wanting a different diet. But the farms along the side of the road were not always what they seemed to be. A farm this far from Horstruff meant the farmer was either poor or someone that didn't want to be disturbed, likely for a good reason. Witches, warlocks and criminals lived in isolation. People, who by the use of spells, had turned into werewolves or other creatures also preferred to be left alone. There was also one other type of creature he knew of. Humans had a cousin along their DNA chain called chimpanzees. Gnants also had a close relative, but they were much more dangerous. Ghouls were the less fortunate cousins of gnants. They were only semi-sentient and liked to live in dark areas, being nocturnal, such as caves and abandoned farm homes.

Daniel was aware sometimes a farmhouse looked unoccupied because the ghouls had attacked and had eaten the original inhabitants. He had heard ghouls usually lived in tribes of six to ten and depended on the consumption of blood and organs as a diet.

It was also known that because ghouls liked to live in the dark their eyes were dark and large to absorb the little light available. Their other characteristic was a small, skinny stature with a sloping shoulder, hands and feet that ended in six-digit claws, and an overly large mouth filled with pointed teeth.

———

Morning came and Daniel led the horse with Sarah riding. She gave him a short conversation this time and he was pleased that she was continuing to gain strength. He was exhausted checking on her every few minutes and doing everything to sustain them. He hoped he could finally relax a bit while she slept on Evado.

He was tempted to ride the horse as well, but he considered that the horse may need all of its energy to carry her to Horstruff. He was pleased when they finally encountered traffic on the road coming the other way, and even happier when he took a closer look. The two older men led a horse pulling a cart full of potatoes.

A few minutes later the men gave a generous amount of potatoes for a few coins, taking pity on the weakened state of Sarah and Daniel.

"Potatoes are good for energy. Eat until your stomachs are full," one of the old men croaked out.

"Thanks." Daniel was willing to eat the potatoes as they were, uncooked and with the peel still on. "What is the road like up ahead?"

"Tis good. Hasn't rained for a couple of days, so the road is firm. With the talk of battles and war, the roads are not busy, even the highway men are not venturing out. Best be careful at night as I heard that a tribe of ghouls has been seen in the area."

Daniel carried on, deciding to eat a small potato. He wished he had salt to put on it but was content with something to have in their stomachs besides the bitter roots and the rubbery flesh of the small creatures he caught.

The road sloped downward and then made a gradual climb. When they reached the top of the hill Sarah called out to him.

"Daniel, I can see a farmhouse up ahead and off to our right."

He turned to her. "Any sign of people there?"

She shook her head. "It's too far to tell. But there seems to be a garden close to the house."

"Okay, let's stop at the road there. I'll go and check out the farm."

"Maybe we should both go."

"No, if there is danger I can escape faster by myself." He grinned. "Heck, when I saw the dragon I thought I could outrun the horse."

"Well I doubt there will be any dragons in the farmhouse."

The farmhouse was small but well built out of dark stone. He understood the need for strength in the remote areas where dragons could visit. A wood structure might fail under a determined attack by dragons. The stone walls were not only strong, but they also resisted the chemical fire the dragons released. The other defence were trees planted close enough to the farmhouse to make landing difficult for the large winged flying dragons. The flightless dragons were more of a concern as they were quick, capable of stealth and would patiently wait for the inhabitants to leave the security of the farmhouse.

Daniel approached slowly, noting that the garden showed signs of recent weeding. That meant at least humans lived in the farmhouse and not ghouls or other creatures that consumed only flesh.

He hesitated at the heavy wood door reinforced with iron straps and knocked. The sound of footsteps moving over a wood floor filtered through the door. A deep voice growled, "Who be there?"

Daniel took a small step back and called out. "A traveller seeking food and a place to rest."

The door slowly moved inward, revealing a wide, dark figure. The man wore animal skins as clothing and with his wild hair and beard looked like a beast as well. His hands and face were spotted with red blisters. "You alone?"

"No, I have a companion with me."

The man, who stood Daniel's height but weighted twice as much, stepped forward and looked around. In his hand he held a machete. "Where is he?"

"Waiting on the road." Daniel looked at the machete. "Beg your pardon for interrupting. I best be going now."

"Wait. Road's not safe at night. You and your friend can stay the night."

"I don't want to cause you any trouble."

"You won't." He looked around again. "Past few days there has been ghouls around here. Even saw them at dusk. I suggest you be here tonight where it's safer. Go get your friend."

Daniel went back to Sarah. "We can stay the night there, but the guy I talked to looked a little odd."

"That's to be expected out here."

"Yeah, I guess so. He also said the road isn't safe at night. Ghouls are around here according to him."

Sarah looked down the road behind her. "You know that makes sense. Whenever there are battles, ghouls often show up to feed off the dead and dying. They could be travelling to where King Charles' men are fighting."

"If he is right, then we best not be on the road."

The farmhouse's door was open, though the man had disappeared. Daniel stood a few feet away and called out. "I'm back."

The same figure stepped back at the door and gazed first at Daniel and longer at Sarah. "Huh, you didn't say nothing about your companion being a woman." He gave a small grin. "Can't say I blame ya." He pointed at the horse. "Best take off its harness and let it be free. If the ghouls come, you don't want the horse to be tied up. Ghouls can't catch a free horse."

Daniel unsaddled the horse and followed Sarah into the farmhouse. His eyes adjusted to the dim light and heard Sarah give introductions.

"My name is Sarah and my husband is Daniel. Thank you for kindly giving us a place to rest tonight."

A woman spoke from the corner of the room. "I am Judith and he is Drake. You are welcome as our guests."

Daniel saw the farmhouse consisted of two rooms, the kitchen and living quarters and a smaller room separated from the main by a leather curtain over a small doorway. The kitchen had a combination stove and fireplace, a table, two sturdy looking stools and a small counter built along a wall where a few pots and utensils were kept. The living area contained two chairs and a small table whose surface was almost covered by a large book.

He looked at Judith and saw a tall, slight woman with pale skin sitting in one of the chairs. She looked young compared to Drake and was dressed in a long, grey gown. He noticed her eyes were almost completely white and he caught his breath.

Drake noticed his reaction. "Do not fear her. She still has control over her hunger." He nodded toward the book. "We are searching for a remedy."

Sarah looked up at Daniel and back at Drake. "May I ask what happened?"

"She was attacked last spring by a vampire. It was a sickly, weak thing that she was able to fend off. Unfortunately, she still became infected. We have followed the advice of a witch and kept her from eating any flesh, cooked or not. We borrowed this book to see if there is a cure in it. We pray there is."

Daniel had heard of the ways of vampires. A vampire once infected is driven by a hunger to drink blood, and once the taste is given into, the hunger increases for more. The usual advice is to avoid giving in to the desire for blood or flesh in the hope the hunger will eventually disappear. There were rumours that some are cured that way. The other search for cure was by trying to read the Book of Spirits. It is believed all spells and counter spells could be found in the book, if one could decipher the strange script within it.

"Her spirit must be strong to last so long." Sarah spoke quietly.

"I do my best. Drake feeds me well from our garden and that helps keep my desires in check. I believe the infection is fading over time."

The four ate a simple meal of bread and squash. Daniel suspected that Drake had decided even milk and cheese would be wrong for Sarah to consume. The vegetable garden was their only substance. He knew that Judith looked younger because of the strange illness she contacted and could not go out in the strong sun, relegating her to a life inside the farmhouse.

Judith and Drake retired to the small room to sleep, leaving Daniel and Sarah to rest on the living area floor with a thin blanket for a cover. Daniel found the wood floor hard and uncomfortable, but exhaustion took over and he fell into uneasy sleep.

Sometime during the night he awoke to the sound of the horse whinnying and galloping away. He listened carefully and heard the cries of the frustrated ghouls. Silence followed a scratching sound at the door and window shutters. Daniel felt Sarah's hand on his chest as she turned closer to him.

"They can't get in, can they?" she whispered.

"I don't think so. I'm sure Drake has had to endure their attempts before."

The sound of the ghouls trying to claw their way in began to fade and finally stopped. Daniel breathed a sigh of relief and looked across the room to see Drake standing in the room holding the machete, staring at them with wide open eyes.

He took a step toward them when Judith entered and pulled at his arm.

"No, Drake, not now. Don't give in to the devil." She pulled at his arm several times and Drake slowly turned toward her.

Drake shook his head. "I'm okay now." He followed her back to the bedroom.

Daniel stayed awake as long as he could before sleep once more washed over him. When he awoke he saw Sarah sitting next to him and Drake and Judith in the kitchen. He slowly sat up, feeling the protest in his back. It was now clear to him that both their hosts were infected. Drake, because of his beard and thick hair, was able to venture for a short period of time to the garden. The leather skins protected his skin from the sun, though where his face and hands were exposed he developed blisters.

Their hosts made no mention of the disturbance last night or of Drake leaving the bedroom. Daniel and Sarah were inclined to leave it that way and after thanking them for their hospitality went outside in search of Evado. They found her across the field and cautiously approached. Her back was covered with small claw marks that weren't deep.

"It's a good thing we let her go free last night." Daniel spoke as he put the harness back on.

"And despite Judith and Drake being vampires, it was good we spent the night in their home. The way the ghouls were acting last night we may have well ended up dead."

Daniel held out his hand to help Sarah up on the horse. "These battles are sure going to attract ghouls and vampires. Drake and Judith are trying to find a cure but there are a lot of vampires who are quite content to feed on wounded soldiers. God help those who are injured.

Their blood will be a beacon for those who like to feed on blood."

# EIGHTEEN

King Charles stood as he heard the footsteps approach. He was alone in the cell, while his sons, high officials of his court and high-ranking soldiers were squeezed into the remaining cells.

Lord Darius with several men behind him approached King Charles' cell and the heavy wood door opened.

King Charles straightened his shoulders as well as he could. "Lord Darius." He gave a small bow of his head.

Lord Darius grinned. "I will be brief as I have more battles and work ahead. I need you to make an appearance on the royal balcony so we can address the masses. You will renounce your rule and proclaim me as king."

"I will, under the condition you spare the lives of my sons and those who were loyal toward me at the end. You have no fear of them. They will serve you as they have served me."

"I promise nothing of the sort. If you fail to do as I ask I will torture them. I'm sure their screams will convince you to quickly comply."

"Have you no honour? Is this a way to start your rule?"

Lord Darius turned to one of the soldiers. "Pick one of those in the next cell and cut off his fingers."

King Charles watched the soldier walk away to the next cell. "Wait, I will do as you ask."

"I'm not asking, I'm ordering you." He pointed at King Charles. "Take him to the royal balcony.

King Charles was led away down the hallway. He heard a scuffling sound behind him and the cry of protest from one of the cells. It occurred to him that Lord Darius never bothered to rescind the order to cut off the fingers of one of the prisoners.

For the final time in his rule, King Charles walked through the throne room and to the balcony. He looked at the masses below him and closed his eyes.

"Let us get started." Lord Darius held the crown in his hands. "Say the words as they are written out this parchment and crown me king."

"Only if you spare the lives of my sons and those you took prisoners."

"I'm getting tired of your demands."

"Then be tired. Kill me if you wish, I am dying anyway. But you dragged me up here to legitimize yourself being crowned king in front of the people. You want witnesses to say they saw me crown you king. There is a price for that and that is the lives of those who you took prisoner."

Lord Darius sighed. "Very well, I will spare your supporters."

King Charles stared at Lord Darius. *I don't trust him but if I don't follow through on the ceremony Lord Darius would claim to be king anyway and would definitely kill my supporters, for no other reason than to put fear in the minds of anyone thinking of opposing him.*

King Charles mouthed the words written on the script set in front of him. With trembling hands, he placed the crown on King Darius. The crowd below did not cheer but watched the proceedings in silence. King Charles guessed they were too scared to verbally protest the crowning of Lord Darius.

The guards led Charles out of the room and back to the cells below as Lord Darius raised his hands in triumph. The lack of cheers and applause did not seem to bother him as he twisted to his left and right as if the masses were giving him an ovation. He turned to a guard. "The former King Charles and his sons are to be put to death tonight and their bodies burned. Do this quietly. I do not want anyone loyal to them to have any symbols or bodies to inspire them." He paused a moment in thought. "Be sure the old man's death is quick and clean. He had at least some balls and never backed down."

"Very good, King Darius. "What about the other prisoners?"

Lord Darius frowned. "I'm in a good mood. If they will swear allegiance to me, spare them. I'm sure we can find work for them to do."

"If they refuse to swear allegiance?"

"Then cut off their heads for being bloody stupid."

———

Sir Sadon woke up with a hangover. He pushed one of the two women he shared his bed with last night out of his way. She swore as she almost tumbled out of bed.

He ignored her complaint and made his way across the room where a pitcher of water sat on a table. *Darius is the new king, thanks to me. And what do I get? More battles to plan. I hope Horstruff doesn't put up a fight. I'm tired of sticking my neck out without a proper reward other than those two bitches.* He poured the remains of ale on the floor from a tankard and refilled it with water. He gulped the water down, let out a burp, and turned toward the bed. "Hey, one of you get me some breakfast."

The one he almost pushed out of bed jumped to grab her belongings. "I'll get it for you, sire."

The other woman lifted her head from the pillow and groaned as she saw Sadon approach.

———

Collin waited until he was sure only the serving wench and the regulars at his table were within earshot. He leaned forward and whispered. "Lads, the king and princes are dead. Murdered last night."

Percy whispered back, "How do you know this?"

Collin gave a smile. "I have me sources. What's more is that you'll never find the bodies. Burned to ashes."

Percy tightened his jaw. "Those bastards. No respect. To win at battle is one thing but at least have honour in victory and defeat."

Collin nodded. "The king never bowed to that tyrant and kept his head up high. God help his soul."

Smitty crossed his arms. "So now we have King Darius. What happens now? I've already been approached to see how many swords I can make. I told them I can't make them out of thin air and that I need decent material to work with."

Collin looked to his left and right. "It is what I expected to happen. You see, Darius can claim to be king all he wants, but what does that matter if he is only king as far as he can see from his tower? He has to subdue any opposition that still resides in the other two castles. They have closed their gates and so far King Darius can't claim they are under his rule. I suspect in a few days they will give allegiance to the new king, providing they are allowed to keep their present status. Then Darius will hit all the small towns around here like Treston and make sure they understand they are under his rule."

Percy put down his tankard. "That still makes it a small kingdom. I suspect they'll want to get after Horstruff. That is the crown jewel."

"You took the words out of my mouth. They need to have Horstruff, but it won't come easy. Lord Perry runs that like it was his own kingdom and he won't have any use for Darius. It could be a nasty fight. Darius has more men and resources, but Lord Perry has the loyalty of the people behind him."

The serving wench bent down to wipe the table. "Horstruff? That's where that dragon slayer Sir Jon lives."

Percy looked up as he worked on his memory. "Yes he does, but I suspect he might be a lord by now. Lord Perry quite favours him after his help in defeating Lord Bennett. Horstruff is also where Council Madoc lives and someone with that much power in magic is nice to have on your side."

Collin tapped his empty tankard with his finger and the serving wench picked it up.

"Like I say, it will be quite a battle if Lord Darius and his dragons go after Horstruff. It will be a legend in the making if Horstruff prevails."

Smitty frowned. "And if Lord Darius wins?"

Collins opened his mouth to answer but was beaten by Percy. "Then we best prepare for a long, dark night."

# NINETEEN

K ing Darius paced the grand hall, taking a drink of whisky he held in his hand. "I love this room. It makes me feel powerful." He laughed. "Of course I am powerful." He looked at the men seated at the long table and stopped his pacing to speak to them.

"The good news is that the lords in this region have agreed to support me as king. We will be able to use their troops, and we will need those troops. I have decided that rather than wait for full order to be restored here, we will claim Horstruff. I believe Lord Perry will be reluctant to pledge allegiance to me but when he sees our troops arrive at his doorstep, he will be convinced to surrender to us. If he is foolish enough to resist our might, then he and any other lords supporting him will be executed." Lord Darius finished off his whisky. "I will also be planning the battle strategy and leading the attack. I want to be there when Horstruff falls. I may even make Horstruff the capital, I hear they have some fine castles I can use." He grinned as his senior officers looked at each other nervously. "Prepare your men to leave in three days time. I want to march on to Horstruff while I have the strong hand."

Sir Gavin left the room feeling it was a mistake to move against Horstruff. It would have been foolish to speak his concern to Lord Darius who didn`t take objections well. *He may think he has all the forces behind him but in truth they will not battle hard for him. They have no real loyalty to a man who forced himself as king. These men for the most part have not seriously trained for battle for* *years. That is one reason why King Charles fell as easily as he did. But Lord Perry keeps Horstruff prepared at all times and he won`t surrender without a battle. Darius' arrogance is going to cost a lot of lives, even if he does win.*

# TWENTY

Nadine carried the paper grocery bag up the stairwell and down the carpeted hallway. She felt too tired to even wrinkle her nose at the smells that emanated from the fabric carpeting. She reached her door, turning when she heard her neighbour across from her apartment exit from her own unit.

"Nadine, how are you doing?"

Nadine gave a small smile as she gazed at the slim but tall brunette. "I'm okay, Anna."

"If you don't mind me saying so, you look exhausted. Here, let me help you with that bag."

Nadine gave up the bag to Anna and took out her key. "You don't have to, I can manage."

Anna shook her head, her short hair tossing behind her. "Look, I know you've been ill for a while and until you get better, I'm glad to help you out." She carried the bag to the kitchen and was immediately followed by a grey and yellow speckled cat. "You go and rest in the living room. I'll unpack the groceries and make you some tea."

Nadine eased into an armchair. A moment later, the cat jumped on her lap, settled down and began to purr. She stroked the cat and whispered, "Rzet, you and Anna are my only friends."

Anna brought in two mugs of tea. "You know that grocery bag had mostly cat food. You look after that cat better than yourself." She smiled.

"I guess that's what makes us human, we look after others before ourselves."

Nadine looked up in surprise as she held her tea.

"Now how are you really feeling Nadine? Have the doctors given anymore information?"

Nadine shook her head. "I'm waiting for some more, Anna, but I fear I don't have much time left. Will you take care of Rzet for me if I can't?"

"Of course I will. If there is anything you want me to do, just ask." She put down her tea. "Now why don't you go and lie down? I'll come by later with some soup for you."

Nadine watched her leave and spoke to Rzet. "Did you hear that Rzet? She said I was human. I may die soon but it will be as a human."

———

Nadine woke up on the couch with the phone ringing. After a moment of hesitation she answered.

"Hello?"

"Nadine, this is Gordon Miller calling. I hope this is not an inconvenient time to call but I wanted to get this information to you straight away. I have been in contact with Jon, well I actually got this young fellow Tuck to do that, but the gist of that is he will be coming to get you."

"Get me?"

"Yes, this Madoc fellow apparently might be able to help by using his magical powers. But to do that you have to come here where we can send you back to Domum. He said on Domum the magic is stronger and also they are in a bit of a war and he can't leave there."

Nadine tried to take in the rush of information. "So this Tuck is coming to take me to Domum?"

"Not straight away. You will have to travel to my castle in Ballymiller first. He will be assisting you on the flight over."

"I'm not allowed to fly. I do not have the documentation that allows people to go to different countries."

"Not to worry. Madoc apparently is going to produce a passport for you. He will use Jon's passport as a guide and Jon also had a photograph of you in his wallet to use."

Nadine nodded, surprised that Jon had kept the picture of her of when they used to go out together. "When will Tuck arrive here?"

"I believe he is scheduled to land in America sometime tomorrow. He will call you when he arrives so you can make preparations to leave. We will make arrangements for you to leave for Domum as soon as you are able."

She hung up, her heart, racing. She had tried to reach Jon out of desperation, not really believing he would care enough to try and help her. *It must be as Anna said, humans try to help one another.*

Nadine tried to relax but the possibility that there might be help for her gave her new hope. She wondered who Tuck was and why he was willing to fly over just to help her. Her mind went through unanswered questions when there was knock on the door.

She opened the door to Anna, who was carrying a tray of food.

"I'm glad to see you're up. I made some dinner for you."

Nadine walked with her to the small kitchen table. "Anna, I just received a phone call. There is a doctor that I am going to see but he is far away. Can I ask you to look after Rzet?"

"Of course. Rzet and I will get along just fine. When will you be leaving?"

"In a day or two."

Anna reached over and touched her hand. "I will be praying for you."

They sat eating dinner without needing words spoken to convey what they were thinking.

———

Nadine made her way to the apartment door to answer the buzzer. "Hello?" She spoke into the intercom.

"I'm Tuck. I'm here to help you, that is, I'm here to escort you to Ireland."

She pushed the button to open the front door of the apartment building, wondering why he sounded so nervous.

Shortly later, she opened the apartment door and let Tuck in. She noticed he had a friendly face, without facial hair. He was average height and also a bit overweight. "Tuck, this is my friend Anna." She went on to explain how Anna was helping her and agreed to look after her cat.

Anna stood up to greet Tuck. "It's so nice to meet one of her friends. It's wonderful that you are going to accompany her to Ireland so she can get medical help."

Tuck nodded. "I'm glad to help out." He gazed around the apartment living room and sat stiffly in an armchair.

Anna looked at Nadine before turning her attention to Tuck. "Tuck, you don't have to go to the airport for a few hours. You must be tired from your flight over here. Why don't you have a rest until then?"

Tuck readily agreed and retreated to the bedroom.

Anna whispered to Nadine. "He seems like a nice young man. Not bad looking either."

"Yes, he is nice. He will be good company for me."

"He must quite like you to come all this way to help you."

Nadine nodded. She didn't know why Anna was so nice to her or why Tuck agreed to travel with her to Ireland. She remembered being a gnant and how rare that another gnant would consider helping another. But she found humans were different and noticed they often did small favours for strangers, such as holding a door open or giving coins to beggars. She found that she couldn't help but feel affection to Rzet and went out of her way to make sure her pet was cared for. She wondered if the Adepts knew when they transformed her to a human that it wasn't just her body that changed, but also the very way her mind worked. As a gnant she found humans ugly, but when Tuck walked into her apartment she saw him as an attractive male despite feeling ill. "I think he was just being nice."

Anna grinned. "I think he was being nice to a pretty lady."

Nadine blushed as she took a sip of her tea. "Thank you. Could you stay here while I visit someone?"

"Of course. Who do you want to see if I may ask?"

"Not so much as someone as some place. I need to go to a church. I need an answer to a question."

Anna smiled. "Go. I hope you find an answer that brings you comfort."

# TWENTY-ONE

Sir Anthony Graham steadied his mount, giving him a few pats on his neck. He looked over at his older brother who was inspecting his sword again.

"Garrett, that sword won't get any sharper looking at it."

His brother continued to examine his weapon. "It may not get any sharper but tomorrow it will be my best friend." He turned toward Anthony, his dark eyes piercing him. "You sit on your horse and act as if you're getting ready for a ride to town. Grow up man, this may be the last day of your life. You think I'm studying my sword too much? I think you would do well to think what we're up against."

Anthony glared at him. "You've never treated me with any respect. I know what's about to happen, you can be sure of that."

"The one thing I'm sure of is that you are the one that avoided the responsibilities of a Graham man. While the rest of us were establishing families and contributing, you were out gallivanting."

"I'm married now."

"Yeah, to a former barmaid." He spat out the words. "Do you know what you put our parents through?" The question was as sharp as razors.

"You bite your tongue, Garrett, or there will be one more battle you wish you didn't have to face."

"Anytime you think you're big enough to take me on, I'm ready to give you a lesson or two."

Anthony gripped the reins of his horse tightly and looked straight ahead, ignoring his larger brother. "Another time, Garrett. It looks like it's time to ride out." He urged his horse forward, joining the other hundreds of horses and men riding out of Horstruff.

The men and horses were divided into four groups to avoid congestion. When it came time to attack the enemy, each group was to hit at a different part, hoping to cause confusion with the larger forces. The battle was expected to be bloody with significant life loss, but it was determined that for Horstruff to have any chance of remaining autonomous they had to take the battle first to Lord Darius. The main reason for attack was to measure the strength and weakness of the enemy and to slow their advance to Horstruff until better defences could be built.

Anthony's other two brothers were in another group. He remembered his father explaining to them, that by keeping his sons in two separate groups it increased the chances that at least two would survive the battle. He further explained that two brothers should be together should one require the aid of the other.

Anthony had listened to his father carefully and looked at his brothers. The brothers began exchanging glances and he knew that none of them wanted to be paired with him.

———

Anthony rode quietly, wondering how he could have let himself drift so far away from his brothers. He had managed to appease his parents partially by behaving more responsibly. They were pleased he did decide to get married but were a bit concerned about his choice. They and the social circles of the nobility accepted Nicole far better than his brothers.

"Anthony."

He turned toward the voice. "Yes, Garrett."

"I was wrong to speak to you that way before a battle. One of us may die and I don't want those to be our last words."

"That's okay, Garrett. I'm sure you were disappointed with my behaviour in the past, but I'm working hard to be a better man."

"That's good to hear." Garrett was silent for a moment. "You do understand the Graham family has a proud tradition and we have an image to uphold that goes beyond being part of the nobility? When Horstruff still had its own king, the Graham family was actually part of the royal family. It was possible under some circumstances that a member of our family could have become king if Horstruff wasn't under the rule of King Charles." He turned to Anthony. "You must ask yourself if you are acting as a future king would. Let that be your guide."

"I will keep that in mind." Anthony had never really thought of the Graham family being part of royalty, but it did explain why his brothers acted the way they did. He supposed his father and mother had tried to set the example of the way to act and he had ignored them. No, he admitted, he hadn't ignored them. He had purposely acted the way he did because he felt he could never reach the high standards his brothers had set and found a different way to attract attention to himself. All very juvenile he decided.

"All I will ask is that you appreciate the high standards our family members must attain."

Anthony nodded, but wondered if his brother understood the chance of the Graham family becoming royalty again was extremely remote. He considered his brother lived in a rather optimistic world.

He also noted his brother still referred to King Charles in the present tense, refusing to accept that Darius had crowned himself king. *Garrett may be stubborn in his views of the world, but no one can ever doubt his loyalty. Next to Father, he considers himself to be head of the family and he should have expected that lecture. Garrett is right about one thing. We better bury the hatchet now because the chances are one of us may not see tomorrow's sunrise.*

# PART THREE

*Probably anywhere they think is safer,*
*but I don't know if there is such a place.*

# TWENTY-TWO

Jon looked out the open window. From his vantage point, it looked peaceful and quiet. But he knew far beyond the horizon a battle loomed. Men were about to die in a fight to preserve Horstruff from the clutches of Lord Darius. Despite Lord Darius claiming to be king, Horstruff served notice it was not prepared to accept his rule without a fight. Jon knew it was necessary to bring the battle outside of Horstruff to show resolve. Otherwise Lord Darius, and the people of Horstruff, would believe that there was no will to oppose him. More than anything else, Jon believed that confidence and attitude were the most important attributes in a battle.

He knew Lord Darius would punish those of the hierarchy for contesting his rule, in particular Lord Perry. Lord Perry accepted his head might be on the block if their opposition failed but believed Horstruff would suffer a worse fate if they didn't show strength. Lord Perry, like Jon, hoped that they could come to an agreement eventually with Lord Darius where they would accept him being king providing Horstruff would be allowed to continue autonomously. That would likely include increased tariffs and taxation but at least the citizens would be able to carry on much the same as before.

Now Jon felt the pain of guilt as he wondered how many lives were going to be lost if his battle strategy wasn't effective.

He found his hands had balled into fists and he tried to force himself to relax. *We need a better way to fight Lord Darius than just sword against sword.*

He walked to the door, addressing the guard. "Get my horse ready and please inform Lady Elizabeth I have gone to visit Lord Madoc."

"Yes, sire. You do not wish a carriage instead?"

"No, I want to feel the air."

The guard smiled, used to the unusual behaviour of Lord Jon.

Jon strolled out of the castle and came to face a carriage. *I thought I asked for a horse.*

Liz poked her head out through the carriage window. "Come on now, you didn't think I was going to let you go to visit Madoc and Angela by yourself did you?"

———

The servant, an older man who stood with perfect posture opened the front door, looked surprised at seeing Jon and Liz.

"Lord Jon and Lady Elizabeth. It is an honour to see you again. I shall tell Lord Madoc that you are here."

Lord Madoc and Lady Angela both greeted them warmly in a sitting room. As they were served refreshments, Angela asked how the decorations at his castle were going.

Jon shook his head. "Every time I look around something is being changed. There are workers in every room moving furniture or hanging something."

Angela grinned. "That's kinda like here. Madoc keeps disappearing all day long so I figured I might as well do something. I'm actually having fun trying to make this old castle homey and cheerful. It's amazing what you can do with the right colours." She stood. "Liz, let me show you around the castle. It has some really neat rooms."

Jon waited until Angela and Liz had left the room and gave Madoc a smile. "So it seems to me that your castle used to be rather quiet. Didn't you have just two servants to look after it?"

Madoc frowned. "That was the situation in the past. Unfortunately, Angela was feeling a trifle lonely and bored. I thought the solution might be to give her permission to make the castle more to her liking." He shrugged. "I didn't realize the extent Angela would change things."

Jon chuckled. "You really shouldn't have been surprised."

"I suppose so. My mind was on the matters concerning Horstruff and wasn't prepared for the mass of servants that suddenly appeared in my castle."

"I can see the flaw in your thinking."

"Flaw?"

"You said "my castle". I think she believes that to be joint ownership now." Jon laughed as Madoc rubbed the bridge of his nose. "What did you think was going to happen when you told Angela to make herself at home? She is not the shy type."

"You are quite right there. I don't really mind the alterations, though it was a bit of a revelation how fast life can change." He took a drink from his wine glass. Now why do I have the honour of your visit?"

"I need some advice and information. As you know the forces to protect Horstruff are undermanned compared to what Lord Darius has. He has managed to bring nearly all of the army under King Charles and put them under his control. In addition he has Sir Nolene and his dragons to assist him in battle. I need to find a way to equal the playing field."

"I see your concern, however we do have a couple of factors in our favour. First, we are defending our homes and that will make most men fight harder. As far as the dragons are concerned, they are difficult creatures to use effectively in battle and may not provide the additional advantage Lord Darius seeks. I will also point out, with all due modesty, that there is no one on the opposing side that can match me in the use of magic. I believe I can make a considerable difference. Lastly, and by no means insignificant, you also add the element of unique battle strategy. Lord Darius does not know what to expect from you and makes it difficult for him to plan an attack."

"I was thinking of using a new weapon. Explosives to be exact."

Madoc raised his eyebrows. "Really? May I inquire how you plan to accomplish this?"

"Gunpowder. It's a mixture of carbon, sulphur and potassium nitrate. I was hoping you could help me get the ingredients."

"I can help you obtain those items, although you may find their properties might cause them to act differently on Domum than on Earth."

"I suppose you may be right there, but we need something to put a bit of fear and confusion in Lord Dauris' men."

Lord Madoc pursed his lips in thought. Finally, he replied, "You are quite right. We put you in charge to come up with new battle strategies and this certainly qualifies in that regard. My own prejudice against using Earth's technology on Domum had me searching for a reason why we shouldn't incorporate explosives against the enemy. I suggest that you allow me a few days to procure the required materials and I will have them delivered to your castle. I will be discrete in doing so as we do not need the means of making explosives becoming common knowledge."

Jon nodded. "I agree with you there. Perhaps only a few individuals should prepare the explosives."

Madoc smiled. "It sounds like an opportunity for me to get my hands dirty."

———

Jon helped Liz into the carriage, his mind thinking of different ways to use gunpowder.

"Jon, have you seen Madoc's castle? I mean have you walked around on the inside?"

He shook his head. "Not really, just the entrance and a couple of rooms at the front."

"It's really interesting. The rooms go pretty far back, much further than you'd think from the outside. I think he uses magic to make the rooms bigger."

"I suppose that is something Madoc would do. As Council Madoc he had to be careful not to show off his wealth and that included the size of his castle. It would have been seen as being rude, and possibly dangerous, to have a castle larger than that of a lord."

"Interesting. So he made the inside of his castle bigger than the outside. He also did something underneath the castle. Instead of a dungeon in the basement there are large rooms. Angela said they were like his laboratories and she didn't go down there much and there were a couple of hallways she didn't know where they went to."

"Madoc can be a man of mysteries."

"That's true. He's still a bit unknown to us but I think Angela has him figured out."

# TWENTY-THREE

Lord Madoc sighed as he carefully poured the chemical mixture into the fist size clay jar. "This is rather tedious work." He spoke toward the long table where he and several others were working in the lower level of his castle. Madoc had obtained the necessary chemicals to make gunpowder, placing them in one of his laboratories.

Lord Perry answered in an amused voice. "If you wish to know what tedious truly is try going through a hundred documents that require your signature."

Lord Kevin Graham chuckled. "I remember those days. As boring as they were at least I had a feeling I was doing something. Hopefully what we are doing today will help in our cause."

Lord Jon spoke softly. "I don't believe Lord Darius' troops will be expecting explosives. Any surprise we can give them will be to our advantage."

Madoc replied. "They will be surprised I can assure you of that. Domum depends on using magic as a means for causing explosions. Because of that during a battle counter spells are used to effectively stop magical explosions. It will be a shock when the explosions do go off."

———

Jon returned to his castle after cleaning up at Lord Madoc's castle. As he made his way to the library where he kept his work for the upcoming battle he was surprised to see Sir Keith waiting for him.

"Sir Keith, what are you doing here?"

Sir Keith gave a nervous smile and raced out his answer. "Pardon the intrusion, Lord Jon, but I was feeling a bit restless and decided to wander down to where I knew you were working on battle plans and offer my assistance.

"I see. Well actually I was just going to relax this evening. The plans are going along very well, and I decided to take a break and look at them again later with fresh eyes. Let us go for a beer instead."

Jon led Sir Keith to a small lounge. A servant quickly brought two glasses of port, a drink he knew Sir Keith favoured.

"How is Lady Karla doing?"

"Very well, Lord Jon. Thank you for inquiring."

"I would guess she's rather concerned about the upcoming hostilities with Lord Darius."

"Yes, as we all are."

"I was curious if she was aware of Lord Darius' opinion of those who practice magic."

Sir Keith sat up straight. "What do you mean?"

"I heard rumours that Lord Darius actually doesn't like or trust witches or wizards. He will use them and their abilities but believes they are only after his power. So he makes sure they are under his control at all times. Not a pleasant existence."

"I hadn't heard that. Are you sure?"

"As I said, just rumours. But Lord Madoc knows of Lord Darius and I'm inclined to believe him." Jon watched Sir Keith's face turn pale.

"Of course, just rumours. Well, I shall not take any more of your time." Sir Keith stood. "It was nice to see you, Lord Jon."

———

Lady Karla crossed her arms and rolled her eyes upward. "That is nonsense. Lord Darius does use witches and others, but he doesn't put controls on them. Lord Jon actually said that? He should know better. People in power don't want to anger those who can use magic for obvious reasons."

"All right, but I was very concerned when he said that, although he did stress it was just a rumour. Perhaps he heard it wrong," Sir Keith said.

"More likely he is an idiot. I am going to my room to meditate."

Sir Keith poured himself another port, wondering about the conversation he had with Lord Jon. *He is not an idiot by any means. Why would he say that to me?*

———

Lord Jon entered Lord Perry's office, acknowledging Lord Madoc and Lord Perry. "I'm sorry for the interruption but I believe we have a situation with Sir Keith and Lady Karla."

Lord Perry rubbed his eyes. "Please go on."

"Sir Keith was at my office again today, inquiring once more if I needed his help. He looked and acted rather oddly, as if he was doing something very uncomfortable. I took him to a lounge instead and during a drink implied that Lord Darius had a dislike for those who use magic. Sir Keith looked very upset with the news and immediately hurried away."

Lord Madoc. "So he believed your ruse."

"Yes, and the only reason I believe he acted that way was because they are in alliance with Lord Darius. I'm sorry to say that."

Lord Perry nodded. "As I am troubled to hear that." He sighed. "We have enough other evidence to suggest they are collaborating with Lord Darius, likely through an intermediate. I will have my guards pick them up and charge both with treason."

Lord Jon closed his eyes for a moment. "Lord Perry, I know the punishment for treason is death. However, I would like to plead to you for leniency for Sir Keith. In the time I have known him, before he met Lady Karla, he seemed to be an honourable man. I believe she has had a negative influence on him, and he wouldn't normally act this way."

Lord Perry studied Lord Jon. "I respect your opinion, but it would not look good if I allowed someone guilty of treason to be spared of his life. An example for all must be seen."

"I may offer a solution." Lord Madoc waited until the others looked at him. "Have your guards pick up Lady Karla who I believe is the one pushing to help Lord Darius. I will pick up Sir Keith and take him to your castle. I will instruct him to make a full confession to you. Perhaps you can spare him his life under the condition that he came to you and confessed his crimes."

Lord Perry thought a moment before answering. "Yes, I believe Sir Keith through his previous behaviour deserves clemency. Lord Madoc, if you would go and pick up Sir Keith and have him make a full confession I will spare his life. I will not give Lady Karla the same opportunity."

# TWENTY-FOUR

Sir Keith heard the door cord striking the bell. Minutes later the servant ushered in Lord Madoc. Sir Keith quickly rose from the armchair in the sitting room.

"Lord Madoc, for what do I owe this unexpected visit?"

Lord Madoc frowned. "I must ask you to accompany me immediately. I will explain en route."

"Of course." He turned to the servant. "Please inform Lady Karla that I am going with Lord Madoc on a matter of importance."

Outside of his castle, Sir Keith found a carriage waiting. So far Lord Madoc had remained tight lipped on their destination and the purpose of his visit. He climbed inside the carriage and faced Lord Madoc. "May I ask what this is all about?"

"We are going to see Lord Perry, the reason which will be very clear in a minute. We are at war with Lord Darius and it has come to our attention you are aiding him. This, Sir Keith, is treason and is punishable by death."

Sir Keith turned pale, and his jaw began to stutter out words.

"Do not speak yet." Lord Madoc held up a hand. "Right now Lady Karla is being escorted to Lord Perry in a separate carriage. Her crimes are clear and without redemption. You have an opportunity to save your life, Sir Keith. Lord Jon and others believe that you have been duped into giving information to Lord Darius. If so, Lord Perry may show leniency.

When you are in front of Lord Perry, I advise you to make a full confession of what you have done."

Sir Keith buried his head in his hands, holding back a sob. "I am so sorry, Lord Madoc. Is there nothing I can do to save Lady Karla?"

"No, her fate is sealed. Yours would be too but for intercession of Lord Jon. I have also spoken on your behalf. But you must now show some backbone. Stand tall in front of Lord Perry and answer his questions fully. Do you understand?"

Sir Keith sat up. "I do."

———

Sir Keith waited in a sitting room with two guards, pacing the room as time dragged on. Finally the door opened, and Lord Madoc beckoned him to follow.

He trailed Lord Madoc to what used to be the throne room of the castle. Sir Keith walked the red carpet up to the steps where the throne chair rested on a pedestal and dropped to one knee with his head down.

"Rise, Sir Keith." Lord Perry spoke in a heavy voice. "You will tell us everything of what you passed on to Lord Darius in your confession to Lord Madoc. You will leave out nothing, is that understood?"

"Yes, Lord Perry."

"I have sentenced Lady Karla to death. She will be executed at dawn. There will be no reprieve and do not waste my time asking for one."

Sir Keith felt weak at his knees, recovering before he collapsed.

"You will receive twenty lashes tonight and be kept in a cell for a fortnight. You will be allowed to keep your castle and your title, under the agreement you never commit an offence against the true king ever again. You have had a serious fall from grace, Sir Keith, but you have a chance to make amends. That is all. Guards take him away."

Sir Keith dropped to one knee again. "Thank you, Lord Perry for your mercy."

———

The first thing Sir Keith noticed in the dungeon was the smell of decay. The low light given by the flickering torches made shadows jump adding to gloom of his cell. After the guard locked the door, Lord Madoc approached.

"Speak."

Sir Keith's jaw worked before his voice came out, cracking as he revealed his guilt.

"I was approached by an agent for Sir Nolene to meet him outside of Horstruff." Sir Keith covered his eyes. "In exchange for the promise of being made a lord, I revealed what I knew of Horstruff's defences and army."

Lord Madoc listened to the rambling, and at times the incoherent confession. At the end of his visit Lord Madoc shook his head at Sir Keith's misguided quest for power and was relieved he hadn't revealed critical information to Sir Nolene.

———

Sir Keith felt the sweat drip down his chest and back as he was led shirtless to the middle of the small courtyard, even though it wasn't an especially warm day. As his wrists were tied to the top of a post, he closed his eyes and let out a shuddering breath. The first strike of the whip came without warning. Each subsequent strike of the whip on his back was called out by one of the guards. After the seventh strike Sir Keith lost all strength in his legs and by the tenth had wet himself. He vaguely remembered being dragged back to the dungeon.

Sir Keith fell to the floor of his cell, almost passing out again from the pain of the lashes. Minutes passed before he managed to crawl to his hands and knees. Tears dripped from his eyes as he gripped the bars of the cell to pull himself up. "Lady Karla," he called out in a croaking voice.

Eventually he heard a reply beyond the stone walls of the cell.

"Yes, Sir Keith." Her voice was calm, without emotion.

"I am so sorry, my love."

"You have nothing to be sorry for, Sir Keith. I used you for my own gains. I got caught and it is my responsibility."

"I still feel guilty."

"Don't. You were good to me and I took advantage of that. I have, to my shame, taken advantage of many people. Sir Keith, you are a good man. I hope the best for you in the future and despite my original goals, I do feel affection for you. But now I must ask you to let me have my last hours in peace. I would like to meditate and prepare myself for the next life."

Sir Keith hung his head and turned to the planks of wood hung by chains from the wall that served as a bed. Slowly he dropped face down on it, feeling like his world had ended.

Sleep wouldn't come to him and in the early light of the morning he heard the guards as they trooped past his cell. He waited, staring past his cell door, and saw Lady Karla in heavy chains being walked between two pairs of guards. She kept her head up high but stopped and gave him a feeble smile. "I am prepared for my next journey. Fear not for me, for I have a place to go." She continued her final journey, giving him a final quick look as she stepped by.

He watched out of the cell door long after she was gone. For a moment he thought he saw the yellow light of the morning sun go brighter. He allowed himself a fragile smile, thinking it was Lady Karla's soul going to heaven.

# TWENTY-FIVE

**D**aniel moved Evado to side of the road, allowing a string of carriages to pass by going the opposite way. "There sure are a lot of people leaving Horstruff."

"I guess they want to avoid being where the battle is going to take place." Sarah grinned. "And we're heading right into it."

"I'm sure we will be safe regardless. It wasn't safe back at Regius, that's for certain"

"True. Where are these people going?"

"We're only seeing those who can afford to go. Most of the townsfolk stay in their homes or a shelter during the battles. Where they're going? Probably anywhere they think is safer, but I don't know if there is such a place."

———

Sarah called out to Daniel, "I think we must be really close to Horstruff."

"Why, because there are more people on the road?"

"No, because of the smell."

Daniel took a sniff of the air. "Yeah, you're right there. That's good because I think we both need rest."

"You more than me. I told you before, I could walk a bit and you could ride Evado."

He shook his head. "That wasn't going to happen after what you went through."

Sarah pointed with her arm. "I can see part of one of the castles. Maybe it's Lord Perry's."

The dirt road widened with the increased traffic and soon changed to cobblestones. Daniel received directions to Lord Perry's castle and followed the main road to his residence. The guard house was manned by an old man who appraised them for a moment and spoke in a reedy voice. "Who are you comin' to see?"

Daniel was expecting a larger force to protect the entrance to Lord Perry but in a careful voice announced, "We need to see Lord Perry on a matter of great importance."

The old man grinned. "No disrespect, sir, but what makes you believe Lord Perry will take the time to see you? There is a war coming here if you haven't noticed."

"That's what we are coming to see him about."

"All right then, but I wouldn't risk a hollow fern he'll see ya." He pointed toward the castle. "Mind the droppings."

Daniel led Evado past the gate. The horse twitched her ears and reluctantly followed him after he gave a stronger pull on the reins. "She doesn't like something here."

Sarah pointed at two almost horse size creatures watching them carefully well away from the brick roadway. "Aren't those valdelupus?"

Daniel peered at the grey and black carnivores. He had heard about oversized wolf-like creatures before but now saw them for the first time. "Oh, shit, I think they are." His heart began to thump in his chest. "I think we're safe." He continued to walk up the road without taking his eyes fully off them and almost stepped into one of the large droppings the guard warned them about.

Daniel helped Sarah off Evado while a stable hand waited to take the horse to the stables. The large double doors had a decorative pull cord that Daniel tugged. He looked at Sarah and sighed. "I hope we get a decent reception."

One of the massive doors swung open, revealing a huge man that strained the large leather belt holding his stomach in. Daniel looked at the blemished face of the wheezing giant who looked straight ahead.

"Yesss?" Daniel jumped, not expecting to see the demon-looking humanoid.

He looked down and saw a gnant dressed in a black suit rubbing his hands together.

"We came to speak with Lord Perry about the battle with Lord Darius." He hoped his voice carried sufficient authority and wished he had better clothes on, deciding looking like a destitute beggar wasn't the way to approach a lord.

"Sssorry, he is busy." The gnant stepped back and the giant of a man began to close the door.

"Wait." Sarah stepped forward. "Please, we have something that will make Lord Perry very grateful to you for allowing us to speak to him."

"How?" The gnant looked from Daniel to Sarah.

"We found something special that will give great power to Lord Perry." Sarah gushed out the words.

"Ssshow me."

Sarah exchanged looks with Daniel. "I will show you inside the castle."

The gnant swayed side to side as he thought. "Insside then."

Daniel followed Sarah and watched her cross her fingers behind her back. The size of the entrance was intimidating with its high curved ceiling. High archways led to other rooms and hallways and he saw a dozen servants going about their various tasks.

Sarah looked at the gnant and spoke in a clear voice. "Daniel, please show him the crystal."

Daniel nodded, slightly surprised at the way Sarah was speaking. He knew she was still tired from their long journey, yet she was displaying a surprising vibrancy. He fumbled inside his pocket for one of the crystals, carefully extracting one from a cloth they were wrapped in. He held it out in the palm of his hand and saw the gnant open his mouth in surprise. He closed his fingers on the crystal just as the gnant reached for it, scratching his hand in the process. "Hey! It's not for you, it's for Lord Perry."

The gnant quickly looked around, noticing several servants were looking in their direction.

"Wait here." The gnant scurried out of the entrance hall and up a curved set of stairs, leaving them in the company of the oversized human.

Daniel looked at his hand and at Sarah. "He was sure excited about the crystal."

"Good thing we only showed him one." She gave him a tired smile. "At least we have a chance of meeting Lord Perry."

The gnant returned with a man wearing a soldier's dress uniform. The bald, dark skinned man frowned as he observed them. "I am Sir Nathan and Lord Perry has instructed me to see exactly what you have in your possession. I understand it is some sort of crystal that may or may not serve any useful purpose."

Sarah gave him a quick smile and a small curtsy. "Please forgive our appearance. We managed to escape from Lord Darius when he raided our village and have been travelling since then. We also have more than just this crystal."

"What else do you have?"

Daniel looked at the gnant that was watching them with keen interest. "Can we show you in a more private room?"

"Very well. Follow me." Nathan led to a small sitting room on the second floor, not looking convinced it was necessary to leave the entrance hall. "Now what is it you need to show me?" He waved at a servant and a gnant to leave the room.

"This." Daniel carefully laid out the five crystals on a table. "We came across them in a field with a torn leather vest. If you touch them you can feel they are alive."

Nathan reached out with his big hand and held them. "They are alive at that. I never thought I would come across these again."

Sarah added, "We thought they may have strong powers and decided we should give them to Lord Perry. He might be able to use them against Lord Darius."

"You did right." Nathan picked up the crystals and turned toward the door. "Wait here. I will return shortly."

Daniel let out a long breath of air. "I guess we wait."

A servant entered the room carrying a tray. "Pardon me, m'lady, sir. Would either of you be averse to having something to eat?"

Daniel sat up straight. "That sounds fine by me."

———

Sarah and Daniel were ushered into Lord Perry's office. Daniel saw Sir Nathan standing by the desk where Lord Perry sat behind.

Daniel dropped to one knee and bowed his head. "Lord Perry."

"Oh, please, no need to be so formal. There is just the four of us here. Are you aware exactly what those crystals are?"

No, Lord Perry. Just that they are alive."

Lord Perry smiled. "They are indeed. The crystals you came across were last seen in the possession of Lord Bennett as he was being carried away by a Fornido dragon. As you may have surmised, these are very powerful crystals. There are actually six crystals and collectively they are known as the Locas Crystals."

"But we found only five. Where is the sixth?"

"Lord Jon alone knows where it is kept. We were concerned what would happen if all six crystals were to fall into the wrong hands."

"What would happen if all six crystals were to be joined together?"

"That is a matter of some speculation. However, it is believed that joining of all six crystals would give the possessor unimaginable power. There is also some danger, that besides giving the owner complete control, it could cause a rift between Domum and other worlds. The ancient Adepts, who created the crystals, didn't leave much information on their actual use."

"So what are you going to do with the crystals?"

Lord Perry sighed. "I will have to consult with Lord Madoc and Lord Jon before I make any decisions. I would prefer if you and Lady Sarah did not converse with others about what you found."

Daniel quickly agreed. "Of course, Lord Perry. We have told no one of the crystals prior to coming here."

Sarah spoke up. "But that gnant knows we have a crystal. He won't keep it a secret."

Lord Perry frowned. "That is a concern. The gnants won't tell humans about the crystals but will quickly spread the word to their own. The situation is that Lord Bennett tricked or stole two of the Locas crystals and they want them back."

Sarah gazed at the crystals on his desk. "I guess they have a point there. Are you going to return them to the gnants?"

Lord Perry sighed. "It is not that simple. I would like to keep the crystals as a safeguard in case Lord Darius obtains the advantage over us. We may need the crystals to assure our survival. There also appear to be two distinct groups of gnants. Lord Jon brought this to my attention that a good portion of gnants have evolved to be smarter, more social and likely have different leaders which are called Adepts. So the question is which gnants do I give the crystals to? The crystals, by the way, are useless unless joined to all the other Locas Crystals. But back to your original question. If I don't return the crystals to the gnants they may perceive that as act of war, and one thing we do not want is a war with the gnants. So far we have enjoyed a good period of peace with them. I wish to keep it that way. So the short answer is yes, I will return two of the crystals to them. The more difficult answer is when."

Nathan cleared his throat. "Perhaps, Lord Perry, we can inform Lady

Sarah and Master Daniel that they are guests here at the castle. Lord Jon and Lord Madoc should be here soon."

"Of course. You two have travelled a considerable journey and I insist that you stay here until the hostilities cease. I will have one of my servants show you to a suite and will also provide you with some new garments. I ask you to refrain from speaking to others about the crystals and not journey outside of the castle walls."

Daniel nodded as Sarah thanked him for his hospitality. Daniel understood they were confined to Lord Perry's castle to make sure they did not reveal the news of the crystals to anyone. He didn't mind, compared to the prospect of trying to find a place to stay in Horstruff or, even worse, being placed in jail until it was deemed safe for to them to be released.

# TWENTY-SIX

Garrett chuckled at Anthony's story as they drank tea and ate a small serving of food. The clearing in the forest provided a good location to dismount and relax. "I didn't know you did all those things. My lord, you got yourself in a situation that time." He shifted his legs as he sat on the log with his ration of stew on his lap.

Anthony gave an embarrassed shrug. "Well, in all honesty that was probably a good indication I should have severely curtailed my drinking."

"I'm glad that you see the wisdom in that. On the other hand, it does make me a bit envious of the life you have led. Tell me about Lady Nicole. How did you meet her?"

"Well, I had first met her acquaintance when I used to inhabit various drinking establishments. At that time she was a barmaid. However it was at Stone Retreat I met her under different circumstances."

"Stone Retreat? You were there on a holiday?"

"No, I escorted Lady Elizabeth there to join Lord Jon."

Garrett sat up straight. "Wait, was that the time the battle with Lord Bennett took place?"

"Indeed. That madman had gone to the roof for his final stand and had taken Lady Nicole as hostage."

"I didn't know you were at that battle, Anthony. Did you see actual combat?

"Not exactly. I rode my horse up the staircase to the roof and took Lady Nicole back down to safety, just as a Fornido dragon attacked."

Garrett's jaw dropped. "I have heard nothing of this before, only of Lord Jon and Sir Nathan battles. Why did you not tell us of this before?"

"I didn't wish to brag about my exploits. Lord Jon deserves the credit for battling Lord Bennett when he had no obligation to do so. Lady Nicole and I know what transpired there and that is sufficient for us."

"There were rumours of a lady tied to a post as a Fornido dragon attacked and that a knight on a white horse came to her rescue. I assumed it was story made up by that silly dwarf Gilbert." He grinned at Anthony. "You as a knight in shining armour." He burst out laughing.

Anthony joined him in laughing. "I was even sober at the time."

Garrett stood. "I think we better turn in early. It is likely we will face battle before noon tomorrow. I must say this journey so far has been worthwhile. I believe I know enough of my younger brother to say I'm proud to ride with him."

———

Anthony waited on his horse next to Garrett. He looked at the long line of horses and men facing the vast army in the field just below them. In too short a time the signal would come, and the battle would begin. Anthony understood that a complete victory by either side was unlikely and casualties would be high, but the battle was necessary. It would help determine strengths and weaknesses on both sides but for Horstruff's army it would also tell Lord Darius that Horstruff was not bowing down to his grasp to being the undisputed king.

Garrett spoke in a low voice. "When we charge, go behind me. Follow my lead."

"I won't use you as a shield, Garrett. I will be by your side."

"I understand your feelings, but I am the oldest Graham here. Please comply with my wishes."

Anthony stared at him for a moment. "Very well, I will do as you ask."

The horns sounded and suddenly the horses began to gallop down the slope. Mud, grass and dust burst into the air under the thundering hooves amid the yells of the men. Anthony directed his horse behind his brother's when the first volley of arrows arrived. He heard the cries of a few men and saw horses stumble as they narrowed the gap between the two armies.

Then they were upon the opposing army, swords flashed and whirled in the close quarters. Screams filled the air from the injured and the dying. Anthony tried to focus on those in front of him while manoeuvring his horse to prevent an attack from behind. His agility and training with swords was giving him an advantage over most opponents. He dispatched another foe and turned to see how Garrett was doing.

Anthony saw his brother was using more strength than skill to overpower his adversaries when a falling opponent struck his sword one final time. The blade slipped under Garrett's guard and into his midsection.

Not a sound came out of Garrett's open mouth as he slumped forward. Anthony moved his horse next to Garrett's and grabbed him to stop him from falling.

"Hang on, Garrett." He led Garrett's horse away from the battle as trumpets sounded on both sides.

Gradually both forces retreated, carefully eyeing each other as they backed away. Battle protocol on Domum demanded that fighting stop at the sound of trumpets on both sides. Shortly afterward, the commanders from both groups would meet to discuss possible surrender, or if hostilities would continue. It would also give time for the grim task of taking care of the dead and the wounded. Both groups knew the dead had to be buried with rocks piled on top to prevent ghouls from feasting.

Anthony pulled Garrett from his horse and held him on his lap as he sat on the ground.

"You'll be okay. Stay strong."

Garrett shook his head slowly. "Sorry." His breath rasped out. "Not going to make it." He took in a ragged gasp. "Tell father I fought well. You, prepare yourself as you're going to be king someday. You're a Graham, do us proud."

Anthony watched as Garrett's body relaxed and life left him. With tears in his eyes, he said, "I promise I will do you honour."

———

Anthony walked about the camp in disbelief, calling out his brothers' names. "Philip, Terrance."

A soldier heard his shouts, stopping him. "I know of them. They be over there." He pointed to an area where several men were lying on the ground with wounds being attended to. A white cloth with a red stain hung from a post, indicating a place where treatment of some degree was available to the injured. As Anthony approached, he heard moans and cries of anguish. The smell of whisky, used as a pain killer and disinfectant, filled the air.

He looked around and spotted his brother Terrance kneeling above Philip lying on the ground.

"Terrance, how badly is Philip injured?"

Terrance, with his thin, chiselled features, looked up at him and gave a small shake of his head. "He is resting right now, barely conscious."

Anthony looked at the blood stain on Philip's right thigh.

"He took an arrow and has lost a lot of blood. The wound looks ugly. As he fell his horse caused the arrow to be ripped out."

"Is there anything we can do?"

Terrance grimaced. "The doctor said we may need to remove his leg to stop infection. I didn't want to make such a decision and waited for you and Garrett."

Anthony placed a hand on Terrance's shoulder. "I'm sorry I must tell you. Garrett has died in battle."

Terrance squeezed his hand into a fist and bowed his head. "Oh, God, no."

Anthony looked at Terrance. The youngest brother seemed ready to fall to the ground in grief. Then Anthony turned his attention to Philip, noting the slow rise and fall of his chest had stopped.

"Terrance," he said in a soft voice, "I believe Philip has joined Garrett. God bless his soul."

Terrance looked at Philip and began to wail. "No, this cannot be. This cannot be."

Anthony stared at his smaller brother, remembering how Terrance was treated differently by their parents. Terrance was smart and artistic, but never was strong in the face of adversity. He reached down and pulled Terrance to his feet.

"Our brothers died bravely and with honour. If their lives mean anything we must act the same. Stop crying out loud and get your back straight."

Terrance swallowed hard and shifted his shoulders back. "I'm sorry, you are right. But it is hard to stop my eyes from wetting so."

"If you must cry, then do so with your head held high. We need not be ashamed to be sad over the loss of Garrett and Philip."

Anthony pulled Terrance away from the area and to a clearing. "Do you know how to fight at all?"

"Not well, I'm afraid."

"Then stay by my side if there is another battle and keep your horse just back of mine. I will protect you."

"I should fight like the rest the men and stand by myself."

"Terrance, that may be what you desire. But consider that if you were to die in battle, how would I tell our parents that three of their sons died?

What would I say to your young wife who is carrying your child? This is not a time to be selfish. For the sake of your family, you must do as I ask."

Terrance nodded. "You speak with wisdom. I will do as you say."

"Good. Now as the oldest Graham I must attend the council meeting that Garrett was to go to."

———

The twelve men sat in an oval inside one of the large tents. A grey bearded man, his battle scars visible on his arms and face, stood at the front. Sir William spoke in a gravelled voice as he looked at each soldier in turn.

"Each of you represents a family of the district of Horstruff. When it is time to give your input, know that besides your families interests you are also honour bound to place the king and Horstruff first." He took a deep breath as a rattling sound issued from his lungs. "We have suffered terrible losses with our battle today, but if it is any consolation, our enemy suffered even more losses. They still greatly outnumber us, however, they know they have been in a fight. Now the question is, do we fight again or retreat? And if we fight, what strategy do we use?"

Sir Edwards, a stocky man of indeterminate age, though certainly past middle age, spoke carefully. "We have done what we set out to do, and that is to tell Lord Darius that we do not recognize him as king. I see no need to lose more lives and little to gain in continuing to battle him here. I say we return to Horstruff where we are needed to defend our property."

Anthony looked around and saw several heads nod, but others remained still, as if still considering the words.

A second man stood, his hair and beard dark, making his small frame look a bit more menacing. "Forgive me, Sir Edwards, but you do not speak my thoughts. It is here where we need to battle Lord Darius. We have already surprised him with our two-prong attack and his losses are heavy. While he still has the manpower advantage we have proven he is no match for our more experienced fighters. I for one do not wish to run with my tail between my legs and return to Horstruff. Lord Darius will attack and lay siege to Horstruff and there he will have complete control. He will merely have to wait until we run out of food and provisions. I say we attack now while our swords have the advantage."

More men nodded their heads and two raised their fists in the air.

Sir William looked around the men again. "Do we have another speaker, or shall we vote?"

Anthony stood. "For those who do not recognize me, I am Sir Anthony Graham, the oldest surviving son of Lord Graham. Both Sir Edwards and Sir Stevenson bring forth valid points. I believe the course of action lies in between them.

"No doubt we did surprise Lord Darius with our attack, but I do not expect he will be so unprepared next time. The men we did kill were mostly those on the perimeter that were inexperienced in how to sword fight. The next time they will not fall so easily. There is also the matter that Lord Darius has the services of a dragon master and has no qualms about bringing dragons to help in his battles.

"However, to fully retreat to Horstruff will give Darius' army an easy route to us and they will arrive refreshed and able to attack.

"I propose the bulk of our men return to Horstruff while a few of us remain to harass Lord Darius' men. A small number of light riding horsemen can cause much difficulty for a large force by taking the high ground and attacking with arrows. Each attack would be short before the riders would disappear again. For example, a few lighted arrows at night, shot at the supply tents."

Sir William rubbed his chin. "An interesting idea."

"I must confess I stole it from Lord Jon. He told me of something they use on his world called guerrilla warfare. Small groups of men can be very disruptive to a larger group."

Lord William looked at the other men, most of whom were nodding. "It looks like we may have a consensus."

Sir Anthony spoke quickly. "I would like to volunteer to stay behind and try to disrupt Lord Darius' troops."

Lord William agreed. "Since it was your idea, it seems to me you are the one deserving to lead it. Pick the men you feel would be the most help to you."

———

Anthony crouched with two other men in the foliage as one of them carefully aimed his crossbow. The arrow had a barbed head soaked in salt water and was designed not to kill but to inflict pain.

The quiet thud indicated the arrow was underway and moments later it sunk into the side of a horse pulling a supply cart. The horse bolted, overturning the cart and charged through a group of men, scattering them as it ignored commands to stop.

Anthony chuckled as they moved to a new position. Several times soldiers had been sent to find the men that had fired arrows from above. So far their efforts had been in vain, even losing a few men to another ambush.

Besides the arrows, a hive of bees had been dropped on them, pits covered with mud and grass lay on the trail and sharp sticks stuck in the ground, which occasionally caused a horse to suddenly rear up. It made travel slow and the men anxious. At night, arrows were shot into the camp and the sleeping men knew the tents offered little protection.

Anthony received word of some of the other small forces that were harassing Lord Darius' troops occasionally were captured or killed. Now he lay hidden in the bush as he listened for men who were searching for them. He heard the voice of the commander, speaking low and was yet close enough to hear his words clearly.

"They are not far from here. Look for broken branches and footprints in the ground."

Anthony slowly tightened his grip on his sword. He knew it would be better to fight and die here than to be taken prisoner where torture and death awaited him.

Minutes passed and the same voice spoke again. "All right back to camp. They must be long gone now."

Anthony waited, still not daring to move. Finally, he decided that it was safe to rise and look for his two companions, who by prior agreement scattered in different directions at the first sign of approaching troops. He kept his eyes on the direction in which the search party had disappeared and slowly stood under the cover of the trees. The soft sound of a foot shifting behind him made him pitch himself forward and roll to a crouching position. Only a few feet away stood one of Lord Darius' men.

The soldier spoke. "Well, I was going to tell you to raise your hands, but you seem to have a sixth sense that I was behind you."

Anthony slowly stood and raised his sword. "You circled back around me."

"True. I must warn you I am an expert in sword fight. I suggest you avoid certain death and surrender."

"I suggest you try and take me if you're so confident about your sword."

"Very well. You have been warned."

Anthony surprised his opponent with several defensive moves that he was able to turn into an attack. His adversary repelled Anthony's assault as well and after a few minutes of fighting both men looked around anxiously.

Anthony spoke. "It would seem we are both wondering when our men might show up."

"Indeed. It seems we are equally matched." He lowered his sword. "Understand I have no quarrel with you personally, but Sir Sadon ordered us to find those who were attacking his men." He looked to Anthony's left. I see some movement behind you and will assume it is one of your men. I will take my leave."

Anthony nodded. "Go before one of them gets too anxious with a crossbow."

The other man began to leave and turned. "Your name?"

"Sir Anthony Graham."

"Sir Gavin Nichols. Perhaps our paths will cross again under better circumstances. Watch your back."

Anthony watched as Gavin disappeared, and was joined by his two companions. "What was that all about?"

"A good soldier on the wrong side. I think he has the same opinion of me."

"Darius' men are getting better at finding us. It's getting harder to surprise them."

"I know. I think it's time for us to head back to Horstruff. We aren't doing much damage anymore and might as well use our efforts to help defend Horstruff." Anthony sighed. "I wish we had better odds. When Lord Darius and his men show up at Horstruff we will be badly outnumbered."

# TWENTY-SEVEN

Father Murray smiled and nodded at the parish secretary.

"Good morning, Father. There is a young woman waiting to see you in the small conference room." She looked up at the middle aged, thin man. Worry lines creased his face but he still managed to look friendly.

"Her name?"

"Nadine Newman. She is not in our church denomination list."

"Perhaps she will be."

He entered the room and gazed at the woman sitting quietly in front of the table. He recognized her from being at a few of his services.

"Miss Newman, how can I be of help?"

She gave a tentative smile. "I want you to answer me a question. It's about religion."

Father Murray smiled as he sat. To his practiced eyed he guessed what that question might be. The woman was obviously ill and nearing the end of her life. He expected her to ask him if he knew for certain there was a soul that went to the afterlife. No surprise there for him. He had his pat answer to bring comfort to those in need. "Please go on. What do you wish to understand?"

"I am not well, Father, and I believe do not have long to live. I have a question about souls."

He smiled and opened his hands palms up on the table. "Ah, you are wondering if you have a soul. The scriptures are very clear on this."

"I know I have a soul, Father. That is not my question."

"What then, my child? Are you concerned about a place for you in heaven?"

"In a way, yes. When I die I know my soul will go to heaven. This was taught to me when I was very young, and I believe it."

"Father Murray became puzzled. "Then?"

She pursed her lips. "I don't know how to say this exactly."

"Just speak as if you were talking to yourself and I will listen."

"Father, for this question, let us say I wasn't born here. Perhaps on another world." She looked up at him, his gaze still soft but his lips had parted.

"Is this what you believe of yourself?"

She nodded. "I also wasn't born human but was transformed into one."

Father Murray nodded. He had seen ill and feeble people having trouble with reality, especially with the drugs they needed for pain. "When did this happen?"

"A few years ago. Since I was changed into human, I have not been completely healthy, and knew I didn't have long to live."

"So you are prepared?"

"Yes, I know there is an afterlife."

"Then what is your question?"

"My soul, when I go to heaven, will it be as a human?"

"Do you think of yourself as human?"

"Yes, I do."

"Then your soul is human."

Nadine let out her breath slowly. "Thank you. That is the answer I seek."

Father Murray escorted out. "Go in peace. God is with you."

"Thank you. If I somehow get well again I will return to see you."

———

Tuck carried his and Nadine's carry-on bags to the waiting area. Neither had any luggage to check in and security didn't cause them any problems. He was worried Nadine's forged passport would be flagged but whatever Madoc did passed all the tests. He watched her carefully walk to the available seats and almost drop on the hard plastic seat. Clearly she was running out of energy and feeling ill, but she didn't complain. She thanked him several times for his help and each time he told her he was glad to do it.

The truth was he was happy to be doing something other than work on a physics problem. He felt needed and felt compassion for the small woman that gave him fragile smiles. She was thin boned and had a gracefulness to her movements. Her face had delicate features with her blonde hair tied in a ponytail that reached her shoulders. Tuck knew she was a gnant at one time, but despite finding those creatures unappealing, thought she was rather attractive.

"Can I get you anything, Nadine? Something to drink or eat?"

"Perhaps some tea with sugar. I feel a bit weak."

Tuck hurried off and returned with a tea and a doughnut for her.

"Thank you." Her hand shook slightly as she lifted up the cup for a sip. "May I ask you, Tuck, how you know Jon?"

"Sure. I helped his sister and Liz with the equipment to help find him when he got lost on Domum. I later worked with his uncle, Gordon Miller, on how the physics of the equipment worked. I only met Jon a few times, but he seemed like a nice guy."

"Well, you are too, Tuck." She reached over and patted his arm. "I don't know if I can ever tell you how much help you're giving me."

Tuck smiled, enjoying the touch of her fingertips on his arm.

When they called for passengers needing assistance to board, Tuck immediately helped her stand up and made the way to the aircraft. He made sure none of the other passengers or staff bumped her as they lined up. He guided her to the seat and helped her with her lap belt before stowing away the baggage.

Nadine looked apprehensive as the plane taxied down the runway. Then as it picked up speed and rumbled down the tarmac, he saw her squeeze her hands.

"It's all right. It's safe."

"I have never been so fast before."

The plane lifted into the air, forcing them back into their seats.

"I'm a bit scared."

Tuck reached over and took her hand.

"Perhaps you should have taken the window seat, Tuck."

"I think you'll enjoy the view once we reach cruising speed."

She nodded and returned to stare out the window. "What makes it fly?"

"Air. The wings have a curved top, which thins out the air above. Then the air below lifts it up. It's how birds fly."

"Oh. It looks very pretty down there."

She continued to hold his hand as she watched out the window. Slowly her head began to nod forward, and her shoulders slumped.

A few minutes later it was clear she was asleep and as he watched her, Nadine twisted. She freed her hand from his, pulled her arms inward and rolled to her side with her head resting on his shoulder.

He felt pleased with her closeness.

Tuck refused to move his arm, not wanting to disturb her and tried to eat his meal using one hand. *I been told I have a big mouth but this time it's coming in handy.*

———

Nadine woke up and looked startled for a moment. "Sorry, I fell asleep."

"That's okay. I didn't mind at all."

She squeezed his forearm. "You're a good man. I feel better around you."

Tuck gave a nervous smile back, not knowing what to say.

The plane landed with a small jolt and after it began to taxi toward the terminal Tuck heard Nadine release her breath.

"You made it across the ocean safe and sound."

"I guess so, it was an interesting experience."

"You have one more interesting experience coming up. I rented a car to drive us to Ballymiller."

"I've been in cars before."

"It was my driving I was referring to." He grinned.

They waited for most of the other passengers to leave and then made their way to the exit. The hostess stopped them at the door, explaining, "We have a wheelchair waiting for you. It's a long walk through the airport."

Nadine nodded. "Thank you. My legs feel weak."

Tuck pushed her slowly along. It seemed to him she was even weaker than she was just a day ago and he was worried if she was going to make it to the Miller Castle and to Domum. He was glad they didn't have to wait to collect any luggage and customs didn't delay them. The rented car was mid-size, and Tuck was thankful for Gordon's generosity in paying for all the expenses of his trip.

He made sure Nadine's seat belt was done up and showed her how to tilt back her seat in case she wanted to rest.

She smiled at him. "You really do care, don't you?"

Tuck gazed at her before replying. "I do." He began the long drive to Ballymiller thinking she was right. He did care about her. Initially he felt only a responsibility to make sure she arrived safely to Domum but that had slowly changed to caring more for her. This was doing something so remote from his life as a graduate student, where experiments were done in a carefully controlled laboratory and analyzed at his desk. Tuck felt as if he had stepped off a stable platform and jumped on a rollercoaster.

Nadine was quiet through most of the trip, sometimes commenting on the passing scenery and occasionally sleeping. Tuck kept the interior of the car warmer than his liking for her benefit and he made sure she had food and drink available when she needed some. When he finally arrived at the Miller Castle, Tuck had to gently shake her to arouse her from her slumber. Worried, he lifted her in his arms and carried her to the front doors, and after a bit of a struggle, stepped inside.

"Gordon, I'm back with Nadine," he called out to the seemingly empty air.

Shortly later Gordon appeared from the kitchen. "You made good time."

"She's not doing well, barely awake."

"Then let us not delay. I can have the array up and running in about half an hour."

"Good." Tuck placed her carefully on the couch, stood for a moment and then dragged an armchair over. He sat with his elbows on his knees and watched her.

Gordon returned with a cup of tea and biscuits, passing them over to him. "The array is charging up and will be ready soon. By the time you finish the tea, it should be ready. Do you believe you can carry her to where Madoc is?"

"I can." His voice came out flat but determined.

Gordon patted his shoulder. "I will call you when it's ready."

Tuck drank the tea and ate the biscuits absentmindedly. He watched Nadine take slow breaths. Occasionally her eyes would open, and she would try to give him a short-lived smile.

"The array is ready."

Tuck turned to Gordon as he stood. "I better get going then." He scooped up Nadine in his arms and walked to the back of the castle.

He approached the crystal array located at the same place as last time. Gordon was close behind, who slipped a crystal around Tuck's neck.

"Good luck, Tuck. I hope Madoc can help her."

"Thanks, me too." Tuck went through the array, paused a moment to orient himself, and hurried through the open field.

"Am I really back on Domum?" Nadine's voice came out as a whisper.

"Yes, we're here."

"I was born here. Perhaps this is where I shall die."

Tuck shook his head. "No, don't say that. I won't believe that can happen."

Gasping for breath, Tuck entered the street and turned toward Jon's castle, the duplicate of the Miller Castle on Earth. The guards standing at the gate stepped forward to block his way.

He looked from one guard to the other. "Get out of my way or you'll be scooping horse shit out of the stable. I'm Lord Jon's friend and this lady needs help from Lord Madoc."

One of the guards nodded and both stepped back as Tuck hurried into the castle.

Puffing he entered through the two main doors and encountered two more guards.

"I'm Sir Tuck and need to see Lord Madoc immediately. If either of you stand in my way I'll speak to my friend, Lord Jon, about your attitude."

"No problem, sir. Do you need any assistance?"

Tuck didn't bother to answer. He rushed on, obtaining a few looks of astonishment at the poorly dressed man carrying a lady to the staircase. Tuck ignored everything around him as he began to climb the stairs.

Fortunately for Tuck, word had quickly been sent to Jon that Tuck had arrived carrying a lady. Jon lumbered down the stairs and met him halfway.

"Tuck, are you all right?"

"Yeah, fine."

"You look ready to pass out. You better give her to me."

Nadine's eyelids flicked open for a moment as she was passed over to Jon.

"Hurry Jon." Tuck plodded behind as he watched Jon race up the stairs.

When Tuck arrived upstairs he found Nadine lying on a bed with Lord Madoc standing by her.

"Can you save her?" Tuck gasped.

Lord Madoc touched her forehead with his fingertips for a few seconds and then turned to Tuck. "I cannot be positive. The Adepts may have used a method of magic to make sure she cannot survive long when they changed her into human. It was not meant to be permanent. I suppose they wanted to make sure she didn't betray their interests. I will try to rectify that part of the spell."

Tuck walked over to Nadine and took her hand. "Please."

Nadine nodded slowly. As she looked at Tuck, she gave him a fading smile.

# TWENTY-EIGHT

L ord Jon arrived alone at Lord Perry's castle, wondering what the latest urgent call to meeting was about. The preparation for upcoming battle was becoming time consuming as every smallest detail was examined. He considered that the emergency meeting at least gave him a break from the studying of maps as he ascended the steps to the front door. A servant quickly escorted him down a hall to a well-appointed room.

Lord Jon looked at Lord Madoc and at Lord Perry, who closed the door to the small sitting room. "I understand you have some important news."

Lord Perry gestured toward the chairs around a three-legged table. Like the chairs and other furnishings the table was made of heavy wood with ornate carvings. "Indeed I do."

Jon watched as Lord Perry made his way across the room and sat heavily as if he was carrying an enormous load. He finally resumed speaking.

"Lord Jon, Lord Madoc, I apologize for asking you to come here on short notice. However I have a situation that needs your input and I don't have much time to make a decision." He took a deep breath. "I am now in possession of five of the Locus Crystals."

Jon's jaw dropped. "How?"

"The crystals were found by a couple escaping from Lord Darius. Thankfully they brought the crystals to me and didn't disclose the information to others, with one exception. The gnants have found out about the recovery of the crystals and are anxious to have their two returned to them."

Lord Madoc nodded. "They were the original owners. It could be argued that they actually were the owner of all six crystals as it is likely their ancestors originally made them.

"That much is true." Lord Perry continued, "But we are now in a situation where the gnants have made it known to me they expect us to return two of the crystals to them. Gnants have an odd sense of honour. They believe it is acceptable to steal or even kill to obtain an item, but not to lie or trick someone to obtain it. The crystals were taken by Lord Bennett under what the gnants consider without honour. To a gnant, something done without honour is a most grievous sin, a serious affront to anyone. I will lay my cards on the table. I want to keep all the crystals until the end of the war with Lord Darius and return two crystals to the gnants. It is possible we will need all the segments of the Locus Crystals joined to give us enough power to defeat him.

"Gentlemen, do you have any suggestions on how to satisfy the gnants sense of honour?"

Lord Madoc rubbed the bridge of his nose. "There are several problems here that need to be addressed, Lord Perry. First, Lord Jon has the sixth and last crystal. I do not wish to speak for him, but he is under no obligation to give that segment to you. It is in fact his to do as he sees fit. I believe you need to discuss with him in private if he is willing to lend or give you the crystal.

The next problem is convincing the gnants to keep the two crystals for an extended time. You will need to convince both groups of gnants of this request because they may not be in agreement with each other. If you cannot convince them to allow you to use the crystals against Lord Darius then you will be waging war on two fronts, and you may find the gnants could be the stronger opponent of the two. The gnants may be leery of you having so much power, Lord Perry. If the crystals allow you to defeat Lord Darius, what will prevent you from using it to overpower the gnants as well? Remember the gnants are very suspicious of humans and there are only a handful of humans that the gnants consider trustworthy.

The final problem is if you were to use the Locus Crystals. The power of the joined crystals is extreme and not well understood. You may be unleashing power you cannot control. It is possible that it will rip open a new gateway between Domum and other worlds. You may stop Lord Darius but create a far worse problem."

Lord Perry frowned. "I had considered that last problem you spoke of. I come back to a discussion we had long ago, and you asked me, in essence, if I trusted you. I do and would ask you to use the Locus Crystals to defeat Lord Darius. It would make you the most powerful man on Domum while the crystals are activated of course, but I trust you not to abuse that power."

"Thank you for your vote of confidence. If it came to that I assure you I would deactivate the crystals at the earliest opportunity."

Jon chewed on his lower lip as he listened to Lord Perry and Lord Madoc. When they turned their attention to him he spoke softly. "It is times like this I am reminded that Domum is a very strange world compared to Earth. At one time, I would have had trouble believing a few crystals could change the outcome of a war. When I first came to Domum there was great fear Lord Bennett was going to ruin Domum by using the Locus Crystals. Now you are proposing we use the same crystals to save it. Lord Perry, I will bow to your sense of honour and what is right and will turn over my segment of the Locus Crystal if you desire it." He heard Lord Perry let a sigh of relief. "But before I do that, I want to tell you of my experience of Earth's problem. We have had our share of wars on Earth, some major and some minor. Some wars were even started by lies to the public why the war was needed. During the wars awful things were done to people. People were tortured to reveal secrets to win the war. No one side was innocent of this behaviour, but both claimed it was something they needed to do. Governments and military leaders are supposed to be honest to the people they represent. They are also supposed to follow rules of engagement of war that we call the Geneva Convention, which stipulates what is allowed.

When the truth comes out after the war, and it always does, the common answer is something along the line that the end justifies the means. To me that always sounded hollow. To fight evil by doing evil yourself makes you no better than your enemy. Lord Perry, I mean no disrespect, but if it is wrong for Lord Bennett to use the Locus Crystal to obtain power, then why is it right for us to do so? Is not the danger of using the Locus Crystal the same no matter who uses it?"

Lord Perry's face turned pale. "You are correct, Lord Jon. In my eagerness to find a solution to defeat Lord Darius I was willing to use tools that could do more harm than good." He sighed. "I will facilitate the return of the two crystal segments to the gnants." He gave a weak smile. "Thank you, Lord Jon, for making the path clear to me."

A few minutes later the three men stood.

Lord Perry announced, "I have a meeting scheduled with the gnant's Adepts. I was going to ask them for an extension to keep the crystals but will now offer to return them immediately."

---

Jon rode back in the carriage deep in thought. He hadn't expected that Lord Perry would have most of the Locus Crystals and was relieved when he decided against their use. He knew now that Lord Perry was even more dependent on him creating a battle plan that would defeat Lord Darius.

By the time Jon returned to his castle he had not arrived at any plans that would help him. Frowning he made his way up to the second floor. He paused as he heard voices coming from one of the bedrooms and deciding to investigate when he recognized the speakers.

Smiling, he stopped in the doorway. "Nadine, it's good to see you're looking better. Is Tuck looking after you?"

Nadine was sitting up in bed, taking a small bite from a sandwich. "Sir Tuck is looking after my interests very well." She reached with her free hand to touch his arm as he sat at the edge of the bed.

Jon grinned, noting that she looked very different from when he first met her and when she first arrived at Domum. Her hair was now long and loose and her figure was that of a woman's now, no longer just slim. More important her complexion showed vitality and there was a sparkle in her eyes. What was also obvious was how protective Tuck was toward her, ready to bring her anything she wanted. "It's great to see both of you looking happy. Tuck, you have a great lady there. You better stay close to her."

"No problem there. I'm just happy she's getting her strength back. How's it going for you?"

Jon gave a shrug. "I have to draw up plans for a battle where we're out numbered almost three to one. I hope I can come with something soon."

Tuck stared at Jon. "You ever play those role-playing games on a computer?"

"No. Would those help me?"

"Too late now, but I've done pretty good playing them. Maybe I can help."

Nadine spoke to Tuck. "You go and help Lord Jon. I will rest in the meantime."

Tuck gave her a long kiss and followed Jon to the room where he was drawing up his battle plans. "You've heard of Sir Alexander the Great?"

"Sure, he was pretty much the ruler of his world at one time."

"Yeah, and he did it by defeating armies several times the size of his own. You see he found a way of getting his enemies to look the wrong way during a battle and would outmanoeuvre them."

An hour later Jon stared at a map with short, heavy lines drawn across it as he listened to Tuck.

"You see, if you bend the two ends down like that it's hard for them to out flank you, and you don't want that to happen."

"I see. It looks like a football play with pass protection for the quarterback."

"I guess so. I don't know much about American football, but you have a horseshoe shape here and Lord Darius is going to have to spread himself thin to cover the entire front. What you want to do here is launch a diversion here on the right and hopefully Lord Darius will fall for it and bring more of his troops there. Then you strike with the real attack on the left. If you can puncture through his lines here he will be in deep trouble."

"I like it. Tuck, you're a genius."

"Don't tell anyone or else they'll expect me to be smart all the time."

# TWENTY-NINE

G ilbert had dropped by the shop only to say hello to Donna and hoped for a drink from Edward, who kept a very good whisky in a back room.

But the sound of voices and footsteps moving past on the cobblestone street interrupted his visit. Someone yelled that a meeting had been called for all of Vegrandis to attend. Gilbert mumbled unpleasant comments as the jostling crowd pulled them toward the cathedral.

Donna squeezed his hand. "Isn't this exciting?"

Gilbert looked upward. He preferred avoiding situations where a crowd was agitated. "Exciting if you like being pushed into a mob-filled room."

The nature of the meeting soon became clear. One speaker climbed a platform at the front and called on all of Vegrandis to help oppose Lord Darius. His speech was greeted with cheers and jeers. Then another speaker said much the same thing only in a louder voice. A third speaker spoke of the need to do nothing in the war in case they picked the wrong side.

Gilbert listened to the speeches, wondering which group would prevail. It may come down to who could shout the loudest or end in a fist fight. Gilbert hoped he could convince Donna to leave with him before then.

A young dwarf with a thin beard climbed on the platform. "We needs a leader who will speaks to Lord Perry and do what's bests for Vegrandis."

That statement at least received an agreement from the crowd.

Gilbert thought that was at least a reasonable thing to say when to his horror he heard Donna yell.

"Gilbert gives advice to Lord Perry. He could talks to him about Vegrandis."

Gilbert suddenly found all eyes directed toward him. Hands began to push him toward the platform. Gilbert immediately regretted all the times he bragged that he gave Lord Perry advice.

"No, I's not no leader." Gilbert's protest was ignored, and he was thrust on the platform.

"Says something, Gilbert." The eager faces looked up at him.

Gilbert closed his eyes and mumbled. "Gilbert is a dead man." He opened his eyes and looked around the room turned relatively quiet as they waited for him to speak. "Okays, I talks to Lord Perry."

A cheer went up.

"But I warns ya all that the battle for a new king is going to involve Vegrandis one ways or anothers."

More shouts came from the hoard around him, but one voice outshouted the rest. "That be okays. Gilbert be our king."

Suddenly shouts of King Gilbert of Vegrandis rang throughout the room.

King Gilbert covered his face with his hands. "I sees trouble. I sees trouble."

Donna made her way to the front, beaming at him. "You's the new king."

"I mays be the new dead king."

———

Lord Perry looked up from behind his desk. "Did I send for you, Gilbert?"

Gilbert remained on a bended knee. "No, Lord Perry, I needs to speaks to you."

Lord Perry sighed. "Very well. Perhaps it will help me to stop thinking about Lady Karla and Sir Keith."

"You means Lady Karla put to death yesterday."

"Yes. It was a decision I made with extreme difficulty. I had to do what was best for Horstruff and not consider my own preference. A sad day for us all."

"I's have a problem too, Lord Perry."

"What is that Gilbert and how does it affect Horstruff?"

"Vegrandis has asked me to speaks to you about the war with Lord Darius. We worried if the war comes to us."

Lord Perry steepled his fingers together. "That is interesting that you have come to speak to me about this matter as I was planning to address that situation in a few days. Horstruff would like the support of the people of Vegrandis in its battle with Lord Darius. Right now, Vegrandis enjoys the protection of Horstruff but that may not be the case in the future if we are not given support in the war."

"We knows. Gilbert now speaks for Vegrandis. What cans we do? Vegrandis people not used as soldiers befores."

"It is time for the people of Vegrandis to step up and help Horstruff. We need men who are willing to fight."

Gilbert swallowed. "We at Vegrandis are willing to help."

Lord Perry stared at Gilbert. "Very well, Gilbert. We will need your men to be prepared for battle."

Gilbert lowered his head and looked up. "The people of Vegrandis may be small but our men are men."

Lord Perry gave a small smile. "I do not doubt that in the least. The measure of a man is not the size of his stature but the strength of his heart."

"I thank thee, Lord Perry, fors his observation."

"Please rise, Gilbert. Now that we have the preliminary discussions done, I would like to know how you were elected to talk to me."

"Well, it be a town halls meeting. People yelled until it decided I be the leader."

"That's an interesting method of choosing a leader, though probably as effective as most I've heard of. Tell me, what exactly is your title?"

"Un, well, that will be, that is, with all due respect Lord Perry, King Gilbert."

Lord Perry looked wide-eyed at Gilbert. "King Gilbert?"

"Aye. It be an honorary title, so to speak."

Lord Perry burst into laughter. "I'm sorry, Gilbert, no offence intended. King Gilbert?" He shook his head. "Well, I must say you have risen in stature past my expectations. The truth is if you are to negotiate with the people of Vegrandis for assistance in our battle with Lord Darius, then you need to be above the title of Freeman Gilbert. King Gilbert might be seen as a bit presumptuous, so perhaps we can refer to you now as Sir Gilbert."

"Sir Gilbert? Yous given me the title of Sir Gilbert?"

"I said so, didn't I?"

Gilbert filled his chest with air. He may have been a dwarf, but he suddenly felt as tall as any man.

# THIRTY

Nadine woke up again, this time longer than a few minutes. She hurt with every breath, feeling pain deep inside where her organs rebelled at being reshaped. But the overwhelming nausea was gone and the headache at the base of her skull had subsided to a dull throb. She stared at the flower decorated ceiling and the walls covered with drapes and paintings. The bedroom in Lord Jon's castle was also overly warm, even in her sickened state. She pushed the bed sheet down to her waist and readjusted her nightgown.

"How do you feel?" Tuck leaned forward over her on the bed, his face creased in concern. Behind him, Lord Madoc stood stiffly.

Nadine considered his question carefully and answered in a soft voice. "Better. The pain is not as strong, and I don't feel as sick."

Lord Madoc spoke evenly. "I believe we have removed the last of the gnant life forms from your body. If there are any left, your human body cells will attack them as a foreign entity. It seems the Adepts had left a fair bit of gnant life forms in parts of your organs as a way to ensure you could not survive indefinitely, or perhaps as a way to ensure loyalty toward gnants.

"Regardless of their reasons, I have used spells to make you fully human."

She smiled. "I like those words. Fully human."

He returned a quick smile. "Unfortunately, that is why you are feeling ill. It will take a while for your body to find its balance and reshape itself.

Your bones have already done so while you were sleeping the past few days, but your muscles will take longer. You will notice you have a different body shape now that there aren't any gnant life forms left to restrain your appearance. I will leave you and Master Tuck now." He gave a small tilt of his head and left the room.

Tuck smiled at her. "It looks like you are going to be okay now, though I guess you will be uncomfortable for a while."

Nadine simply nodded. "My body does feel different already." She shifted in the bed. "Do they look too big to you?" She pushed her breasts together with her hands.

"Oh no. They look fine to me, just the right size."

"It feels strange to have such big lumps in the middle of my chest. I guess I'll have to get use to it." She looked at Tuck's face. "Male humans are attracted to such things, aren't they?"

Tuck took in a deep breath. "Oh, yeah. We are very attracted."

She gave a wider smile to him. "That is good, because I'm attracted to you too."

"You are?"

"Yes." She stared at him. "I think you should kiss me now."

# THIRTY-ONE

Sir Gilbert stood on the platform and faced the crowd. The people of Vegrandis filled the cathedral and shouted questions at him and at each other. It was rare for Vegrandis to discuss something as serious as war and their involvement in it, and as a result decorum was being tested to its limits.

Gilbert wiped his brow with his sleeve and looked down at Donna who was smiling away at him. He gave a forced smile back as he inwardly groaned at the responsibility he faced.

He started his young adult life as a thief, bravely entering the world outside of Vegrandis to steal items that he would trade. Using his wits he managed to avoid being caught and eventually became known as a man who could be depended upon to get what you wanted, as long as one didn't care about its source. To help avoid being declared a thief and a criminal, Gilbert learned the art of telling stories and tall tales. He became so good at spinning yarns sometimes, he forgot what the truth really was.

Now he recalled how he had gotten himself in the mess he was in and it started with one stolen crystal that almost led to the destruction of Domum. That error forced him to find the courage to correct his mistake, which meant he had to make up a good reason why he failed to meet Donna when he was supposed to. That story implied he was helping Lord Perry on a secret task that Donna accepted. However, when Vegrandis was looking for a man to represent them to Lord Perry about the upcoming war, Donna pushed for his nomination and suddenly Gilbert found himself in a very precarious situation.

Gilbert cleared his throat and began to speak. "Me hads a long talk with Lord Perry and Lord Jon about what Vegrandis could do to helps with the war with Lord Darius. If we do nothin' then it be bad if Horstruff wins. Horstruff wonders why they allow Vegrandis to exist when we don'ts do nothin' to helps it. If Lord Darius wins, it be worse."

"What yous says we do, Gilbert?" someone shouted.

"I says we ask for volunteers to help fight Lord Darius. Lord Jon has a plan where we be useful. Nots too dangerous, mostly firing arrows."

Another voice called. "You wants us to risk our lives? What ifs Lord Darius wins? He be mad at Vegrandis."

"He be mad at us anyways. Be better we fight, win or lose battle."

"What difference does it makes? We not do much goods. What benefit we fights against bigger men?"

"Benefit?" Gilbert repeated slowly. "I tells you." He sought the one word the people of Vegrandis desired from Horstruff. "It be respect. No matters what the outcome of the battle, no ones can say Vegrandis didn't do theirs best to help."

That unleashed a lot of shouting back and forth around the cathedral. The tide was turning toward Gilbert and helping in the battle. One old man looked up at Gilbert and shouted, "Tells me, Gilbert, has any Lord in Horstruff shown yous any respect?"

Suddenly there was a quiet in the room as all eyes looked at Gilbert.

Gilbert shrugged. "Of course. I not wish to brag, but Lord Perry himself has given me the title of Sir Gilbert. That be enough respect for yous?"

A cheer went up and the news spread, "We's going to battle!"

Gilbert grinned and looked around before he turned his gaze at Donna. Tears poured down her cheeks as she smiled up at him.

Another voice shouted out. "Vegrandis be fighting and Sir Gilbert goings to leads us!"

Gilbert's grin disappeared.

# THIRTY-TWO

The great hall in Lord Perry's castle looked empty with only two dozen noble men sitting along one table. Still Lord Jon understood the significance in the room with the paintings of battle scenes, coat of arms secured high above on the walls and the rich tapestries hanging from the ceiling. This was the room where the fate of Horstruff was to be decided and the history of the region was going to be a strong influence. Lord Jon looked at Lord Perry as he spoke at the head of the table. While the other lords and prominent sirs would also have their say it was Lord Perry who would carry the most weight. There was talk that if the battle was victorious for their side, there would be little opposition to Lord Perry being crowned the new king.

Jon was mildly surprised to see Gilbert representing Vegrandis and even more so to learn Lord Perry had made him a Sir. He thought it was a remarkable climb in social standings for the one time thief. He also knew as a Sir he was entitled to a small income from the king and that should offset his need to steal. As a lord, Jon received a larger allowance from the king through the office of Lord Perry.

Lord Perry finished speaking on the need to consider all options and gestured to Lord Jon. "Lord Jon has spent many days devising a battle plan that we believe will be victorious for us. I will now ask him to explain it to you."

Lord Jon walked to the front of the room. "It is of our belief that Lord Darius plans to use his larger number of men and horses. However we can overcome that advantage by changing how we confront his army." He drew two black lines on a large parchment hanging from the wall. The lines were parallel to each other and spaced slightly apart. "Let these two lines represent the battle lines between us and Lord Darius. Lord Darius has two advantages. One is the use of dragons to help scare men and horses opposing him." He looked at Lord Madoc. "Lord Madoc has assured me he will be able to neutralize that advantage."

Lord Madoc nodded as the others turned their attention to him. "Rest assured I can prevent the dragons from helping Lord Darius. In fact I believe if he does try to bring the dragons into the battle they will cause him more harm than good."

Jon spoke again. "His second advantage is he has more men and horses. When the battle begins there is not much of a benefit for him to fight straight on. He will want to use his greater resources to outflank our lines. We can counter that by bending our ends and making it more difficult to surround us." Jon drew two more lines at an angle to the first parallel line and slightly below it. "Lord Darius will try to follow that bend with his men. Notice that when he does so it will cause a small weakness where the line bends as the troops are stretched to cover the wider area. The next part is critical in timing." Jon pointed to a hill to the right and behind Lord Darius' troops. "Sir Gilbert and his men from Vegrandis will fire arrows at their troops. At the same time, a small group of men and horses will launch an attack on the same side, creating an appearance that we are trying to breakthrough. As soon as Lord Darius reacts to that charge, we launch a second attack on the left side." Jon pointed to the other side of the map. "Men with long pikes will push forward, creating a wedge at where the battle lines bend. Men on horses will ride through at that point and attack the command of Lord Darius. There will be little defence past the front lines and we should be able to defeat Lord Darius then."

Questions were raised and serious talk was given to how the battle would work. At the end Lord Perry stood. "It seems the plan is to use a ruse to get Lord Darius to overreact and to attack at a weaker side. I know of Lord Darius as a skilled swordsman and have seen him battle in competitions many times. If he has a weakness it is he is arrogant and doesn't believe he can ever lose." Lord Perry smiled. "He rarely wins those competitions. Despite his skills with a sword he often puts himself in a vulnerable position by overreacting to a deception. I support Lord Jon's proposal."

Many noblemen at the table nodded and with a show of fists in the air the support for Lord Jon's plan was unanimous.

Lord Perry, in a voice loud enough to fill a room twice the size, spoke. "Gentlemen, we are going to battle not just to fight Lord Darius but to crush him completely. We will, God willing, be victorious."

The men in the room stood with swords raised and shouted in unison. "To victory!"

———

Lord Jon arrived back at his castle feeling exited and confident about the upcoming battle. He entered his study and saw Liz standing facing the window. "Liz." He broke into a grin as she turned around.

Liz crossed her arms. "You lied to me. You said you wouldn't be in any danger and that you wouldn't be doing any fighting. Now you're going into battle."

Jon spread out his arms. "When I said that, I didn't have any intention of going into battle. But things changed. I can't ask the others to go into battle if I don't."

"Jon, this isn't our world and it isn't our battle either. Let someone else do this. Surely they don't expect you to die here."

"I'm not planning to die here, Liz. Please be reasonable. I planned this battle and it would be bad if I left without being part of it."

"It would look worse if you were killed. And what do you mean be reasonable? I'm being unreasonable in wanting to keep you alive? I'm being unreasonable in sticking to what I say I'm going to do? Exactly how am I being unreasonable?"

"I didn't mean it that way." He sighed. "Look, I'm sorry circumstances have changed. I don't want you to have to worry about me. I will avoid the fighting as much as possible."

Liz opened her mouth for a moment and closed it. She looked up at Jon as he stood looking formidable by the door, looking like an immovable object "Look, I love you and I will support you in what you feel you need to do. But I want and need you to be honest with me."

"You know that I am."

"Okay. Big question. After this battle, where do you want to live? Domum or Earth?"

Jon looked like a caged animal as his eyes darted left and right. "Can we talk about this later?"

Liz frowned. "all right, but only because I want you to concentrate on surviving this battle. But we will be discussing this later."

———

Angela hugged Madoc in the front hall as he stepped inside his castle. "I missed you. I feel all alone here."

"I'm sorry, but this upcoming battle is taking a great deal of time to prepare for."

"What exactly is your role in this battle? You're not going to have to fight with a sword are you?"

He shook his head as he led her into a sitting room. "Hardly. It would be a waste of my other talents. I will be using magic to help neutralize the dragon attack."

"Does that mean you won't have to go to the battlefield?"

"I will be near the battlefield but not within it. Magic is a tricky thing when there is more than one person performing magic. The spells can easily interfere with each other and cancel each other out. I am sure Lord Darius will have witches or other practisers of magic on hand to help in battle. I should be able to overpower them and still initiate a spell to stop the dragons from attacking us."

"But you won't be in any danger will you? Maybe we should both go to Earth until this battle is over."

"Of course I will be in some danger, more so if Horstruff was to lose the battle. But my risk is small compared to those in battle. I intend to do my part in ensuring safety for all those living in Horstruff." He looked at her eyes. "I told you I will be willing to live on Earth if that is where you want to be. If I must leave Horstruff, then I will feel good in the knowledge I have done my part to allow it to survive." He looked around the sitting room. "I am not sure if I approve of all the soft colours you have used in this room."

"I like yellow and pink. Since you're not here long enough to offer any suggestions, I used my own judgement."

"But a pink tablecloth?"

"Okay, maybe I went a bit overboard there. But wait until I show you what I did to the bedroom." She took his hand and began to lead the way. "I think it looks beautiful, much better than the dark wood you had before."

Madoc closed his eyes momentarily. "I am sure it will be interesting."

# THIRTY-THREE

N ervously, squeezing his hands together, Gilbert stood at the front inside the largest cathedral in Vegrandis. Towering next to him stood Jon, who seemed in a better state of mind than the groom.
"Relax Gilbert. Everything is going to be fine," Jon whispered.
"Easy for yous to say. Gilbert be the one who is giving up freedom."
"So is Donna."
"But she don'ts wants freedom. Donna after Gilbert for a long time."
"Gilbert, you're lucky she wants you at all."
Suddenly bells chimed and two men carrying poles with branches attached entered through the front doors. Attached to the branches were bells of various colours and sizes. They walked slowly, shaking the poles to generate as much sound as they could. Behind the two men walked Edward, giving small waves to some of the people crammed into the seating area. He looked proud as he stepped forward, knowing this was the best attended wedding in years in Vegrandis. Edward was amazed that a lord was not only attending the wedding but had agreed to be Gilbert's second. He wondered how he underestimated Gilbert all those years, thinking he was not much more than a thief. A thief in Vegrandis was not a criminal, but he wasn't normally considered at the high end of the social ladder. A thief who was caught was considered stupid, or clumsy or both. It was clear to Edward that Gilbert was a thief who also mastered the art of slipping into the company of the rich and powerful.
Behind Edward walked Trudy, feeling giddy with the crowd and

excitement of her last daughter being married. She knew Gilbert was more of a talker than a doer, but Donna loved him. She understood that perfection in a man was not possible but hoped that Donna would be able to get Gilbert to be more responsible, much like she had to do with Edward. *At least*, she mused, *Gilbert had friends in high places.*

———

Liz sat near the front of the cathedral and watched Jon. He was acting calm and was giving Gilbert whispered reassurances. It seemed to her that Jon was in complete control. He looked authoritative and she understood why others looked up to him whenever he entered a room. There was no lack of confidence in his demeanour or his manner of speaking. Compared to Earth there was a world of difference on how he carried himself. She was concerned how she was going to convince him to return to Earth to live and if she did, how he would react.

Liz swung her attention to the bride.

Donna clutched a bouquet of flowers so tight that it looked like the stems would all break. Her dress was a bright yellow, representing the sun and the start of a new life. On the dress were swatches of coloured material sewn in a pattern of a backwards "a" with a line through the centre. The symbol meant life's journey and the centre strike that went through the middle showed the there was still more to come.

Each coloured patch represented a part of the bride's life. Her first memories as a child, her friends, the passing of her grandparents, various accomplishments and the last patch represented Gilbert. She choose that carefully to represent his strength, picking the colour of forest green. That meant one who was close to nature and lived within it. The shade was special as well, and showed he encompassed a caring personality as well. Gilbert, Jon and most of the men wore brown, the traditional colour for the groom.

Liz considered that like most women, Donna was seeing something in her man that eluded the attention of others. Although in Jon's case, she believed she was being objective about his character.

Liz joined the others in clapping and cheering that followed Donna on her slow walk down the aisle. She smiled at the small woman and her obvious excitement. She wondered about her own wedding with Jon. She looked back at Jon at the front and wished he could be just as happy and confident on Earth as he was here.

Her thoughts were interrupted by a man speaking in front of Gilbert and Donna. She recalled they called him Ductor, and thought he looked like a miniature Einstein, though with a bald spot in the middle of his head. For such a small man, his deep voice easily filled the noisy cathedral.

"Why are we gathered here today?"

The congregation replied, "For a union between two people."

"Between which twos people?"

"Donna and Gilbert."

"Is it true love that brings thems together?"

"Yes it is."

Liz watched as Donna and Gilbert joined hands and the Ductor placed a hand on each of their shoulders closest to each other. He tried to push them apart.

"Can theys be separated?"

"No, theys together forever."

Liz understood the people of Vegrandis had their own set of beliefs. They acknowledged sixty-four gods, of which thirty-two were mostly good and the others largely bad. Of the thirty-two good gods, sixteen directly affected human life. Eight of those could understand words spoken by people but only four would normally consider answering prayers. One of those four, the Goddess Diligo was the one who overlooked marriages. She guided couples together and nurtured their love but was adamant the union was never to be broken. Thus the people of Vegrandis never accepted divorce. Even if a spouse were to die, a second marriage was not accepted. So when the congregation shouted out they were together forever, Donna and Gilbert knew this was their first and last marriage.

"Thens they be togethers for ever more. Donna and Gilbert, Gilbert and Donna be ones now." The Ductor then had a group hug with Donna and Gilbert. Shortly later Donna and Gilbert turned around, beaming. They walked to the exit, followed by Edward, Trudy, Jon and the bride's second.

Without much in the way of decorum the crowd followed after them, singing a song of being together that Liz had trouble understanding. But they sounded enthusiastic as they sang if not exactly in tune with each other. The happy couple stood outside as flower petals and seeds were tossed over them to ensure a good life together.

Liz considered her own wants and wondered if she was being too selfish in insisting Jon move back to Earth. *He is truly happy in Domum and if living here means a successful marriage I would be foolish not to reconsider it. What is the point in marrying him if I insist on him leaving a place where he is content? Am I being too selfish here?* She gave him a grin when she noticed Jon looking at her and pushed through the crowd to give him a kiss.

"So that was an interesting ceremony."

Jon laughed. "Yeah, short and direct. Want to use it in ours?"

"Oh no. As nice as this was I think I like spoken vows better."

"I thought you would say that. Still, think of the time we would save in a church."

Liz shook her head. "Nice try. We're having a full service."

# THIRTY-FOUR

Gilbert led a group of several hundred Vegrandis men down the dirt road. There was a big send-off for the army as they marched down the streets of Horstruff. Gilbert was given several hugs from women and handshakes from men when they reached the imaginary boundary between Vegrandis and Horstruff, including a tearful kiss from Donna.

After a period of time the reluctant leader turned off the road and into the bush. Gilbert considered that just a few weeks ago he was happily stealing items, such as cutlery, from Lord Perry's castle. So far, he was elected as representative of Vegrandis to meet with Lord Perry, promoted to Sir Gilbert, married and now was the leader of an armed force to help save Horstruff. Gilbert couldn't figure out how the chain of events led him to this predicament, but he was going to have words with the gods later.

The tree and plant growth made travel slow and Gilbert quickly appointed two of the strongest men to help make a path first. The journey was slow but eventually Gilbert came across the field where Jon wanted the battle to take place. To Gilbert's right was a steep hill where trees had trouble establishing roots but was covered with ferns and other low-lying plants. He sighed and pointed to the hill.

"We goes there and waits."

The men grumbled as they made their way up the hill. Careful not to disturb too much of the plants, they half buried themselves into the ground. Then they waited under the cover of the plants for the battle to begin. Gilbert clutched his bow and hoped Jon was right that Lord Darius would not expect an attack. He knew the small men of Vegrandis would be hard to detect compared to normal sized people of Horstruff, and that it would be difficult for Lord Darius to send men up the hill to respond to the attack. Of course, he also understood if Horstruff were to lose the battle that protection would mean little, and Lord Darius would punish Vegrandis for their efforts.

Gilbert rested his head on the sandy soil and tried to focus his thoughts on his recent marriage to Donna. He then gave a small prayer of thanks to the Goddess Diligo and made one to the God Catha, asking for protection and victory.

———

Jon sat on his horse, making small talk with Sir Nathan and Sir Anthony at the front of Lord Perry's castle. Soon he would be leading the thousands of men into battle, and despite the enormity of the situation, felt relaxed. He understood too well the consequences if he failed to defeat Lord Darius but felt confident that he had done the best he could and there was little point in second guessing.

With a wave of his hand he led the men and horses out past Horstruff. The troops followed in a thunder of hoofs and dust. Jon's thoughts turned to Liz and he pursed his lips. He didn't like their conversations of late. He knew she wasn't happy in Domum and wanted to return to Earth, not understanding why he was compelled to go to battle in this strange world. Jon tried to explain but felt he stumbled over his answer to Liz. As far as living on Earth or Domum, he hadn't really thought out which he preferred. *There are advantages to both worlds to me, although Liz has already made up her mind. I'm going have to figure out what I want soon.*

It wasn't a long ride to the area where Jon wanted to confront Lord Darius, and if they were to lose it wouldn't be long after Horstruff itself would be attacked. Jon believed that fighting near Horstruff would give their troops the advantage of fighting harder to defend their home. It also meant their troops would be fresher from a shorter journey and he knew he needed every advantage he could get to defeat the larger army. He noticed Anthony had pulled alongside of him and he acknowledged the son of one of the most powerful families in Horstruff. Anthony had changed recently from a man who seemed to enjoy the easy life of partying to a hardened soldier. *No doubt,* he thought, *a battle where two of his brothers died would do that.*

"Lord Jon, I have a minor concern about your battle strategy. I was wondering if I may elaborate."

"Of course. Your opinion is invaluable."

"You are proposing to lead the charge into Lord Darius' army and that as the leader you feel an obligation to do so. However, such a charge has risks and I believe it would be better if I were the one to do so. I am not trying to usurp your authority, but please understand I am an experienced horseman and excellent swordsman. I can handle unexpected situations better than you could be expected to do so. If one of us has to fall during that charge, it would be better if it were me for then you can improvise a new strategy.

"Lord Jon, you are an excellent fighter, but you would be in difficulty if you were to confront Lord Darius. I believe I could dispatch him in a fight and that is another reason why I should lead the charge."

Jon mulled over what Anthony said. "Very well. You are the better horseman and fighter. You have been in battle before and I have not. It seems to me it is logical a man of your skill and courage should lead the charge."

Sir Anthony bowed his head. "I thank thee for your compliment."

———

Jon made camp a short distance from where they planned to do battle with Lord Darius. He looked at the hill overlooking the broad field but didn't see any sign of Gilbert and the other men from Vegrandis. He nodded his approval. If he couldn't detect them then it was unlikely Lord Darius could either.

He sat with Nathan and Anthony for a final meal before retiring for the night. He had already walked among his men and gave words of encouragement. Now it was a time to try to relax.

Nathan clamped his big hands together as he sat on a log. "Lord Jon, I like our chances tomorrow. We may be outnumbered but we have heart on our side and a surprise attack in our favour. Of course, if we do win, that will lead to a serious problem."

Jon looked puzzled. "What would that be?"

"Now old Nathan may not be privy to all that is said in the high circles, but it's my understanding that Lord Perry has no desire to have a greater role than he has now." Nathan stood. "If Lord Darius is defeated, we would be having to find a new king. Now Lord Perry has a lot of influence on choosing the next king, and I suspect he believes a younger man of intelligence and strength of character would be best." He gave Jon a grin. "Something to consider. Good night, gentlemen."

Jon looked at Anthony. "I think Nathan has a good imagination."

Anthony laughed. "Maybe, but Nathan does always think before he speaks."

———

Jon walked among the troops, taking deep breaths of the morning air. He could almost taste the nervousness as the men began the task of preparing for battle. The horses sensed the unease as well, not wanting to stand still for long. There was little talking among the men and when they did speak it was in short, quiet sentences. He stopped where a young man, still in his teens, sat hunched over as he stared at the ground.

"What is the problem?"

The young man looked up and sprung to attention. "Nothing, Lord Jon, nothing at all."

Jon wasn't sure if he looked scared because of the upcoming battle or because he was speaking to him. "Relax. It looked to me that you were deep in thought about something. Do you wish to share a concern with me?" Jon noticed that several other men were taking a quiet interest in their conversation.

The young man's face was breaking out into a sweat. "I was worried about the battle today. I'm ashamed to say I am worried that I could die today."

Jon nodded. "To be frank, you'd be a fool not to be worried about going into any battle. But destiny and circumstances has put us in this place." Jon raised his voice slightly. "We cannot know our fate, but I do know this of us. We are all brave men, willing to fight for what is ours and Lord Darius will know our fury at the end of the day." He pointed to the battlefield and shouted, "This is our land and we will win the day. I don't care how many men he has under him. I will personally raise the flag of Horstruff at the end of the battle and kick Lord Darius' ass while doing so!"

Cheers broke around Jon as he turned back to the young man. "Your name?"

"Freeman Connor."

"Have a good battle, Freeman Conner. I know you will do yourself proud. Now keep your head held high."

Jon walked away, but now felt a ripple of excitement following him. Nathan caught up with him and slapped him on his back.

"That was a hell of a speech. What inspired you do that?"

"I don't really know. I think that poor boy who looked so scared made me want to get everyone perked up."

"Well, it sure did the trick. Those men now believe we're not just going into battle but that we're going to win it."

Jon swung his arm around Nathan. "I tell you, my friend, for some reason I don't have a doubt of that in the world. Sometimes you just have to believe."

———

Lord Madoc kissed Angela. "Please do not be worried for I shall not be in any danger. My task is a simple one and I will be well away from the battle."

"Then take me with you. If there isn't any danger, I could be with you."

"The work I am going to do is best if I was alone. I will be able to set the spells faster without having to worry about your where-abouts."

He kissed her again and turned to head downstairs. After a long walk down the hallway he exited through another door that led to a tight spiral of downward stone steps. He breathed in the damp air and took a lighted torch to see along the gloomy stone walls. The stairs emptied to another hallway, which was barely tall enough at its rounded top to allow him to stand up straight and the width would make it difficult for two people to pass each other.

Madoc walked slowly but confidently along the tunnel he had used many times before. Occasionally a small creature would scurry out of the way and he brushed aside spider webs and flying insects. *Is this to be the last time I have need to use this tunnel?*

He felt amused at his folly all those years ago, believing at that time he was taking steps to rule the world and grow rich and powerful.

He smiled. *I used magic to help direct my path to where I would be most content. Clever me! I thought events would unfold that would take me to the top. Instead I was exiled to Earth! I wondered how that could possibly lead to contentment. How naive I was, thinking I was sent to Earth as a way to develop more magical prowess.*

*No, my path took me to Earth where I found contentment. It wasn't more power I needed to be happy. It was love— it was Angela.*

Madoc came to the end of the tunnel and pushed open the small door. When sunlight flooded inside, he hung the torch on the wall then stepped outside.

He walked for half an hour until he heard the sounds of people talking. Once he found the exact location of the upcoming battle, he picked a quiet spot to wait. He felt the aether, detecting several wizards and other practitioners of magic. Some were trying to affect the battle while others were merely trying to add a protective spell for individuals. Almost all the spells were interfering with each other. The end result was very few spells would be effective today. Madoc had little concern that his own magic spell would fail.

Madoc gave a thin smile as he chanted out the spell. He had studied dragons and learned that they had eyes of a hunter and could see all the colours humans could, plus the infrared and ultraviolet spectrums. Madoc took advantage of their ability by creating the image of a Fornido dragon that was visible only in the ultraviolet. He knew that other dragons were frightened of the monstrous dragon and would want to vacant the area as quickly as possible. Because the human handlers could not see Fornido dragon, they would be unaware of why the Patiri dragons had become unruly.

Satisfied he returned home. Angela was waiting for him and after hugging him, stepped back.

"What's wrong? You feel tense."

"Nothing, other than I was thinking that this may be the last time I will be in some parts of the castle. After this battle is over we will be living on Earth. I will miss this castle."

"Well maybe you can have your cake and eat it too."

"What does food have to do with this?"

Angela laughed. "Silly. I mean this." She stepped closer. "Let's say I'm in Domum right now." She jumped sideways. "Now I'm on Earth." She jumped back and forth. "Domum, Earth, Domum, Earth. Madoc, we can live on both worlds if you want. Maybe Domum can be our vacation world or something like that."

He smiled "I would like that."

# THIRTY-FIVE

S ir Gavin steered his horse behind Lord Darius and Sir Sadon toward the meeting point, halfway between the two battle groups. He knew the meeting was just a formality and it was unlikely to the extreme the Horstruff leaders would agree to surrender. He doubted anything surprising would happen at the short meeting. He was wrong.

Gavin watched Lord Darius stop his horse opposite of the three members from Horstruff and point to Sadon, then to Gavin and finally to himself, calling out their title and name as he did so. He immediately recognized the three men. Lord Jon had seemingly come out of nowhere and had become a legend as a dragon slayer and an honourable man. Sir Nathan he had heard about as one who could be counted on to win any tournament he entered. For the last man, Sir Anthony, he gave a slight nod of acknowledgement. He was surprised to know the man he battled to a standstill a few days ago was now one of the leaders.

Lord Darius spoke in an offhand voice. "This is Sir Sadon, Sir Gavin and I am, of course, King Darius."

Gavin was taken aback by Darius using the title of king. It sounded like a deliberate attempt to provoke the Horstruff leaders by using the disputed title. He saw the flush of anger in Lord Jon's face as he responded and followed the angry exchange between the two leaders.

"This is Sir Nathan, Sir Anthony and I am Lord Jon. Lord Darius, do you wish to surrender now?"

"Surrender? I warn you, do not insult me."

"Then do not assume a title that you have not earned."

Lord Darius sneered at Lord Jon. "I have a larger army and when this battle is over you will know who is king."

Lord Jon pointed at Lord Darius and at his own chest. "Why bother with all these men? How about you and I settle it right now, here?" He directed a hand toward the ground. "That is if you have the balls to do so."

Gavin looked at the shocked face of Darius and back at the aggressive look of Lord Jon. The big man had earned the additional title of dragon slayer and Gavin had reason to believe he could handle just about any opponent by sheer force. Gavin understood what Lord Jon was doing. He had made a show of challenging Lord Darius in front of both sides and while it would have been foolish for Lord Darius to accept, it still was inspiring to his men.

Lord Darius shook his head. "This meeting was a waste of my time." He turned his horse and rode away, making Sir Sadon and Sir Gavin hurry after him.

———

Sir Gavin felt useless sitting on his horse next to Darius and Sadon. His job was to provide advice if asked but in truth he knew he was there to protect the other two men from a possible attack, even from their own men. He considered that was a sad testimony to the loyalty to the leaders. He watched as Darius began to raise his sword.

They waited behind the left side of their line, believing that would give them the best vantage point of the battle as the ground rose slightly before sharply rising to become a hill. The hill was briefly inspected at its base by Sir Kaden who informed them the ground was a mixture of sand, rock and earth that only low-lying plants could grow on. It was virtually impossible for a horse to ascend and a man would have to use his hands and knees to climb it.

"We'll soon show the Lord Jon what he's fighting against." Lord Darius spitted out the words.

Sir Gavin heard shouts and saw that Horstruff troops had already launched an attack. It obviously caught Lord Darius off guard, and he hesitated before yelling to his men to attack. It was a poor start to the battle for Lord Darius' men and Gavin hoped there weren't going to be too many more surprises like that.

The battle started as he expected, with the battle line forming more or less along a straight line. Gavin knew Lord Darius believed his greater numbers would overwhelm the Horstruff troops and that all he had to do was to outman his enemies at the point of attack. Gavin didn't like that strategy in that it meant he was merely reacting to whatever the Horstruff troops did. He watched as the Horstruff troops began to bend at the ends to prevent the Lord Darius troops from getting behind them. It was difficult to see the details with the dust filling the air, but it seemed to Gavin the Horstruff troops seemed to bend on one side a bit too easily. As arrows flew around them a trumpet sounded three times. Suddenly more arrows pierced the air from the Horstruff troops.

Lord Darius moved his horse back behind Sir Sadon and yelled for more men to move to the side of attack. "This is where they want to battle, so be it. Let's flood them with men and it'll soon be over."

Gavin frowned at Lord Darius hiding behind Sir Sadon, only because he was the biggest body and most likely to intercept any stray arrow. He looked on as Lord Darius' men poured to the one side, firing arrows back. The Horstruff troops after an initial surge began to fall back. Gavin thought that was a rather strange manoeuvre from Lord Jon, considering it looked like he planned the attack in advance by the sounding of trumpets. He saw the Horstruff troops had now pushed forward in the middle of the battlefield. Gavin suddenly realized most of Lord Darius' troops were at their left side of the battle zone. A pocket had formed where the right side of the Horstruff troops had retreated and the centre had pushed forward. It looked wrong to Gavin and he considered it might be a trap. He moved his horse over to Lord Darius to say so when the first explosions filled the air.

Horses reared up and men dived for cover, not sure of the nature of the explosions. Gavin knew in theory the magic used to counteract explosive spells should have made this impossible. He considered the wizards would be in deep trouble after the battle. The noise, smoke, the sulphur smell, screams and horses galloping without riders made it difficult to understand what was happening. Gavin noticed Lord Darius had moved to the other side of the battle ground, leaving Sir Sadon in charge of the chaotic left side. Before Lord Darius left, he ordered Sir Kaden to have Sir Norlene bring in the dragons.

"If they want to use magic, then we will use dragons. That will teach them!"

Gavin looked at the retreating back of Lord Darius. *He acts like he's ready to piss himself. Coward.*

The arrows flew past them with two of them hitting Gavin's shield before bouncing away. Like many of the men, Gavin also wore chainmail draped over his shoulders and tied together at his waist, effectively protecting him front and back. He knew it would take a very lucky shot to hurt him this far from the frontline. Near the edge of his vision he saw the flutter of a wobbly arrow. The green feathers of the arrow caught his attention as it curled toward them in a slow arc. Gavin turned to see where it landed and looked at the open mouth of Sir Sadon. His mouth closed then opened again without a sound coming out as he slumped to his side, the arrow sticking through his neck.

Gavin didn't have time to worry about the last moments of Sir Sadon's life as he fell off his horse. Out of the sky, arrows starting raining down on them and Gavin felt one arrow deflect off his helmet. He quickly covered his head with his shield. The arrows were coming from near the top of the hill and were decimating the troops caught in the pocket on the left side. Gavin raced his horse to where the longbow and crossbow men were positioned well behind the front line.

"Sir Oliver, you need to get your men to fire on that hill. The arrows there are killing us."

Sir Oliver looked surprised and bewildered. "Explosions and dragons have made a mess of trying to figure out where to shoot. At least the hill is a target we can be sure of."

Gavin followed his gaze to the hill. He saw one problem. They couldn't see the targets below the green plants. That made it guesswork where to place the shot.

Gavin waved at Sir Kaden and raced over to where Lord Darius waited. He looked up to see Sir Nolene's dragons race away, seemingly not wanting to have any part of the battle. He wondered what could have scared those killers so much.

He was about to inform Lord Darius of the problem of the left flank when he saw the charge on the right side by the Horstruff troops as they burst through the now thin battle line. Most of the Lord Darius troops fell in disarray as arrows rained down, forcing them to give up defending the battle line. They were no longer fighting as organized troops but had turned into panic mode.

The centre was still secure but now the advantage was to the Horstruff troops. Lord Darius' longbow and cross bow men were no longer supporting the centre attack and they were retreating as Horstruff longbows were able to shoot without retaliation.

The biggest concern was to the right side as the Horstruff horsemen raced unimpeded to where Lord Darius waited. *It's over. King Darius, you had a very short reign.*

———

Gilbert checked his bow and arrows, his belt knife, short sword, a second knife secured to his pant leg, a third knife strapped to his back and finally, his shield that hung loosely at his shoulder. He tried to find a comfortable position under the green foliage but no matter which way he moved one of weapons pushed back at him. Gilbert wasn't sure if his weapons would be any use in this battle, but he wasn't going to take any chances, at least anymore than he had to as the commander of the Vegrandis forces. But it did make finding a comfortable position and obtaining good purchase on the steep slope difficult.

What was abundantly clear to Gilbert was that none of his men had ever been in an army or seen battle. That wasn't too surprising considering the Vegrandis consisted of dwarfs that weren't the first choice for a soldier. The people of Vegrandis were also known for not wanting to venture much past the boundaries of their town site other than for hunting. Visits to Horstruff, which surrounded Vegrandis, were not uncommon but rarely happened past daylight. Gilbert was an exception and learned how to live in both communities.

Gilbert turned to one of the men near him, a young man with blond-reddish hair. "Tommy, pass the words around to keeps below the plants, even when shooting. Someone sees yous, they cans shoots ya."

Gilbert watched as Tommy swallowed hard and passed the information along. He wondered if Tommy was going to be too scared to even fire an arrow.

It wasn't that Gilbert wanted to fight but waiting as the two armies prepared for battle was becoming boring. Horses and men moved into position. On Domum it was customary for the commanders on both sides to meet first to offer the other side a chance to surrender. Gilbert recognized Jon approaching Lord Darius near the middle. Both men were flanked by their commanders. After a short discussion, the meeting broke up.

Gilbert watched as the silence and tension grew. He saw Lord Darius start to raise his sword in the air, but in a sudden move Jon quickly raised his own sword and yelled, "Charge!"

Lord Darius' troops looked confused for a few seconds with some of the troops responding to the Horstruff attack while others stayed in line, waiting for an order.

"Good fors yous, Jon," Gilbert muttered to himself.

———

From his vantage point Gilbert could see the battle lines play out. At first it looked like chaos, but gradually a pattern emerged as the greater numbers of Lord Darius circled around the ends of the Horstruff troops. The Horstruff troops began to fold back, making a U shape.

Gilbert heard a trumpet sound three times and the Horstruff troops with pikes surged forward. The Lord Darius troops responded by moving more numerous troops into the middle. Another series of trumpets sounded and the Horstruff's right side launched an arrow attack. Then troops of Lord Darius responded the same way from the centre, the new area of contention. From Gilbert's perspective it looked like Lord Darius was using sheer numbers to overwhelm the Horstruff troops.

Gilbert placed an arrow into his bow and looked to where Jon sat on his horse. Within moments he saw the reflected light of the sun on the shiny metal mirror Jon held in his hand. The signal.

Gilbert yelled, "Fire!" He launched his own arrow and quickly reloaded the next. He saw the arrows arc nicely above Lord Darius' troops and come down on them almost vertical.

Suddenly explosions filled the air, turning the left side of the Lord Darius troops to a mass of confusion.

———

It was not unexpected to Gilbert that Lord Darius would use dragons in the battle. Jon had spoken to everyone about that possibility before but had promised that the dragons would not be a factor. When Gilbert saw the dragons in the sky, he wasn't surprised, and kept firing his arrows. It looked like madness on the field as Lord Darius' troops tried to respond to the arrow attack from the Horstruff troops. At the same time, sudden and mysterious explosions were maiming horses and men. To add to the confusion, arrows poured down from the Vegrandis men.

Troops with longbows and crossbows moved toward the steep hill where Gilbert's men hid. They fired at the unseen attackers. Occasionally there was a cry as one of the arrows hit. Then shortly after, a body would tumble down the hill. Still, for everyone hit they made it was small compared to the damage the Vegrandis troops were doing.

Gilbert was about to shoot another arrow when he heard Tommy cry out. He looked and saw an arrow had punctured Tommy's lower leg. As Tommy reached for the arrow he began to slide down the hill.

For a moment, Gilbert hesitated before diving for Tommy. He grabbed the collar of the young man and pulled him back to safety. For a second, his back went above the plants. "Don'ts worrys, I gots yous." In that moment Gilbert reflected back when he first met Jon and how the big man had saved him from sliding down a riverbank by grabbing him by the collar, likely saving his life. *Perhaps I be evens with the Gods now.* Then something slammed into his back. As his face hit the dirt, Gilbert groaned and went limp.

————

Longbows man, Freeman Delbert, anxiously turned his attention to the hill. It made as much sense to shoot at those hiding in the hill as any battle plan he heard so far. From the back of the battle he could see how the Horstruff troops were first massing on the left side and when Lord Darius overreacted by sending a mass of troops there, they were met with a devastating arrow attack.

Delbert slowly pulled his arrow back. It was the extreme range of the longbow, but he knew he could still be effective with his arrows. The problem was the lack of a target. Those shooting the arrows were hidden under the green plants and he thought most of the arrows shot were not hitting anyone.

He heard some of the men leave the position and go to safer ground. Freeman Delbert was proud to serve in King Charles' army and took pride in maintaining his skills even though the army fell to disrepair. When King Darius assumed the throne, he accepted the change in leadership like a good soldier. His faith was shaken by the wanton disregard the man had for decorum and the lives of those under him. Now he as he shot his arrows, he wondered if he was fighting for the good of the kingdom. He had trouble believing Horstruff and Lord Perry were real enemies.

His eyes detected a movement in the plants and the back of a man became briefly exposed. It was all a trained marksman needed. Freeman Delbert heard the snap of the string as it unleashed the arrow. As soon as it was released, he knew it was a good shot. For a moment, he felt sad for the man about to die.

Now it was time for him to retreat as well and to be concerned about his own life.

————

Sir Nolene took his flute from his assistant with a shaking hand. He wasn't comfortable standing in the battlefield. The dragons were hard enough to control and watch without worrying if a stray arrow was going to hit him. The dragons were restless as they circled the sky, not responding well to the battle below. The noise and smoke made them wary of landing.

Sir Nolene continued to blow the flute. He wanted them to land, establishing his dominance.

Freeman Owen watched the dragons land and he cast a nervous glance at the other assistant. The young man look petrified, whether it be from the battle or the dragons. *Perhaps both,* mused Owen. *I know I am.* Their wings hadn't folded yet and with their legs fully extended looked ready to take off again. Finally they gave in to Sir Nolene's influence and began to settle down. Owen knew the tricky part was yet to come. Using the right notes of the flute would establish the perimeter of the area the dragons would defend. If he did it right the dragons would attack only the Horstruff troops located past Lord Darius' troops.

Owen fidgeted as he watched the dragons slowly redirect their attention. Both he and Sir Nolene were within easy striking range if the dragons were to attack. He drew in a breath hoping the yellow vests and Sir Nolene's flute would keep the monsters at bay.

Then suddenly in unison the dragons turned their heads up to the sky, their eyes transfixed on something high above. They screeched and whipped around in a frenzy, ignoring the frantic flute playing of Sir Nolene.

A tail from one of the larger dragons hit Owen below the knee sending a fiery shot down his leg before lifting him momentarily in the air. He landed on his back. The pain from his broken leg ripped through his body. He gasped in disbelief as he saw white bone stick out his torn pant leg. He looked over to where Sir Nolene stood transfixed as a dragon clamped his jaws across his chest and shake him before tossing the lifeless body in the air. The other assistant fared no better as two of the smaller dragons grabbed him and pulled him apart in a shower of blood. But the dragons weren't interested in eating, leaving the carcass behind. They struck at anyone within the range of their long necks, screeching and growling as their agitation grew. Suddenly they took flight, their wings beating the air as they flew low to the ground, escaping the battle.

––––––

Sir Terrance looked up at Sir Anthony as he saddled his horse.

"Anthony, I hope both of us survive this battle, but if..."

"There is no if Terrance. We will both be standing at the end." Anthony turned to his younger and smaller brother. "Just do as I say and stay well behind the main group when we charge. I will be in the lead and if it goes according to plan there won't be much fighting."

"I should be near the front."

Anthony shook his head. "Why? You're not a trained swordsman, Terrance. Leave the fighting to those who train for it. Your strength is brains, something that seems to be in short supply here." He put a hand on Terrance's shoulder. "You're being brave going into battle. Being dead won't gain you any more respect than that."

––––––

Sir Anthony waited for Lord Jon to give the signal to charge and he kicked his heels into his horse. The white stallion needed little urging and sprung forward, leaping over small mounds of dirt.

Anthony observed that while some horses shied away from loud noises and the commotion of a battle, Fortis seemed to relish going into combat. The stallion, a hand taller than most horses, was a weapon by itself as its hooves sprayed clumps of dirt behind it.

He swung his sword at those too slow to get out of the way but did direct Fortis away from those who had dropped their swords and were running away. They would no longer be a factor in the battle, and he didn't want to take a life needlessly. But if a man wanted to stand and fight, he would make it a short clash. He was proud to be leading this charge, a role he relished for more than one reason. He had told Lord Jon the truth that it was safer for him to lead in case there was a trap or if quick thinking was needed.

If they were to defeat Lord Darius, they needed to be sure Lord Jon survived the battle.

But Sir Anthony also had another reason he wanted to lead the deciding charge in the battle. His parents were waiting a long time for him to grow up and accept the responsibilities of a man especially of a Graham. If he was to die today he would finally fulfill their wishes in that way. He also remembered Lord Perry's speech telling all that it was time for those in Horstruff to step up and help save the kingdom. He saw Sir Jon being promoted to Lord Jon in the short time he was on Domum and felt the pain of jealousy and regret of his own wasted life. When the woman he loved and admired the most, informed him he was no better than a whore and an easy lay, he felt as if ice water had been thrown on him. Even Liz urged him to step up and be a man. It was at that moment he knew he had to shed his childish attitude and stop ignoring the responsibilities facing him.

He pushed hard to be included in the battle plans and be an integral part of the battle. He was surprised at the change in attitude of those he met. It was as if they could sense there was a change in him and treated him differently. His wife, Nicole, now acted warmly toward him, dropping her hostile manner, as if she had completely forgiven him for his past indiscretions.

Now as he pushed his mount hard toward Lord Darius a new feeling of hate welled up inside him. This was the man responsible for the death of two of his brothers, two men he wished he could tell he was now a man and a brother they could be proud of. He hoped Lord Darius wouldn't surrender. He wanted to kill this man for doing what he did for power and greed.

He stopped his horse next to Lord Darius who began to speak. Sir Anthony didn't listen to the words. *You talk to me like an arrogant bastard. I will not negotiate with you on any terms.*

Sir Anthony laughed at him, hoping to make him angry enough to fight. "You are an idiot, Darius. Get off your horse and toss away your sword and surrender."

"I will do no such thing. I demand your respect. Now get me Lord Jon."

*Demand my respect? Respect this!* Sir Anthony took his sword and swung it hard at Lord Darius' shield. "Surrender or fight. Choose now." He raised his sword again.

Sir Anthony was pleased when Darius took a swing at him. *Good, you have just decided to die.* He urged Fortis forward and his horse quickly moved to bully the other horse backward. As Darius struggled to maintain a fighting position, Anthony saw an opportunity to pull Darius to the ground.

It was not a significant advantage for Anthony. He had little doubt he would defeat Darius on horseback, especially with Fortis as a mount. But battles on horse sometimes ended with the loser merely badly injured. He suspected that as Lord Darius began to lose the fight he would use his horse and run away. He would be humiliated and captured but still be alive. On the ground it would be impossible for Darius to turn tail.

He began to pummel Darius with hard blows with his broad sword. Darius was able defend himself but had little opportunity to strike back. Now Anthony could see the smaller man weakening and was becoming slower. A mistake by Darius left his sword arm exposed a fraction of a second too long and he took advantage of it, slicing nearly all the arm off at the elbow.

He watched with satisfaction as Darius clutched his useless arm and screamed in pain. As blood spilled out of the gushing wound, his knees buckled. Anthony didn't hesitate. He rotated his shoulders and swung his sword again, cutting off his head.

Sir Anthony took a deep breath, feeling the air fill his lungs. Cheers broke around him. A few seconds later, he felt Lord Jon clasp a hand on his shoulder.

"I guess that's game, set and match."

Anthony looked at him. "That sounds like an Earth saying meaning we won."

Lord Jon nodded. "Is there anyone here who feels they can represent Lord Darius' army?"

A man slowly stepped forward among the crowd casting a glance at the body of Lord Darius. "I will, if you need someone to formally surrender the troops."

Sir Anthony gave a smile. "Sir Gavin. I am pleased to see you survived the battle."

"Me as well. A fine battle Horstruff fought and well deserved of victory." He looked at Lord Darius' headless body a second time. "He died without a friend or respect. A very poor man indeed." Gavin stood straight and lifted his sword. He slowly extended it with the hilt first to Lord Jon. "On behalf of Lord Darius' army I hereby surrender." He dropped to one knee.

"Rise."

Sir Anthony watched as Lord Jon formally took control of both armies. *Now I wonder if I have just witnessed who the new king will be. King Jon would be a fine and worthy king, one who the people would respect and love.*

---

Jon took the handle of the sword. "I accept the surrender of your troops. Now please rise. We have much work to do to clean up this battlefield."

He looked around. "Is there a Freeman Conner within hearing distance?"

A few moments later, the young man made his way to Jon and dropped one knee.

"You wished to see me, sire?"

Jon smiled. "I am pleased to see you survived the battle. Congratulations on your first engagement. Now I want you to ride to Lord Perry's castle and let him know Horstruff has been victorious. Go in haste."

"Yes, Lord Jon." He ran to where his horse waited and raced away.

Jon walked over to where Sir Anthony and Sir Gavin were exchanging a conversation when a lightly armoured young man slowly approached them.

"Sir Gavin, do you remember me?"

Sir Gavin looked puzzled for moment and smiled. "Of course I do. It appears you made it safely to Horstruff and contributed to the defeat of Lord Darius. How is your wife?"

"She is alive and well. We both are, thanks to you."

"I am pleased to hear that. The thanks are appreciated but what saved you was your own courage and strength."

"We will always be in your debt. I will tell Sarah that you are alive and well. She will be pleased to hear that."

Jon looked at Sir Gavin. "That sounds like a long story."

Sir Gavin laughed. "I will tell you about it someday over a few pints. That small man has the courage of men twice his size."

Jon made his way to where the soldiers from Vegrandis had congregated. Immediately several stood up and bowed when he entered their camp. "Relax please. I am looking for Sir Gilbert."

One of the dwarfs pointed to the centre of the camp. "He be theres."

Jon saw Gilbert lying still with his eyes closed. "What happened?"

Gilbert opened his eyes. "I be injured, Lord Jon."

"I can see that. How?"

"I stands up to help me friend Tommy ands suddenly Gilbert is slams into the ground."

Another member of the Vegrandis troops spoke up. "I sees what happens. An arrow goes right tos Gilbert's back buts at the last second bounces aways. Gilbert falls and hurts his head."

Jon looked at the colourful lump on Gilbert's forehead. "So the arrow didn't actually hit you?"

Gilbert shook his head. "Nay, Lord Jon. You sees Gilbert has a spell tattooed on his back that stops weapons from hitting me back. Knifes and arrows cannot stick in me back, but I still feels their impact. Me feels like I was punched."

"But you are alive, Gilbert."

"Aye. Me thinks I needs a drink."

"Only water, Gilbert. You have a bit of a concussion and better take it easy."

Jon left the Vegrandis camp to visit as many men as he could and thank them for their part in saving Horstruff. *It will be a long day.*

———

Liz huddled with the others on the second floor of Lord Perry's castle. She was angry and worried that Jon had insisted on leading the troops in battle. As she paced she smiled at Nicole, who was pacing herself.

"This is killing me, not knowing."

Liz agreed. "I know what you mean. I feel helpless waiting for a battle to end that I cannot see nor understand."

Nicole took her arm. "Come, let's pace together."

"Honestly, I respect Jon for wanting to see this through and wanting to help Domum. But he's risking his life and that I don't understand."

"Jon is going to be behind the front lines. He's also pretty big and strong and can take care of himself."

"I hope so. I also hope your Anthony is going to be okay."

Nicole smiled. "I have to tell you I was worried about him. But he has been a different man these past few weeks. It's like a cover has been pulled off a table and his true character has emerged. I know in my heart he will be okay."

Liz gave her a hug. "That's wonderful to hear. I'm really happy to know that."

They heard a shouting from outside and hurried to the balcony that opened to the courtyard below. Already a crowd had formed around the horse and rider that carried the Horstruff flag. He paused as he looked up to the balcony.

Liz and Nicole stepped aside as Lord Perry made his way to the front of the balcony with Lady Beatrice holding his hand.

"Speak. What news do you have of the battle?"

The rider removed his cap with a flourish. "Lord Perry, I have news of a great victory for Horstruff." He waited for the cheers to subside before he continued. "Lord Darius is dead, and Lord Jon has claimed victory for Horstruff. Long live King Perry!"

The cheers continued as Liz turned to Nicole and gave her a hug. "Thank God."

Nicole responded with a grin. "And all the men who fought today for Horstruff."

Liz broke apart and looked at Lord Perry with his upraised arms. "He called him King Perry."

"True. A region cannot be without a king. There is no one claiming to be King of Horstruff right now so the title goes to the closest contender. There isn't anyone who would challenge him as king right now. On the other hand, from what I heard, Lord Perry doesn't want to be king."

"So what happens if Lord Perry doesn't want to be king?"

"The lords all get a say on who will be the next king but ultimately Lord Perry will pick the successor. If the lords don't support the king he will have a very short reign. Some like Darius try to rule by intimidation and bribing others for support but that only works for so long."

"So for now Lord Perry is the new king. When do the men arrive back to Horstruff?"

"Not until tomorrow. First they have to bury the dead and tend to the wounded. That will take the rest of the day and then they will spend the night near the battlefield."

"I can hardly wait to see Jon again."

Nicole laughed. "Don't be too eager. Men usually come back from battle dirty, sweaty and with bits of blood and muck on them. What's more they would rather drink ale than to wash up. I'm going to change into something I don't mind having ale spilled on. If you want to come with me I suggest you change as well. Be warned that the men usually are drunk and don't always appreciate that you made the effort to see them."

Liz sighed. "Maybe I will pass on going to the celebration. I'm not much for being around drunken soldiers. I guess I shall be patient, but now that this battle is over I hope Jon will want to go home."

Nicole thought. *I guess that depends on where he thinks home is.*

———

Nicole approached the street, side stepping a drunk staggering out of the entrance of one of the taverns. She scanned the mass of singing, drinking, laughing warriors that had spilled out of the taverns and taken to the street. It looked to her that half the town had joined them in drinking and celebrating.

There were several taverns on the street and Nicole went into what looked like one of the better drinking establishments. She squeezed by tables and chairs, receiving a few grabs along the way. Once she was pulled on a lap where a hand quickly covered her breast. Her memories of being a waitress came flooding back and she reacted the best way she knew of getting away. First she laughed with the man holding her, leaning back into him. Next she grabbed a mug of ale sitting on the table and began to pour the contents on his head. Seconds later she escaped as he sputtered under more laughter at the table.

She found Anthony, quite drunk, sitting on a table with his legs dangling off the edge. A few others grouped around him, including Gilbert who was singing a bawdy song that was generating howls of laughter. Nicole's attention was drawn to two women who were standing on either side of Anthony with their hands touching him lightly. They were dressed as serving wenches with high slits along their skirts and revealing tops, a style she remembered wearing as a server.

"Hi, Anthony."

As he looked up in a slow motion, a grin appeared on his face.

"Nicole. You made it."

"Yes, and by the looks of it just before you're ready to pass out." She gave him a kiss, smelling sweat and spilt beer on him.

He laughed. "Just celebrating a great victory." He raised his mug. "To King Perry!"

Everyone around him raised their glasses and repeated the cheer.

Nicole ginned at him and shook her head. "I guess you deserve drinks after the battle." She took a mug from a passing server and took a long drink of the bitter ale. She knew the drinks were going to be paid for by King Perry and the taverns were trying to serve as much as possible to take advantage of the busy night.

As Nicole finished her second mug, she heard a thump and saw Gilbert pass out face down on the floor. That meant more laughter as two drunken soldiers picked him up and placed him in a chair to sleep. She looked around and found the tavern owner, opening another keg behind a crowded bar.

"Hey keeper." She tossed him a silver fern.

He reacted quickly, grabbing the coin in his thick hand. "What's this for?" He studied the currency that was as much as he made on a quiet night.

"Make sure Sir Anthony wakes up in a bed in the morning. I don't want him telling me he had to sleep in the tavern."

"Aye, miss. He shall have the best bed in the inn. After all he did put an end to the war by chopping off that bastard's head."

Nicole made her way out of the tavern and to the street, although the distinction wasn't great between them. Both had drunks, toasts and song. *The singing,* she mused, *was of the quality only drunks can manage, with words forgotten as much as the tune.* Still everyone was in a good mood and she smiled at the celebration.

She stopped long enough to have another drink, this one of red wine. It had been cut with water, but the dry wine was still potent with alcohol. A soldier made a pass at her, but she simply laughed at him and quickly moved away. She kept away from the street where the worse drunks were and stayed close to the sidewalks. She felt a little unsteady but the man who stumbled out of a tavern was definitely in worse shape.

"Jon!"

He turned to look at her, stumbled and fell to the ground.

"Hey, Nicole. How's you doing?"

"Better than you I think. Where are you going?"

"Home. I thinking I had enough to drink."

"You think you can walk home in your condition?" She shook her head as she helped him to his feet. "Let's get you a room."

Nicole helped him back into the tavern that had an inn attached to it. After a brief negotiation with the inn keeper she helped Jon climb the stairs to the second story rooms.

"Come on Jon, if you fall we'll both take a tumble." She fought to keep their balance as they made their way upstairs. His arm pulled around her waist and she reminisced back to the first time she had met him. That time he was also drunk, and she had to guide him upstairs to a room. Her server's attire didn't hide much of her body and he took advantage, moving his hand down her backside. In the room he tried unsuccessfully to pull her top down. She was not impressed by his behaviour but to his credit he apologized profusely in the morning, even as his hangover was on the verge of making him ill.

It was an odd friendship they had developed she considered, especially since she tried to seduce him later.

They made it into the assigned room, and she pushed him toward the bed. He sat down hard on the thin mattress and tried to remove his shirt with clumsy fingers.

"So warm in here."

It was warm, she agreed, and maybe more so for a man of his size. "I better help you or you'll be sober by the time you get it undone."

She pulled off his shirt and he mumbled thanks. His eyes were half closed, and she pushed him back to lie on the bed. "Jon, you're going to be in some pain tomorrow." She pulled off his boots and asked him, "Do you want your pants off too?"

"Yeah. Still too warm."

The pants were of thick leather, meant for protection in battle, and she struggled with them. His own efforts were more of a hindrance and she finally slapped at his hands. "Stop helping me. I can do this faster by myself. She finally dragged the pants off and saw his underwear came along with them, sitting around his knees. She removed those as well, deciding it would be near impossible to pull them up under his weight. "It's not as if I haven't seen you naked before," she muttered.

"Thanks, Nicole." He mumbled through closed eyes and looked dead to the world.

"No problem. Now what do I do?" She didn't relish the thought of trying to get past the drunks along the street and the long walk home. In the morning, she could send a messenger to obtain her carriage but tonight even the messengers were inebriated. *Maybe I'll rest here a bit and leave in the early morning.*

Nicole removed her dress, keeping on her light petticoat and bodice. She loosened the laces of the front of the bodice and found enough space next to Jon. Nicole closed her eyes, sleep rapidly coming.

———

Her dream was interrupted by a weight on her and she quickly became aware of a hand pushing underneath her bodice. The loose lace holding the top together was not a match for his determined effort.

"Jon?" She gasped as he pushed his hips between her legs. "What are you doing?" It was, she knew, a rhetorical question. However, she was surprised at his aggressiveness.

"The dragons are not here. We're safe." He spoke in a loud voice.

She knew resistance to him was not possible, or she considered, even desirable. Still he was acting rather odd and she pushed against his shoulders, trying to slow him down.

"Don't worry, Gilbert is guarding the door." Jon pushed himself forward on her.

Nicole moaned. "You're dreaming, Jon."

A few seconds passed and he suddenly stopped. "Nicole?" he whispered.

She slipped her hands behind his shoulders, pressing her fingers into his skin. "Yes. Don't stop. Keep going." She guessed he was still halfway between dreaming and being awake, but at least he knew he was with her.

There was a moment of hesitation before he continued. Later when he finished and rolled back off her to sleep, Nicole softly cried before drifting off to restless dreams.

The morning light stirred her, and she quietly slipped out of bed, dressed and stopped at the door.

"Goodbye, my love."

———

Jon groaned as slid his feet to the floor. He held his head with his hands, trying to push the headache out of his skull. "What is it with Domum ale that it gives me such a hangover?"

He slowly stood and saw his clothes lying next to the bed. Vague details of the night came back to him, but most of what transpired hid like the moon behind clouds. He mumbled out his thoughts. "Nicole. She helped me up to the room. But did she stay the night? Did I dream making love to her? Had to be a dream. There were dragons wandering around the castle." He shook his head. "It felt so real though." He dressed in slow motion. "I sure wish Domum had coffee. And aspirin."

# PART FOUR

*Live long and prosper. It's an old Vulcan saying.*

# THIRTY-SIX

King Perry sighed as he read. This document put forward two names that suggested these men should have their title upgraded due to their efforts in battle. As far as King Perry was concerned, the very act of being willing to fight for the kingdom automatically allowed a man to carry the title beyond that of Master. Master was usually reserved for a very young man but when he reached adult hood would normally adopt the title of Freeman, providing he wasn't under contract for his services.

The suggestion of a promotion from freeman to sir was a bit more difficult. Being a sir meant you had to be an honourable man that was usually recognized by the king or the king's representative. Other than serving well in battle, King Perry felt he did not know enough of one of the men to grant a promotion. He shook his head and wrote denied next to it. He then made a written note of Freeman Pearson for future reference.

"Perry."

He looked up and saw Beatrice. His face broke into a warm smile. "My love, I am sorry I have been neglecting you."

"I understand. But you need rest if you are to continue to make all these difficult decisions. Put away the paperwork. They will still be waiting for you in the morning."

He slowly stood. "You are quite right. I am dealing with people's lives and should not make them when I am tired." He gave a small smile.

"Would you care to have a nightcap before retiring? It will give me a chance to converse with you about something I've been meaning to discuss with you."

"Of course, Perry. I do miss our talks."

He nodded. "It is a sad reality that almost all my time and energy has been used first to take over the administration of Horstruff when Lord Bennett was killed and then to prepare for war."

They made their way to the main floor and sat in a small drawing room. A servant quickly poured two glasses of brandy and disappeared.

"What did you want to talk to me about Perry?"

He was scared to speak at first, worried that his voice would catch. He cleared his throat. "I feel like I should have found a way to ask you this long ago, Beatrice." He shook his head ruefully and smiled. "You are my candle in a dark room. You give me the vision to see where I need to go. You give me warmth and you are someone I want to keep close to me for the rest of my life. I cannot promise you I will have enough time to be always around you, but I will promise never to have you out of my thoughts. Beatrice, my love, let us get married. Let us formalize our relationship now. You have moved into my castle, but I want to show the world I don't want you to ever leave me."

"Perry, I think I was waiting half my life for you to ask me. I shall be the happiest woman alive to marry you."

He held her, kissed her and said nothing for long minutes. They slowly parted and he took her hand, leading her out of the room. They walked down the hallway that went past the double set of doors for the main library.

Perry stopped and looked inside. It was almost deserted, save for a gnant that was sorting a pile of manuscripts on a table. "Hello, Resx. Are those new acquisitions?"

"Yesss. They arrive today."

Perry looked at the papers. He employed staff specifically to search and find books and documents of his special interest, information on the physics and mathematics on how different universes can co-exist together. He was also interested in any information on how the ancient Adepts created the crystals that seemed to have a small circuit inside. While many documents were located, a problem was they were written in a language no longer used.

"Fascinating. This paper here has a diagram showing the field a crystal generates when activated." He let out a long sigh. "I doubt I will ever have the time to study in the library again."

Beatrice slipped her hand under his arm. "And why is that, my love? Is it because as king there won't be any opportunity to do what you love to do?"

"Yes, my priorities are to the people of Horstruff. There is much to do in the coming months to set everything in order. Perhaps in a few years when things are set up, I will have time to dabble in research again."

"There is another solution, Perry."

He looked at her. "What would that be?"

"Abdicate the throne. Perry, you have served Horstruff well and you can be proud of what you did. No one else is able to do this research. I think this is your calling, to study and learn so others can benefit."

"I never thought of it that way." He frowned. "I was a bit blind thinking I was the best choice as king. There are plenty of other fine men who can lead the people."

"So you would be willing to step down as king?"

"Indeed, it is something to consider."

As they left the library his footsteps became a bit faster and lighter.

———

"You wished to see me, King Perry?"

Perry looked at the tall young man with his hands folded respectively behind his back. In his dress uniform, Sir Anthony looked like a confident man, willing and able to take on any task. It was a far cry from his behaviour two short years ago when his own father, Lord Kevin Graham, had to accompany his son when he was charged with stealing one of king's horses.

"Indeed I did." King Perry got up from his desk and walked over to a cabinet. From a crystal decanter he poured two glasses of a dark liquid. As he offered one to Sir Anthony, he spoke. "There are some matters of great importance I must attend to. The first matter of business concerns you directly. I spoke with Lord Jon about what occurred on the battlefield. He told me you personally led the charge across the battle line. You also were the first to confront Lord Darius in battle. I understand part of your motive behind your actions was to avenge the deaths of your brothers, but nevertheless you stepped up as a soldier when we needed you the most. The decisive way you defeated Lord Darius left no doubt which side won."

"Thank you, King Perry. I was fortunate to be put into the position where I could help Lord Jon win the battle."

"Well put, Sir Anthony. You are a man who speaks modestly of his own accomplishments." King Perry looked at Sir Anthony carefully. "In fact I see a man who will someday achieve many things." He took a drink of his port. "I spoke with Lord Jon and your father about you a few days ago. We find it hard to believe your transformation in the past weeks. It is as if a spell was put on you."

Sir Anthony took a slow drink of his port and responded. "I suppose I was given a verbal slap on the face. So hard that it knocked me to my senses." He smiled. "It hurt at the time, but I finally saw myself as others see me. It was not a pleasant image."

"Well, whoever did that would be pleased to hear that you are to be promoted to Lord Anthony."

Sir Anthony's jaw dropped. "King Perry, I don't know what to say."

"Your face tells me all I need. Congratulations."

"Thank you. It is an unexpected honour."

"The ceremony will take place in two weeks time along with other announcements. Now I would like to ask you about Sir Gavin. I understand he is currently staying at your castle until he returns to Regius in a few days time."

"Yes, the first time we met on the battlefield and fought to a standstill. I believe we both saw each other as kindred spirits. When Lord Darius was defeated, Sir Gavin was the one that took the responsibility to surrender the troops to Lord Jon. After that we shared a few stories and laughs together. I asked him to stay at my castle until he returns home. I must say I am impressed with his character and he's a fine fighter as well."

"That is good to hear. You see, I do have a problem with the administration of what used to be King Charles' castle and the surrounding district. My thoughts are to replace at least part of the administration with new people. Sir Gavin strikes me as a man of intelligence and good character. I met him briefly during a meeting of what to do with the former Lord Darius troops, and was impressed by his demeanour. I am strongly leaning toward promoting him to Lord Gavin and have him take over the administration of Regius. Your thoughts?"

Sir Anthony paused before speaking. "I do not know who lives in Regius that would be better, but I do know it would not be a mistake to have him representing you in Regius. He is honest and would be loyal to you."

"Excellent. Please do not inform him of this conversation until I speak with him." He refilled the two glasses. "What are your feelings on Lord Jon as a leader?"

Sir Anthony was silent as he thought. "King Perry, he is a fine leader. I can think of no reason why he shouldn't be given the opportunity to extend his role as leader of men. He is not too young in that he has life experiences. He is also intelligent, honourable and would serve Horstruff to the best of his abilities."

"That is certainly a fine endorsement."

"Lord Jon is a good man."

"Don't sell yourself short, Sir Anthony. You may have taken the long journey, but you are here today as an honourable man as well."

———

Sir Gavin bowed as he entered King Perry's office. "King Perry, it is an honour to meet with you again."

"Thank you, Sir Gavin. I have a proposition for you. I know about your ability as a fighter, but I'm also impressed with your ability as a leader. From what I can gather you possess a good sense of right and wrong."

"Thank you, sire. I believe people do better at a task when they aren't forced to without a good reason."

"Good to hear that. Sir Gavin, I would like you to take over the administration of Regius as Lord Gavin."

Sir Gavin stood silent in astonishment.

King Perry smiled. "I believe you deserve this chance to move up from the fighting ranks. You will have to follow my directions, of course, but would be free to appoint others in the capacity in the running of Regis."

"King Perry, I will do my best to serve you. Thank you for the trust you have given me."

"The ceremony will be done here in less than two weeks time. I suggest you use that time to talk to Lord Jon and Lord Kevin Graham about how a kingdom needs to be run. It will help you to know what to look for."

Sir Gavin left the room, wondering how King Perry had learned about him. *I guess you never know whom you will meet and how they will have an influence on your life.*

# THIRTY-SEVEN

Sir Keith stood as the jailer opened the cell door, surprised to see King Perry standing behind the overweight guard.

King Perry gestured with his hand. "Come. I want to discuss your situation with you."

Sir Keith gave a small bow and followed King Perry. After a few steps along the straw covered hall he spoke up. "I have lost track of time and didn't realize I was being released today."

"You are being pardoned early. I see no need to keep you prisoner now that the conflict with Lord Darius is over."

"I am pleased to hear the conflict is over. I would like to offer my congratulations on your victory."

"Thank you. I wasn't sure which side you were hoping to prevail, but I suppose now you have few options."

Sir Keith heard the sarcasm in King Perry's voice and felt shame wash over him. "I deeply regret what I did to cause distress to your kingdom. However, I will not deny my love for Lady Karla. I hope you understand the dilemma I was under. Please forgive my lapse in judgement."

"I do." King Perry sighed. "You actions and behaviour caused me to have many a sleepless night. I have known you for many years and was shocked to hear you betrayed us to Lord Darius. I decided your character allowed you a second chance. I trust you will reflect on the path you must take to re-establish your reputation."

"I will. Thank you, King Perry for sparing my life."

Sir Keith shielded his eyes as he stepped outside. The sun blinded him, but he soon adapted to being outside the dark of the dungeon. He felt dirty and unkempt after his time in prison and walked along the quieter side streets with his head down until he reached his castle.

He opened the front door of his home, startling a servant cleaning the front hall.

The woman quickly curtsied, looking flustered. "Sir Keith, we weren't expecting you to return so soon."

Sir Keith looked at the petite, young blonde. "Neither was I expecting to return at this date. However, I have been pardoned early."

"Is there anything I may get for you, sire?"

"Just fill my tub with hot water. I need to get cleaned up. I fear I smell worse than I look."

———

Sir Keith dressed in clean clothes and instructed a servant to dispose of his earlier clothes. "I will never feel clean in them again no matter how well they are washed. Please bring me a bottle of brandy to the second level library."

The elder servant bowed. "Would you like your dinner served there as well?"

"Yes, and it would be best that I be left alone."

———

Sir Keith poured another goblet full of brandy and stared at the flickering flames of the fire inside the stone fireplace. "Why my love? Why did you want to embark on such a dangerous journey?" He took a long drink of his brandy, coughed, and took another swallow. "I have trouble believing you are gone from my life forever. I would feel better knowing that you are all right and at peace."

He continued to sip and stare at the dwindling flames. He took a final drink and then rose unsteadily to his feet. He was about to turn toward the door of the library when the fireplace suddenly was engulfed with flames for a few brief seconds before settling down to its previous quiet state.

Sir Keith stared at the fireplace and smiled. "Thank you. It was all I needed to know."

———

The young servant entered quickly into the second level library room, curtsied and spoke in a rush. "Sir Keith, Lord Jon is here with Sir Gilbert. I have them waiting in the drawing room."

Sir Keith stood from his chair where he had been watching the flickering flames. The library had become his favourite spot in recent days as he isolated himself from the rest of the world. "Thank you. Please make sure you take them refreshments. I will greet them shortly."

Sir Keith quickly fixed his shirt, wishing he had shaved earlier. He walked to the drawing room, straightened his shoulders and forced a smile. "Lord Jon, Sir Gilbert. For what do I owe this unexpected visit?"

Lord Jon spoke. "We haven't seen you in weeks and wanted to make sure you are doing all right. We also want to express our sympathies for events that occurred recently to you."

Gilbert chimed in. "Yeah, we hopes you be doing okay."

"Thank you for your sentiments and your concern. I have been doing some reflection."

Jon nodded. "My friend, I and others are a bit concerned about you. You seemed to have vanished from the social circles you used to attend. Now I hear that you won't be attending the ceremony when the promotions to lords are officially announced. I am hoping we can convince you to change your mind."

Sir Keith took a drink from his glass of port. "I appreciate your concern, but I would feel awkward attending such an event. No doubt people would look at me with disdain as a man who tried to betray the kingdom. I am certain it would be a most uncomfortable experience, knowing that they see me who was recently placed in a dungeon for crimes against the kingdom."

Jon shook his head. "If King Perry forgives you, and he has, then others will follow his example. You made a mistake, as we all have done in our lives. Now the past is done, and it is time for you to live again."

"I don't know, Lord Jon, if I am up to the scrutiny of other nobility."

"There is only one way to find out." He smiled. "By the way, Gilbert and I are not leaving until you do agree to attend, so I hope you have a lot of liquor on hand."

———

The ceremony for the promotion of Lord Anthony and Lord Gavin had taken on the life of a party. It seemed the people were also celebrating the victory of the battle. Lord Jon smiled with a lopsided grin as he watched Liz hug Lord Anthony. He found Liz's excitement contagious. Lord Anthony himself looked like he was on the verge of tears. He had been hugged and congratulated by a dozen people before Liz had a chance to step forward. At first Lord Anthony just smiled and accepted the accolades that came on him, but when his parents hugged him he looked strained and Liz seemed to put him past being able to hide his emotions.

Jon knew he had too many drinks but considered this may be one of the last times he could celebrate on Domum and he intended to take advantage of it. He stepped forward and shook Lord Anthony's hand. "Way to go. You deserve this more than anyone I know. Congrats."

Anthony mumbled words of thanks, looking a bit lost.

Jon put his hand on his shoulder. "Come with me for a minute. You need a proper drink." He pushed Anthony to a waiter and took two glasses with whisky from the tray.

"To Lord Anthony. May he live long and prosper." Others raised their glasses in salute.

"Thank you, Lord Jon." He tossed back his drink and looked like he had regained his composure. "That is a fine toast."

Jon laughed. "It is not original. Actually, it's an old Vulcan saying."

"Vulcan?"

"A fine, alien race." He laughed as Liz punched him on the shoulder.

Jon saw Sir Keith, who was talking to two women across the room. Both women stood close to him seemingly hanging on to his every word. At first Jon was worried he was going to have to spend the whole evening trying to keep up Sir Keith's spirits. He had shown up not dressed up to his usual standards and even had a bit of a shadow on his face, and Jon quickly tried to get his spirits up. It wasn't long before several ladies came up to Sir Keith and Jon gradually left him alone. He turned his attention to Nicole and touched her arm to draw her attention to him.

Nicole smiled warmly and took a step away from Lord Anthony and those wanting to have a word with him.

"How are you, Jon? Besides drunk I mean."

He chuckled. "Good. Happy. Satisfied. And definitely a bit drunk. How about you?"

"I'm not drunk but feeling really good. I hear you are planning to leave Domum."

"Yeah. Gotta go back to Earth and make an honest living."

"I'll miss you.

"I'll miss you too. Very much, to be frank."

"Really?"

"Yeah, somehow I fell in love with you." He closed his eyes and swayed on his legs. "I don't think I should have said that. I mean, I do love you but..."

"I love you too, Jon. But you have Liz and I have Anthony."

"Very true. I don't regret saying Liz is the one for me, but if I had met you under different circumstances..."

"I know. Let`s go for a walk." She hooked her hand under his arm. "You need some fresh air to clear your head. The evening is going to end too soon for you if you don't slow down your drinking."

"I think you're right." He looked over at Sir Keith. "Can you tell me what the hell is going on with him? All those women hanging around him who wouldn't give him the time of day a month ago."

"Jon, women are complicated."

"Tell me something new."

She laughed. "A month ago Sir Keith was with Lady Karla. Not many women wanted to go close to them, and with good reason. Now since then, he has lost weight and has become available. He has also suddenly developed a reputation as a dangerous man. He has served time in the dungeon, been whipped and looks a bit scruffy. He still is a Sir with some wealth behind him. Women suddenly find him attractive."

Jon shook his head. "Mostly because he was guilty of a crime against the kingdom."

"Yeah, some women find that enticing." She laughed. "You always were a bit clueless about women."

"True." He put his arm around her briefly. "But I have been lucky to have met some very nice ladies anyway. When I go back to Earth I'll miss you. You have made a big difference in my life on Domum and I remember how much you helped me the first time I was here."

Nicole gave him a smile. "I'll always remember you too." *He doesn't remember that night. Probably thinks it was just a dream.*

# THIRTY-EIGHT

King Perry smiled at Lord Jon. "My friend, it is so good to see you. It seems to me that the only time in the past few weeks when we saw each other we were scrambling to get our army ready for the ceremonies. It will be nice to relax and have a drink with you."

"I agree." Jon lowered his body to a leather armchair in one of the drawing rooms of King Perry's castle. "I believe we both deserve some time to get reacquainted with our regular lives."

King Perry tilted his glass toward Jon. "That is actually a topic I wanted to discuss with you. You see I have been placed in a position that is removed from my comfort zone. When I first met you, I was responsible for finances of the kingdom, representing King Charles. When Lord Bennett was killed, I took over the administration as well. These duties have taken away from what I wanted to do, and that was to do research in my library. Now I have been made king, which not only eliminates any opportunities for working in the library but has also taken time away from my courtship of Lady Beatrice."

Jon smiled. "It sounds like destiny is taking you for a ride. I must say you do make a great king. You are intelligent, honest and care about what's best for Horstruff. I admire how you pay attention to the small details of running a kingdom."

King Perry chuckled. "I think that is more of a curse than a blessing. I wish I could stop looking at every detail before making a decision."

"Well, I suppose that is how you work. It probably helps a lot when you are doing your research."

"Except I don't have the opportunity to do research anymore." King Perry gave a short smile. "Actually, that is what I want to talk to you about." He let out a long breath. "I have to consider who will be taking over for me eventually, and I believe I have to make that decision soon."

"Are you all right? I mean you're not feeling sick or anything like that?"

King Perry laughed. "No, no, no. I mean to say I am planning to step down as king. I want to go back to doing research and to spend time with Lady Beatrice."

"You had me worried there." Jon chuckled. "When are you planning to step down as king?"

"As soon as I am able to find a suitable replacement, and that is not an easy task. I am looking for a man who is young enough that he will be able to serve as King for a long time, but also mature enough to make difficult decisions. He must also be honest, sincere, and be respected by the commoners as well as nobility."

"That is quite a list of qualifications."

"Indeed it is but believe it or not there are suitable candidates."

"That is good to hear."

"The one I prefer to take over for me is you."

"Me?"

"Yes, I can think of no better man than you to take over as king. You, Lord Jon, have the all the characteristics we need. What do you say?"

# THIRTY-NINE

L iz thought about Jon as she finished dressing. She was pleased that his stomach had shrunk considerably, and his arms and chest had become bigger since they arrived on Domum. He was in the best shape since she met him. The reasons why didn't please her as much. Domum had transformed him into a man of confidence and the physical exertions of fighting had changed his body.

The problem was Domum was good for him, but it was not a place she wanted to live. She was bored and frustrated on Domum.

She was tiring of the layers of clothing she had to wear as Lady Elizabeth and the trouble she had breathing with the corseted dresses. She understood after the battle there was a lot of work to do. As the leader of the Horstruff troops, he had to help with the numerous tasks that followed for the new king. She was willing to be patient until after the promotion ceremonies. But after that she decided she would give Jon a deadline. She was going to return to Earth. If he was reluctant to do so, then it would be a difficult goodbye, but she wanted to live where she was more than just a lord's wife.

———

Liz saw Jon enter the carriage and waved goodbye to him wondering what Lord Perry wanted to talk to him about. *I just hope Lord Perry doesn't try to find something else that would entice Jon to stay in Domum.* She waited a few minutes, then went back inside, and found Nadine sitting with Tuck in the main room. She didn't look like the half dead woman that arrived here a few weeks ago. She had colour in her face, her long hair had waves in it, and she had gained weight. *A lot of the weight may have gone into her boobs. She has quite the hourglass figure.* Liz was at first concerned with Jon's former girl-friend Nadine staying in their castle, but quickly saw Nadine and Tuck as a couple. Jon acted as a friend to both and didn't show any lingering romantic notions toward her.

"Hi Nadine, Tuck. How are you feeling now?"

Nadine smiled. "Much better thank you. I'm actually feeling good enough to go for walks. Tuck has been so good to me. I am very lucky that he cares for me so."

"You're looking much better as well. I was wondering if you would like to go with me to Lord Sussex's castle? Just a few of us girls are getting together to talk and relax a bit. We would likely come back late tonight."

Nadine looked at Tuck with a question on her face.

"I think it will be good for you to go." He smiled. "I'll be here when you get back."

Nadine grinned. "I think it would be nice to meet some other people. It's been years since I saw Domum."

———

Liz watched Tuck help Nadine into the carriage and kiss her goodbye.

Nadine stared out of the window. "You know, it is how I remembered Horstruff but still different. When I was a gnant I smelled things differently. We used our tongue to taste the air. As a human, I find the scents so weak and the ones I do smell harder to fix the direction it is coming from."

"You mean gnants know where a smell is coming from?"

"Yes, the tongue is forked so it's like using two ears to hear where a sound comes from. Gnants also have better hearing and I'm missing some of the sounds I used to hear. That's okay. Humans have something gnants don't possess."

"What's that?"

"Compassion. Gnants are selfish by nature. Our natural tendency is to care for ourselves first."

"Humans can be selfish too."

"I know. But where a human would sacrifice themselves to save their

child, a gnant would not. The gnant self preservation is too strong."
Nadine smiled. "I think humans understand that by caring for another as
much as for themselves, they are happier. I was rarely happy as a gnant
and never felt for someone as much as I feel for Tuck. You must feel great
joy when you are with Lord Jon. When I first met him I was still partially
a gnant. He scared me because he was so big. Now as a human female I
understand why you care for him so. He is a very attractive male and his
size probably attracts a lot of interest from other females." Suddenly she
bit her lower lip. "I don't believe I should have said that. I am not very
good at understanding the boundaries of human conversation. I do not
mean to offend you with my openness."

Liz smiled. "It's all right. When men aren't around, we woman can be
pretty frank about the men in our lives. We talk a whole lot differently
when they're around though." *I wonder if I am being too selfish in demanding
Jon come back to Earth with me. Maybe I need to try to understand what will make
him happy that I can live with.*

———

Liz was happy to see Patricia and the other ladies at Lord Sussex's castle.
Patricia wore a long, loose flowing pink gown that showed off her figure
quite well by clinging to her body. The other women were dressed in the
familiar attire of the castle with most of them wearing only a simple skirt.

"You must be Nadine. We have heard about you and it is so nice you
have made it to our castle. First things first. I will show you to our guest
room where you can change into something more comfortable. Then we
can share a few drinks and talk."

Patricia led Liz and Nadine to one of the guest bedrooms. "There are
lots of gowns in the closet. Help yourself and join the rest of us on the
second level dining room."

After Patricia left, Liz looked inside the closet. "Wow. I think there are
a lot of choices here." She went through several of the gowns and pulled
out a white, lacy gown. "What do you think?" She held it up against her.

"It is very pretty."

Liz carried it to the bed and reached behind her to undo the strings
holding the upper part of her dress together. "Soon I can breathe again."
She pulled her top open and down. Gradually she managed to step out of
the pile fabric. Liz hooked her thumbs in the waistband of her panties
and saw Nadine was watching her closely.

"Is something wrong?"

Nadine suddenly looked away. "I'm sorry for staring, but I have never seen a naked woman before, other than myself. I was curious. I was comparing you to me. I didn't mean to upset you."

Liz gave a small smile. "That's okay. I understand why you're curious, though if you hang around at Lord Sussex's castle for any length of time you will see a lot of naked women." She continued to undress.

Nadine let out a long breath. "Thank you for not being upset. I have never seen a naked man before either. I am getting very close to Tuck, but I'm scared about mating with him. I don't know what to expect."

Liz put on the nightgown. "Let him make the first moves and just go along."

"How do I arouse him?"

"Oh that's easy. Just take off your clothes."

"Just take off my clothes?"

"Always works." She handed a nightgown to Nadine. "This is pretty. Do you want me to leave while you change?"

"No, please stay. Can you tell me what a man looks like? I understand they can be quite a bit larger than gnants. I guess I'm a little concerned about that."

"Don't be. Men and women are meant to—well, let us say it will fit."

———

Patricia finished her drink, putting it down just as she burst into laughter at Angela's joke. "Oh my. That really happened in that bar on Earth?"

Angela giggled. "It did. She claimed she was in the men's room by accident, but that didn't explain why her top was off."

Liz grinned. "Angela, you have more stories than you can shake a stick at." She reached over to Angela who was sitting next to her on the loveseat and patted her bare leg exposed by the slit in her gown.

Angela grinned. "When you work in a bar, strange things happen after midnight. But I seem to attract odd things." She laughed. "Like Madoc."

"What is the deal with him? Are you going to be living on Earth or on Domum?"

Angela grabbed her hand. "It is both. He was willing to move to Earth to be with me, and that was good. But I thought here was the perfect man for me and he was even willing to give up his world just to be with me. I felt, well flattered, but also maybe a bit selfish. I mean it wasn't fair for him to give up Domum just to be with me. So I suggested we live a while on Earth and a while on Domum until we figured out what works for both of us."

Liz took another drink of her wine. "You mean you're willing to live some of the time on Domum? Even after he offered to move to Earth?"

"Of course. I mean I like Earth better but Domum isn't so bad. I get to decorate the castle and believe me there are a lot of rooms that need work, and there is Lord Troy's castle and the famous parties. I would feel selfish to take him away from his home just like that. Marriage is give and take and where you live has to be a compromise."

Patricia raised her eyebrows. "Marriage? Is that official?"

Angela blushed. "Okay, not official, but we talked about living together and maybe having kids and to me that's almost a proposal. I know he's the one."

Liz laughed. "I think I hear your heart talking there."

Angela stuck her tongue out at her. "He loves me. That's all that matters.

Patricia looked at Nadine. "How about you? What's going on between you and Tuck?"

Nadine sat quietly in a well-cushioned chair and looked reluctant to say anything. "Tuck is being very nice to me. I think he wants to have sex with me but I'm not sure if I'm ready yet."

Liz spoke up. "I think Tuck is a very nice man. I also think he's in love with you."

"Really? I mean, will a male love a female before they have sex?"

Liz laughed. "I don't know if the two are always related. Men want sex all the time. It's up to the woman to decide if he gets it or not. But in the case of Tuck, I think he's thinking past the sex."

"I hope so. You see he has offered to let me live at his place on Earth. I think I will say yes because it is hard for me to be by myself. I have so much trouble understanding how to act around people and being with him would make it a lot easier."

Angela nodded. "That makes sense, except how do you feel about him? I mean, it wouldn't be right to live with him just to make it easier on yourself and not care for him too."

"I like Tuck a lot. He smells nice and I would like to have sex with him, except that I'm scared to. I have never had sex with a man before."

Patricia looked surprised. "You're a virgin?"

"Only with humans. I had sex before when I was a gnant."

Liz listened to the conversation. Her thoughts drifted to her own situation with Jon. "I have a question for you girls. Do you think I'm being reasonable in wanting Jon to move back to Earth? I know he likes it here and he feels strong and powerful. But I want to live on Earth. I was thinking of asking him to choose me or Domum."

Nicole gasped. "Are you serious? You would give up Jon just because he wants to live here? What's wrong with living here?"

Liz shook her head quickly. "Nothing really, but I have to finish my university classes."

Angela poked Liz on the shoulder. "I don't believe this. University classes or not, you would give Jon an ultimatum on where to live? What's the truth?"

Liz sighed. "It's hard to explain. I grew up in Ballymiller and it was expected I would live there, marry a local lad and raise a family there. My mom is a wonderful, smart lady who spent her life making a home for us. Her life was centered around the home without many opportunities to enjoy time outside it. Dad was a hard worker, but he had more freedom and occasionally went to the pub with the boys. I vowed I was not going to spend my life doing what Mom did. I was going to have a career and live in a city where I could do things. So I went to university, determined to break free of the role Mom had to endure, returning during summer to be with my parents. I refused to get involved with the local boys, no matter how charming they were, because I knew I was going to live else-where. I met Jon and I had visions of being with a man who was going to live in a city." She took a drink of her wine and continued. "So now I see Jon is happy, confident and in his element here in Horstruff. He's even more attractive to me than when we were in Ballymiller. But to me Horstruff is like Ballymiller. Women stay at home and try to make sure their man is taken care of. I know I sound selfish, but I know I will be miserable here. I need more out of life than what my mother had."

Angela tilted her head to the side. "Can I ask you something?"

"Sure."

"Have you asked Jon where he wants to live? Seems to me you're assuming he wants to stay in Domum."

Liz frowned. "Well, why wouldn't he? I mean everyone here looks up to him. He's respected, has his own castle and controls his own destiny."

Angela smiled. "All the same I think you better talk to him about this. He loves you and I would bet he would be willing to go to Earth for you."

"But I don't want to do that to him. I love him very much and he deserves to be where he would be the happiest."

"Okay, but I still think you should ask him where he wants to live. Don't assume you know what he's thinking. Men can have the oddest thoughts at times."

Liz nodded. "All right, I'll ask him. I sure want to stay with him."

# FORTY

Liz put on what she considered the prettiest of the dresses available to her from her closet. After checking her make-up, she went to the study where Jon was sitting, drinking a glass of whisky and looking at an unrolled scroll in front of him.

"Hi."

Jon looked up and a smile broke out on his face. "Hi there yourself."

"Jon, I want to talk to you about something important." Liz walked up to him as he stood. "I need to know something."

"Sure, ask away. I want to tell you something too."

"Oh, what is it? You go first with your news."

"I had an interesting meeting with King Perry. He has informed me that he is planning to step down as king, to abdicate the throne."

"Oh, my gosh. Really? When is he going to do this and who will take over as king?"

"Well, I suppose he won't give up being a king until he has a replacement ready." Jon paused before continuing. "He asked me to be the new king."

Liz was silent for several seconds and buried her head in his chest. "Jon, I love you more than you can imagine. I know you will make a wonderful king and that Domum is a place that makes you feel strong and confident. You are happy here and I wish you all the happiness in the world, but I can't stay here with you. I hope you don't think of me as being selfish, but I need to live on Earth." She let out a sob. "I wish things had turned out different and we could stay together." She turned away from him and began to hurry out of the room.

"Liz, wait! I told him no."

She spun around and looked at him, tears running down her red cheeks. "You told him no?"

"Yeah, I said I needed to return to Earth. I didn't go to university to learn how to be a king after all, and you still have a year left on your studies. If we have kids, I don't want to raise them on Domum. Earth is our home, Liz."

Liz closed her eyes. "Now I feel like an idiot." She walked up to him and punched him on the shoulder. "Do you think you could have started with telling me you turned him down first?"

"Sorry, but how was I to know you were going to say what you did?"

She sighed and gave him a kiss. "So when do we go back to Earth?"

"How about a couple of weeks? We need to have a farewell party before we leave and there is the problem of our castle. Who do we leave the keys to?"

Liz laughed. "Maybe we can place an ad to rent it out."

———

Lord Madoc smiled as he lifted his drink from the table. "You do have a nice port here, King Perry." He inhaled the aroma and took a small drink. "I have not been in your main library for quite some time, but I do not recall it being this quiet before." He gazed around the shelves filled with books and scrolls up to the second level. "As a matter of fact, the last time I was here there were half dozen clerks and one or two gnants. There doesn't seem to be any one in here besides us now."

King Perry nodded. "Your observation is quite correct. Usually I do have some activity here, however I asked for the room to be vacant for our discussion. This library used to be the centre of my life."

"The responsibilities of being a king can be enormous and time consuming."

"The truth is I was finding my time in the library dwindling ever since I had to take over the duties of Lord Bennett. Then of course I have wanted to spend time with Lady Beatrice. As a king I can rule the kingdom but not my own life."

Madoc swirled the port around in his glass. "I have heard you are planning to step down as king."

King Perry chuckled. "You still have the ability to ferret out information. I just hope you are still discrete with your knowledge."

"Of course, King Perry." He smiled. "You can trust me."

King Perry laughed. "Those words have come back to haunt me. But now, Lord Madoc, I was wondering if I can have the service of Council Madoc. I need some advice."

"You are relinquishing your title as king, so perhaps I should surmise you are wondering who should be taking over as king."

"That is perceptive of you."

Lord Madoc rubbed the bridge of his nose. "The suitable candidates will need certain qualifications. One being young enough so the possibility of needing a new king again in a few years will not occur. He, of course, must be a leader of men, resourceful when it comes to dealing with problems, be honest and respected by those around him."

"I agree with you there."

"Perhaps I am being hasty in forwarding a name, but it seems to me Lord Jon meets all those requirements and should receive serious consideration."

"Well, that is part of my problem. I offered to support him if he wanted to be king, but he turned me down. Lord Jon, despite my efforts, has decided to return to Earth. I cannot blame him. It is apparent Lady Elizabeth is not comfortable here and he will do what it takes to ensure her happiness."

"That does make the process a bit more difficult. Lord Jon certainly would have the support of the lords and would make a fine king. Fortunately, we do have other lords to consider for the position."

"Yes, though my preference is to pick someone from the region of Horstruff. I do not feel comfortable in championing someone from Regius. We do not know enough about them, other than they may have been part of the downfall of King Charles."

"That was obvious when you appointed Lord Gavin to oversee the region of Regius. I must say I agreed completely with that move. Regardless of the merit of other lords there, Lord Gavin's loyalty will most certainly be with you and Horstruff." Lord Madoc took a long drink of his port, stood and walked around the central area of the library. He turned and addressed King Perry. "By appointing Lord Gavinas administrator of Regius, you have made it known you are not afraid to make a bold move to ensure the stability of the kingdom. I have heard that already Regius is changing back as a prosperous county."

"I had heard good things about Lord Gavin and liked him immediately when we met. To me, he provided an ideal solution to a difficult problem. Someone from Horstruff would have needed time to understand what was going on at Regius. While Lord Gavin served under Lord Darius, he had been in contact often with Regius to understand the goings on there."

Lord Madoc walked to where King Perry sat. "Your decisions as administrator of Horstruff, and now as king, have garnished tremendous respect among the people and nobility. Whoever you choose to be the new king will likely receive little opposition from the other lords." He smiled. "There are exceptions, of course, such as myself. I am still surprised you managed to have me appointed as lord."

Lord Perry smiled. "I can be convincing when making a presentation. I did briefly consider you as king as well. But my understanding is that you wish to live on Earth, at least part of the time. Secondly, I believe you are much like me and a bit tired of all the politics and details a king must always consider whenever he makes a decision."

"You are quite correct there. At one time, not so long ago, I would have been excited at the prospect of being king. Now I am excited at spending time with Lady Angela on Earth. During my time on Earth earlier, I avoided many of the treasures it had to offer for fear I would find it too enticing. I told myself at the time it was because I feared the aether being contaminated, but that wasn't true. I was scared Earth would draw me in and I wouldn't want to leave. Odd isn't it, how life and your desires can change so rapidly?" Madoc sat again at the table, looking at the polished dark surface of the wood.

"Yes, that is true. People can change unexpectedly under different influences."

"We have seen that with Sir Keith, under the manipulation of Lady Karla. I hear he has suddenly become a bit of a social player and has been seen in the company of various women." He smiled. "Not the same man of a year ago when he merely pretended he was a man of the world. Now he actually seems to be that man."

King Perry chuckled. "I do believe he is having the best time of his life. But speaking of changes in men, there is one man who has gone under a remarkable transformation recently."

Madoc nodded. "I know who you mean. I do believe he may be the best option as king."

King Perry took a drink of his port. "When you used to go by the title of Council Madoc I remember asking you for information and advice. At the end of our conversation you would often leave me with advice or ask me to consider a certain direction. I often had the feeling you were leading me to a path that benefited you, even though your recommendation was sound. In fact, I believed you already knew my questions before you entered the room and already had an answer. You would draw out the conversation so it gave the impression you were carefully considering the facts and come up with an answer." He put down his glass and leaned forward. "Lord Madoc, why do I have this feeling again?"

Madoc took his drink and smiled. "As Council Madoc, I had to take pains to look like I was unbiased when I gave advice. Yes, I had my own agenda and it was true I often knew what advice I was going to give before I met anyone. Part of the reason was to help myself in my role as Council Madoc. My greatest asset was the ability to perceive what someone was going to do next. As to your question, yes I knew you were going to seek my opinion on who might make your best replacement."

King Perry grinned. "You already knew Lord Jon had turned me down?"

Madoc nodded. "I did." He broke into a grin.

"You scoundrel." He shook his head. "So you already had this name you thought was best and waited for me to mention it first." King Perry laughed.

Madoc laughed with him. "I knew eventually you would figure out how I worked. All the same, your choice is valid and the best you can make."

King Perry raised his glass. "To the new king then. I'm glad we agree on him."

Lord Madoc raised his glass. "To the new king, Lord Anthony."

# FORTY-ONE

Tuck walked with Nadine along the hallways. He was pleased how much stronger she had become in the past week and how close they had become. He led her to a dining room where Jon and Liz were already waiting for them.

After exchanging greetings they settled down around the long table as servants placed food on their plates.

Liz smiled at Tuck. "You and Nadine are looking much better now. It's good to see."

Nadine replied in a quiet voice. "I am very fortunate. I have been given a second chance to live and Tuck has been very nice to me."

"So have you decided where you are going to live?"

Nadine gave a smile. "I'm going to live with Tuck on Earth. His friend Tom and his girlfriend Marisa know about Domum so I'll know people I can talk to and help me adjust to Earth. I need to return to my apartment first and get my cat. My neighbour is looking after it and I think she will be happy that I am no longer sick."

Liz smiled. "That is wonderful to hear that you and Tuck are staying together. Jon and I are going to live in Ireland until I finish university and decide where we want to live. I told him anywhere on Earth is fine with me."

Jon nodded. "It will be good to go home again. I travelled a long distance to find out where I needed to go."

Liz looked at him. "I'm happy to be with you on the rest of the journey."

Nadine looked over at Jon. "Lord Jon, I understand that you know several of the gnants here on Domum."

"I guess so. Some I've made friends with."

"I am hoping to find a gnant named Rzet, at least that's how humans pronounce his name."

Jon looked surprised. "I know him actually. Do you want me to send a message to him?"

Nadine gave a hurried response. "Please. I would like to speak to him before I go back to Earth."

# FORTY-TWO

Jon held Liz's hand as they stood with the other invited guests inside Lord Perry's castle. The main ballroom was filled with well dressed guests as they stood on either side of a walkway that led to the throne on a raised platform. Jon had one of the best positions to view the crowning of the new king, near the front and along the walkway.

Liz looked up and whispered to him. "When does this start?"

"Soon I guess. I wished they used time pieces here, but things happen when someone feels it's time it should."

"I hope it starts soon. My feet are getting sore."

"Has it occurred to you wearing high heels to a medieval world wasn't the smartest thing to do?"

"Yes, well, they make me taller and that's worth the pain. Besides it makes me closer to your height and easier to kiss."

"I see something happening at the front, it's Lord Perry."

Lord Perry walked up to the throne.

"This is a day that will be remembered as the day the throne has been restored to the rightful family. The Graham family was the royal family before and now that honour and privilege has returned. It is with great satisfaction I introduce your new king, King Anthony Graham the Second."

The crowd applauded as King Anthony Graham and Queen Nicole walked slowly up the aisle between the people. Jon felt his hand being squeezed tight as Liz looked on, her attention completely focused on the new king. Jon had expected Anthony to look nervous as he was crowned, but he gave the appearance of a confident man. Jon looked at Nicole and her expression was a mixture of anxious and relief. He thought she had made a rather spectacular rise from a barmaid to queen in less than two years. *Nicole has a good heart and she deserves what she can get.*

———

Jon and Liz pushed their way out of the main ballroom and to a private room at the back. There they waited with a dozen other special guests for the appearance of the royal couple. He watched as Lord Kevin Graham and his wife approached them. Lady Graham was smiling as she looked at Liz.

"My dear, it has been a long time since I've talked to you." Lady Graham reached over and touched Liz's arm. "You certainly have managed to succeed in life."

Liz grinned. "Yes, I have been fortunate. The last time we talked was when I was employed as a hostess at the Rosemore Castle. I am so excited for Anthony. I find it hard to believe when I met him he was also working at the Rosemore Castle."

Lady Graham laughed. "As a stable hand, no less. But you have helped guide him to his potential and for that I will be forever grateful." She turned to Jon. "You have a wonderful lady here. Be careful you don't do anything to upset her."

A guard standing at the entrance announced in an overly loud voice, "His royal highness, King Anthony Graham the second and Queen Nicole." He snapped his heels together and stood stiffly as Anthony and Nicole entered.

The king's first action was to shake hands with his father and hug his mother. He eventually turned his attention to Liz and Jon.

Jon grinned. "I hope they don't announce you like that every time you enter a room. That could be a little overwhelming."

The king laughed. "I guess it would make it difficult to sneak into a bar for a quick pint."

Nicole wagged a finger at him. "Those pints of ale could get you in trouble again."

Liz held up a small silver box. "I was wondering if I could take your picture."

Anthony's forehead creased as he stared at it. "What is it?"

"A camera." She pointed at Anthony. "Smile."

Anthony blinked at the sudden flash of light. "That little box has a fire inside it."

Liz giggled. "That was just the flash." She turned the camera around and let him see the LCD display. "See, you take a good picture."

Anthony shook his head. "That is magic. You have put my likeness inside that little box."

Liz nodded. "Would you mind if I take a few more pictures?"

"Go ahead."

Lord Madoc joined them. "Ah, another infernal device that upsets the aether." He smiled. "I guess I better get used to them."

"He will." Angela slipped her hand under his arm. "I'm going to make sure he gets the full Earth experience. We will have a TV, a stereo, a dishwasher, vacuum cleaner and all kinds of electronic stuff."

Jon chuckled as Madoc rolled his eyes upward. "Hey, you may like some of that stuff. At least when I talk about football you may understand what I'm talking about."

Angela laughed. "I like football too. I'll explain it to him. Well, maybe you better. I just watch them throw the football." She looked at Liz. "How's the wedding plans going?"

"Good, catering is a bit of an issue for the reception in Boston. I'm depending on Jon's sister, Sandra, to help us. The problem is the best one was fully booked that Saturday so we're looking for an alternative. Jon's parents are paying for the reception there, so I want to be careful with the costs. Everything is worked out for the wedding in Ballymiller next month and the small one in Horstruff the following week."

"We're looking forward to attending the one in Ballymiller and the one here. I think this is the first wedding ever in Domum where gnants are to be invited. It'll be interesting to see how they react at the buffet table."

Liz laughed. "It's Jon I'm concerned about. Don't stand between him and his dinner."

Jon smiled at Liz's joke and turned to see Anthony and Nicole approach. He shook Anthony's hand. "I'm not sure of protocol here. Am I supposed to kneel, bow or salute?"

Anthony laughed. "Anything but curtsy. You, my friend, will never have to do anything but treat me as your equal."

Nicole hugged Jon. "Thank you so much for returning to Domum for the ceremony. It means so much to me to see you here."

"I'm glad to be here. You will make a wonderful queen."

"Thank you. The next time you come to stay at Horstruff, you can stay with Anthony and me."

"Thanks, though we do have a place to stay."

Nicole smiled. "Lord Jon's castle. It has been officially reserved for guests from Earth, but you and Liz are welcome to stay at the king's castle. We have tons of room and that way we can spend more time together." She squeezed his hand.

Liz tugged at Jon's arm. "Dear, we have to get going. Madoc has to return to Earth, and we need to catch a ride with him." She looked at Anthony. "Well, Tony, it looks like you're all grown up now."

Anthony laughed. "You're the only person in Domum who calls me Tony. I like it. It brings me back down to earth when I start thinking myself as king."

"That is why you're going to make a great king. You have humble roots and have proved yourself to others with your courage and strength."

# FORTY-THREE

Collin took a long drink from his pint, wiped his mouth with his sleeve and looked at Smitty and Percy sitting at the table. "Well, lads, it sure has been an interesting turn of circumstances. Lord Darius gets his ass kicked and loses his head when he tangled with King Perry."

Percy snorted. "Well, good riddance to him, but it don't change much here. We still have the same nobility here that let Lord Darius to take power in the first place."

Collin let a smile creep across his face. "Then you haven't heard the news. King Perry has appointed a new lord to run this kingdom. A Lord Gavin is supposed to get this kingdom back in working order."

Smitty nodded. "Got to say anyone Lord Perry appoints has to be better than what we got."

Collin tapped his finger on the table. "I've heard talk that this Lord Gavin will get things done the right way. No more of guards catching a nap at mid-day. About time some of these people learned to do the jobs they get paid to do."

———

Collin threw some straw into the corner of the stall and took a breather. He leaned on the pitchfork by the open doors and glanced at the sun, determining he could head to the Dragon's Egg in another hour. *Just enough time to put on some shoes for one of the nags.* He watched as a man dressed in the attire from the royal court approached him from the cobbled road leading to the stable. Collin frowned at the lightly built young man, his light brown hair hanging down to his shoulders. A wisp of a moustache ran along his upper lip.

"Freeman Collin Ferguson?"

"That is I. Are you looking for a horse? Most go to the upper stables for one."

"No, it is not a horse I seek. I am Sir Georges, appointed to oversee the royal stables. I was here yesterday an hour before sundown, and no one was here. Can you explain that?"

Collin gulped. "I was out, inquiring about a horseshoes for one of the bigger horses. The ones here don't seem to fit him."

Sir Georges pursed his lips, letting the silence continue for several seconds. He raised his eyebrows. "Are you saying the blacksmiths are not providing you sufficient material?"

Collin shook his head vigorously. "No, just one horse causing some problems. It has been looked after."

"Well, Freeman Colin, this time I shall not pursue whether you are telling me everything I should know. But I have noted that the taverns often have those working for the King visit their premises well before sunset." He paused, letting the last sentence linger before continuing. "I want you to know that on occasion, I will be dropping by to see how well the royal horses are being cared for. I do expect to see you doing work when I arrive." He looked at the pitchfork. "Am I being sufficiently clear?"

"Yes, Sir Georges. I take my job at the royal stables very seriously. All the horses are well looked after."

Sir Georges smiled. "I do expect that of course. I just wanted to introduce myself and let you know of my expectations. I look forward to seeing you again in the coming days."

Collin watched him leave and let out a long breath. *This is not good. The lads will be wondering where I am and will be disappointed I cannot be around anymore at our usual time.* He looked back inside the stable, deciding he had enough time to clean up the back corner before shoeing horses.

# FORTY-FOUR

Rzet made the two-day journey to Lord Jon's castle. Lord Jon had spared his life last year and he was able to return the life favour by warning him of impending danger of an ambush. Now when he heard Lord Jon asked to see him, he didn't hesitate to travel to see one of the few humans the gnants respected.

As it was the custom in Lord Jon's castle, Rzet was given the same service and acknowledgement as a human would. Rzet waited in a small sitting room with a tray of food and drink of his choosing. He looked up as Jon and Nadine walked into the room.

"Rzet, thank you for coming here. My friend Nadine wanted to see you. I will leave you to talk alone."

Rzet looked puzzled at Nadine. "I do not know you."

"Not as a human. When we were younger. We were both studying as Tyreel followers. Do you remember Ctze?"

Rzet looked at Nadine for several seconds and spoke slowly. "Rzet remembersss her. She was Rzet's partner. Adeptsss take her away. Ctze never return."

"No, she never will. The Adepts made her into a human to spy on people. She is still a human."

"How you know thisss?"

Nadine replied in the gnant's language, mispronouncing words that her tongue could no longer make. "I used to be Ctze. Now I am Nadine. I tell you this because I always care for you very much."

"Truth? Human lie?"

"Truth. You once broke a finger jumping from a tree."

"It is you, Ctze. I glad you alive. Miss you, but have new partner now."

"So do I."

Nadine and Rzet exchanged small bites when it came to say goodbye. *I won't tell him I named my cat after him. I don't believe he would understand.*

––––––

Father Murray looked up at the secretary standing at the doorway. "Father, do you remember a Nadine Newman that came here a couple of months ago? She was thin and not in good health."

Father Murray thought a moment. "Yes, I do. She asked me a question on souls." He smiled at the memory. "I hoped I helped her to put her mind at ease. Has she passed on?"

"No, she's here to see you again. I have to say she looks so different, I barely recognized her. Shall I send her in?"

He stood as Nadine entered and was surprised to see a vibrant, healthy woman in front of him. "Miss Newman, it is wonderful to see you again. I have to say you are looking well."

"Thank you. I promised you I would return if I recovered. I am fully recovered now and wanted to fulfill my promise."

"It seems you have discovered a miracle. Your prayers must have been answered."

"I have more good news. I will be getting married to a wonderful man. I have been very fortunate."

"I am happy for you."

She turned to leave. "I hope I didn't trouble you before when I told you I wasn't born as a human."

Father Murray smiled. "That doesn't concern me at all. We are all God's children. Go in peace."

––––––

Nadine knocked on Anna's door and gave a smile to Tuck. "I miss Rzet, and it will be great to tell Anna everything is fine."

Anna opened her door cautiously at first, but then swung it wide as she recognized Tuck and Nadine. She covered her mouth in surprise. "Nadine, I hardly recognize that it's you." Anna stepped forward and gave

Nadine and Tuck a hug. "My Lord, Nadine, you look absolutely wonderful. What did the doctors do to you?"

Nadine shrugged. "Something to do with my organs, but I'm completely healed now."

Anna ushered them into her apartment and began the process of making tea. She called out from the kitchen. "That is wonderful to hear. You look like you have never been sick." She walked into the living room and looked at Tuck. "Now are you two a couple?"

Nadine bent down to pick up Rzet who had come over to her and made noises. "Yes we are. In fact we will be getting married."

Tuck sat quietly, devouring the cookies on the plate as Nadine and Anna talked. He wasn't keen on having a cat in his apartment but concluded it was part of the package with Nadine. He felt content for the first time in his life and one small cat was not going to disturb him.

# FORTY-FIVE

Daniel stopped the horse, leaning on the plough. He waited for Sarah to make the way across the field, giving her a smile.

"You look tired, Daniel. Do you want to stop to eat now?" She carried a clay jug filled with water.

"One more row, then I'll stop." He lifted the jug to his mouth and took a long drink.

"You have half the field done already. Maybe you can slow down a bit."

"I need to get this done as soon as I can. We've missed part of the growing season already."

"That was very generous of Lord Perry to give us the land."

"It was. He also gave us a horse and some tools. It was a good thing we went to Horstruff."

"I do miss our old home, but I guess if we went back there, we would find our farm taken over by someone else. I have some really good news. Our neighbour Irene came over and she said next week a few families are going to come over and help build a house for us."

He grinned. "No more living in a tent. It looks like we're here to stay."

# FORTY-SIX

The ballroom was still filled with people even though the hour was growing late. It was the last of the three wedding receptions for Liz and Jon and it seemed everyone wanted to make sure it was a celebration.

Jon walked over to Nicole. "Can I buy you a drink?"

Nicole laughed. "No thanks. I'm just having juice. How are you doing?"

"A little drunk, but good. I'm going to miss this place."

"We'll miss you too." She smiled. "I think there's part of Domum in you now wherever you go, and in a way there's part of you that will be in Domum."

"Thanks." He gave her a quick kiss. "Hey, I want to talk to Gilbert before he passes out. Talk to you before I go."

Jon walked to where Gilbert sat, his back against the wall, his legs sprawled out in front of him. A tankard rested on the floor next to him.

"Heys, Lord Jon. 'Tis a fine party you and Lady Liz threw."

"Thanks, Gilbert. Mind if I join you?"

Gilbert grinned. "Don'ts minds at all."

Jon dropped to the floor next to him and lifted his glass in a toast. "To friends."

"To friends, Lord Jon." Gilbert slurped his ale and burped.

"Gilbert, you are a good friend. I remember when I met you. We didn't get off to the best start, but I think we understand and respect each other now. When I think about my time on Domum you are a big part of it. You helped me survive and come out a better man than when I came in."

"Thanks, Lord Jon. You helped me too. I's a better man too. You taughts me to be honest."

Jon took another drink of his ale. "Well, Gilbert, let's chalk that up to the mutual benefit of being friends."

"I drinks to that." Gilbert took another drink. "So tells me, Lord Jon, does all your weddings end up likes this one?"

"I don't know about that. The other two receptions on Earth had less drinking." He thought a moment. "Music. We had bands playing and danced a lot more. But I guess all wedding receptions are pretty close to being the same. People talking, drinking and congratulating the married couple."

Gilbert chuckled. "Congratulations, Lord Jon. I hopes you and Lady Liz be very happy togethers."

"Thanks. I think Liz and I will do all right. I have to say this is the most fun I've had of the three wedding receptions. I've certainly had the most to drink."

"You really goings to lives on the Other-side from now on?"

"Yeah. It's where I need to be, but Domum will always be part of me." He looked over to his left. "I see Donna is coming over."

Gilbert sighed. "She probably wants to dance." He quickly finished his ale. "I don'ts know if I cans. I feels a bit unsteady."

Donna put her hands on her hips. "Gilbert, yous drinks too much." She shook her head. "Comes with me. You need some strong tea."

Gilbert staggered to his feet and with Donna's help made his way to where food and refreshments were set out.

Jon smiled as he looked up at the ceiling and the gold trimmed scenes of the Graham family history filling the sections of the huge dome. The last section portrayed the battle with Lord Darius. In the final scene, it showed King Anthony the second, Lord Jon, Lord Madoc, Sir Terrance, Sir Gilbert and Lord Gavin. Lord Darius was shown only as small figure lying dead on the ground. In the background of the battle, painted as ghosts, were Anthony's two dead brothers, Sir Garrett and Sir Philip.

*That was quite a battle and it's hard to believe I was part of it. I'm so glad Anthony became king. He's a good man and I sure wouldn't want the responsibilities of ruling a kingdom. As much as this is fun living here on Domum, I need to get back to reality and to Earth.*

"What are you thinking about?"

228

Jon didn't notice Liz's approach and quickly turned to where she stood, to his right. "Just reviewing the past few weeks I was on Domum. You're still wearing your wedding dress."

"This will be the last time I will ever wear it, so I figured I'd wear it as long as I can. Isn't your tux going to get dirty sitting on the floor?"

Jon considered the question for a moment. "Na. The cleaning staff here keeps the floor clean enough to eat off of."

"Well I was wondering if you wanted to have a dance with me. I told the band to take a break and I have the boom box ready to play some of our music."

Jon climbed to his feet. "Sure. It will be interesting to see how those living on Domum will react to Eric Clapton and the AC/DC."

Jon held Liz close as they danced. He watched as smiling faces came and disappeared from his field of vision. He saw Nicole trying to teach Anthony to dance, laughing at his attempt. It seemed to him the people of Domum were doing their best to improvise their dance to the odd music. A few were studying the portable player, trying to understand how it worked. He glanced at Nicole once more, thinking she had almost a glow to her. Then he recalled she had turned down any drinks offered to her. *She's pregnant.* He closed his eyes as he thought back to what she said earlier. "...and in a way there's part of you that will be in Domum." *I wonder if that dream was not just a dream.* His thought was interrupted by Liz.

"Lost in thought?"

"Yeah, just thinking about what I'm leaving behind." He looked at her. "But I have made a choice and it's you and Earth I want."

He spun Liz around a final time around the dance floor, trying to capture the last night on Domum. *The next time I come to Domum it will be only as a visitor, not as someone who lives here. So be it. Good-bye Domum. It has been a grand adventure.*

––––––––

**Don't miss out on your next favorite book!**
**Join the Melange Books mailing list at**
www.melange-books.com/mail.html

**THANK YOU FOR READING**

Did you enjoy this book?

We invite you to leave a review at the website of your choice, such as
Goodreads, Amazon, Barnes & Noble, etc.

**DID YOU KNOW THAT LEAVING A REVIEW...**

- Helps other readers find books they may enjoy.
- Gives you a chance to let your voice be heard.
- Gives authors recognition for their hard work.
- Doesn't have to be long. A sentence or two about why you
  liked the book will do.

## ALSO BY JH WEAR

### Novels

*A Taste Of Murder*

*Play Dead*

*Witches and Warriors*

*Shadows And Sensations*

*A Hole in the Universe*

### Castle Series

#1 *Fall to Domum*

#2 *The Curse of the Dacron Gem*

#3 *The New King*

# ABOUT THE AUTHOR

For a few years I wanted to try my hand at writing but too many obstacles prevented me from having the time to do so; three boys and a darling wife that loved home renovations to be more specific. Now the boys have "grown up" and left home I have time to do a bit more what I want to do, such as writing.

My other interests include wine, reading, astronomy, photography and convincing my wife that our home is actually fine the way it is. I have actually lost that battle. She wants our deck replaced; apparently rotten boards isn't considered safe anymore.

www.jhwear.com

 twitter.com/JH_Wear

www.ingramcontent.com/pod-product-compliance
Lightning Source LLC
Chambersburg PA
CBHW060154180626
46813CB00007B/2751